ASSASSIN OF SECRETS

ASSASSIN
OF SECRETS

Q. R. Markham

MULHOLLAND BOOKS

Little, Brown and Company

New York   Boston   London

Mulholland Books / Little, Brown and Company
Hachette Book Group
237 Park Avenue, New York, NY 10017
www.hachettebookgroup.com

First Edition: November 2011

Mulholland Books is an imprint of Little, Brown and Company, a division of Hachette Book Group, Inc. The Mulholland Books name and logo are trademarks of Hachette Book Group, Inc.

The characters and events in this book are fictitious. Any similarity to real persons, living or dead, is coincidental and not intended by the author.

The publisher is not responsible for websites (or their content) that are not owned by the publisher.

Library of Congress Cataloging-in-Publication Data

Markham, Q. R.
  Assassin of secrets / Q. R. Markham. — 1st ed.
    p. cm.
  ISBN 978-0-316-17646-0
  1. Intelligence officers — United States — Fiction. 2. Assassins — Fiction. I. Title.
  PS3613.A7542A92 2011
  813'.6 — dc22   2011017861

10 9 8 7 6 5 4 3 2 1

RRD-C

Printed in the United States of America

To SR and LR, the original Markhams

"Young Men, life is before you. Two voices are calling you—one coming out from the swamps of selfishness and force, where success means death; and the other from the hilltops of justice and progress, where even failure brings glory. Two lights are seen in your horizon—one the fast fading marsh light of power, and the other the slowly rising sun of human brotherhood."

—John P. Altgeld, former governor of Illinois, in an address to the Boy Scouts of America

ASSASSIN OF SECRETS

The brightness that is the sun or from the sun passes the silver telescope many times as it drops its undeveloped film to earth. From end to end, along its fault lines, it's wired. Impulses respond to impulses. Somewhere deep in the big structures, below ground level, men at long tables study the printouts. These men have named it Keyhole-7 and they are intent on capturing information, storing it, sifting it, integrating files, and cross-indexing salient characteristics. For them, input is hard to discard. The cigarette someone dropped at the Severodinsk shipyard might be important. Or the man who stood too long at the Aswan Dam. All are joined in a common dance. Every hand holding a ballpoint pen, every finger pressing a button; each sends out shock waves to whose collective rhythm the world structure is vibrating.

At 1.9 miles per second Keyhole-7's life is perfectly ordered and void as a chess game. It glides through space and time in a brief wedding where data and expressive form bounce off each other like electrons. The stars are silent and unchanging and none of the men below can guess how much this concerns them, any more than they can imagine that one particular spurt of blips might be the wedge that makes an immediate nuclear confronta-

3

tion possible. That would be the mad scientist's dream, the plots of science fiction for years past.

But if you could see what Keyhole sees you would quickly become dizzy. The vertigo of the web laid bare; the writhing intertwining unity of all the secret transactions on which the world is built.

Prologue

Whenever he could, Number One traveled by train. He liked the solitude of a sleeping-car compartment, the chance to read while the countryside flashed by, the mechanical sounds and the sheer inertia of the experience. In Paris, after his flight from New York, he booked a place on the night train to Berlin. At dinner he was seated by the headwaiter with a young woman who was also dining alone. Her eyes were fixed on the menu. She wore a wedding ring. The choices were mushroom soup or grapefruit, roast chicken or "sole" (meaning flounder), salad, and caramel custard or cheese.

The woman put her hands in her lap and studied the menu card. "Chicken or fish, how dreary," she said in French. "What do you think?"

"The flounder," Number One replied.

She had not yet looked at him. Now she lifted her eyes, which were large and blue with violet flecks, and examined him without smiling. The waiter arrived with his pad. She put her hands back on the table. Her wedding ring had vanished.

"The soup, the fish," she said. "A small carafe of Muscadet. Cheese."

She had a long aristocratic face that glowed bronze, the color of autumn beech leaves. The contrast of colors—the skin and her striking white blond curls cut close—made this woman not only acutely desirable, but also an object lesson in unblemished, classical beauty. She dressed modishly, a Chanel jacket over a blouse with a many-stranded necklace of beads at her throat. She was tall for a Frenchwoman, slim. Number One did not take this inventory. With little gestures she presented it to him item by item. She was an amusing talker. She spoke French with a faint Niçoise accent, lifting her voice at the ends of words and adding a final Italianate vowel that was not present in the written word.

They talked about the Côte d'Azur. She recommended restaurants in Nice and Cannes and their surrounding villages. She recommended Provençal dishes as if he had never heard of them. She liked swimming, sailing, and—in the winter—skiing in the Maritime Alps and sometimes in Cortina and Megève.

"Do you sail?" she asked.

"Not as much as in the past. I don't live close to water."

"You live in Paris?"

"For the moment."

"But you ski, surely."

"Why surely?"

"You look like a skier."

Number One talked with her about skiing in Switzerland and Austria as he finished his food and arranged the knife and fork on the empty plate. She asked about movies. What did he like? Mostly American movies, he said. Why American films, of all things?

"Because the girl never takes off her clothes and dies in the end."

"Which part of that French cliché do you object to?"

Number One smiled and drank the rest of his Evian water.

Brewster had taught him when he was young to drink good wine or no wine at all. He understood that this was a rule for snobs, but he didn't like bad wine. On a train, which was a giant over-heated cocktail shaker, there was no such thing as good wine, no matter what the label read. The Muscadet had brought a flush to the woman's cheeks. She was talking more rapidly.

"Me, I prefer French films," she said. "Sometimes Italian, if they're funny. I adore Claude Lelouch—*Vivre pour Vivre, Un Homme et une Femme,* everything."

The dinner, rapidly served, was not bad. They ate their cheese. The waiter asked if they wanted coffee. The woman said yes, Number One declined.

"It keeps you awake?"

"Yes."

"Me, too," she said, drinking. "Sometimes all night." Her eyes were wider now and shining.

Number One had brought a book to the dining car. It lay face-down on the table, dust jacket removed. "What are you reading?" the woman asked. Number One showed her. It was a novel in English. She turned the pages until she came to the one she was looking for. She rummaged in her purse and found a pencil. With it she drew a circle around the page number, closed the book, and handed it back.

"Hide and seek," she said, and rising to her feet she walked down the aisle, swaying with the train and the wine. Her legs were spectacular like the rest of her. At the door she looked over her shoulder, a glance full of meaning.

Number One knew it was bad form for an agent of I-Division to permit himself to be picked up by a stranger on a train. He went back to his own compartment and started to read his novel. A moment later he put the book down and thought to himself: *It's been three weeks since the last one was delivered to us. The com-*

puter whizzes have gamed every possible combination of data — does the kidnapper strike when the moon is full, do his crimes coincide with the anniversaries of outrages against the Arab nation, is he trying to drive us crazy by running an operation that has no plan or purpose? I need some of Chase's golden opinions. There has to be something obvious in this situation, something hidden in plain sight. Another purloined letter.

Sometime later he came to the page in his book whose number the woman had circled in pencil. It was, he knew, the number of her compartment. He put the book down and went out into the hallway. He knew most agents in his position would have resisted going this far. Number One chalked it up to boredom and loneliness, and, giving himself a small boost to his ego, to his expertise with the opposite sex. He knocked lightly on the appropriate door.

"What do — oh, hello," she said.

She held the door open and gestured for him to enter. Number One sauntered in, pausing to run an index finger along her chin as he walked by her.

He turned to her and put his arms around her. She looked up at him, her mouth parted. Her lower lip trembled a bit, and he could feel her shaking. Number One brought his mouth down on hers and roughly held her against him. She submitted with a soft moan, then opened her mouth to receive his tongue. They kissed passionately until he felt something sharp jab into his neck.

Number One's eyes dilated in terror. His hands grabbed at his neck and pulled out the long glass barrel of the syringe planted in his posterior external jugular vein. He knew he had approximately 30 seconds before the drug reached his bloodstream.

Before he had a moment to think, the blond woman — with a perfectly executed maneuver — kicked him in the face. Recovering quickly, Number One head-butted the female assassin in the stomach. Both figures tumbled onto the railcar bed, ending up with the woman on top with her hands around Number One's throat.

Jesus, she's strong.

With a superhuman effort, he thrust his arms between her elbows and delivered dual lightning-quick hand chops, which made her lose her grip. Then, with split-second timing, Number One jerked his head forward against her nose, breaking it and causing her to cry out in pain.

With a shout, he delivered a kick to the blond woman's chest, knocking her back. The blow was meant to cause serious damage, but it landed too far to the left of the sternal vital-point target. Number One was momentarily surprised that she didn't fall, but he immediately drove his fist into her abdomen. That was his first mistake—mixing his fighting styles. He'd been using a mixture of karate and traditional Western boxing, whereas the female had picked a system and stuck with it. He kept on, though, lunging away, and smelling her stinking Je Reviens perfume, but he knew these sensations were only a dream. In reality they were floating in a skiff down the Seine, listening to a tinny phonograph record of a girl singing in French. How beautifully the girl sang, how the river smelled of the flowers that turned its torpid waters into perfume, how much like his own mind and voice were the mind and voice of this chanteuse! It was uncanny.

Someone seized his lower lip and twisted. The pain changed his idea of where he was. His right eye focused, briefly, and he glimpsed the blond woman's eyes. She was on top of him now, thrusting her forearm into Number One's neck, exerting tremendous pressure on his larynx. With his right hand, the American fumbled in his pants pocket, attempting to get at his insurance policy. The blond managed to elbow him in the ribs, but this only served to increase his determination. She managed to get her hands around the man's neck, but it was too late; Number One deftly retrieved the twenty-ounce Mk 2 "pineapple" fragmentation grenade from his trousers and pulled the pin.

She dived through the compartment door and fell to the floor in the hallway. Afterward, the assassin known as Snow Queen thought that she remembered the flash of the explosion lighting the flat face of the American spy and the blast lifting his thick black hair so that it stood on end. The noise was a long time coming. Before she heard the explosion, like the snap of a heavy howitzer, she saw the whole body of the train car swell like a balloon full of water. The glass blew out and the compartment door cut through the rest of the car like a great black knife.

Concussion sent blood gushing out of her broken nose. She could hear nothing except a high ringing in her ears. All around her, mouths opened in noiseless screams of terror. She lay where she was with her eyes open.

In a few hours a policeman wearing a lacquered French helmet liner leaned over her and spoke. The blond woman pointed to her ears and said, "I'm deaf." She heard nothing of her own voice but felt its movement over her tongue. The policeman pulled her to her feet and led her out of the debris. She would have been killed by the fire truck that roared up behind them if the Frenchman had not pulled her out of the way.

ONE

ONE

–1–

His step had an unusual silence to it. It was late morning in October of the year 1968 and the warm, still air had turned heavy with moisture, causing others in the long hallway to walk with a slow shuffle, a sort of somber march. Clad in a lightweight navy blue racing jacket and white pants, Jonathan Chase seemed relaxed enough, his face entirely free of perspiration. He merely wondered to himself about the latest directive to all officers from I-Division advising "constant vigilance, even when off duty" and if it had something to do with his appointment today with Brewster.

The boxy, sprawling Munitions Building which sat near the Washington Monument and quietly served as I-Division's base of operations was a study in monotony. Endless corridors connecting to endless corridors. Walls a shade of green common to bad cheese and fruit. Forests of oak desks separated down the middle by rows of tall columns, like concrete redwoods, each with a number designating a particular work space.

Chase's brown loafers made a sudden soundless left turn into a heavily deserted wing. It was lined with closed doors containing dim, opaque windows and empty name holders. Brewster sure knows how to pick his HQ, Chase mused, as he turned right into Room 32, a small office containing a massive black vault, the kind found in exclusive Swiss banks. Reaching into the front pocket of his gingham shirt, he removed a small card. Then, standing in front of the thick round combination dial, he began twisting it back and forth. Seconds later he yanked up the silver bolt and slowly pushed open the heavy door, only to reveal another wall of steel behind it. This time he removed a key from a small compartment inside the heel of his left shoe and turned it in the lock, swinging aside the second door to reveal an interior as bright and cheery as noonday sun.

"Over here, Number Two," called Brewster across a gaggle of attractive secretaries in op-art miniskirts and harassed-looking analysts in horn-rimmed glasses.

Brewster was a big man, tall, broad, bearded, with an expansive personality—"a big bearded bastard," Brewster's secretary and mistress, the petite, blond Tabitha Peters, was often heard to remark. Not the usual kind of person who made it to a responsible position in the clandestine services. They tended to prefer what were commonly called "invisible men"—ordinary, gray people who could vanish into a crowd like illusionists. Yet somehow, at forty-eight years old, Virginia-born Brewster had spent his entire adult life studying, practicing, defining the black arts of espionage and counterintelligence. Six years earlier, during the autumn of 1962, Brewster had been appointed the chief and sole employee of a secret new organization responsible for monitoring—"watchdogging," in the new president's words—all of the other intelligence services: the CIA in particular.

Jack Kennedy had been an admirer of the writer Ian Fleming, and Brewster had seemed at the time to be his perfect "M." By the summer of 1965, Brewster's one-man task force actually had employees, including three field agents. Jonathan Chase had been the second one recruited. In the years that followed, the study of spies for the purposes of entertainment had become a universal vocation. But never for an instant did Jonathan Chase believe himself to be anything like James Bond. The popularity of the espionage melodrama had codified the notion of the British spy who was a courageous fighter for justice. Chase himself was an American who had only ever played an abstract, nihilistic game.

Because people who had seen him remembered his size and his beard, Brewster remained in Washington. He was a natural administrator; he absorbed written material at a glance and never forgot anything. He knew the names and pseudonyms, the photographs, and the operative weakness of every agent controlled by Americans everywhere in the world. Brewster rarely met with any of them, and few of them knew he existed, but he designed their lives, forming them into a global subsociety that had become what it was, and remained so, at his pleasure. He was outranked by only three men in the American intelligence community.

"Couldn't even wear a suit to work, Number Two?"

"You're aware of my predilections, chief."

"Tabitha needs to put you on the heart attack machine before we can talk. Find me in my office."

Leaving the chief for the moment, Chase followed Tabitha behind a reinforced steel door. Before every new mission all of the agents of I-Division submitted to a lie detector test. The machine measured their breathing, the sweat on their palms, their blood pressure and pulse, and it knew whether they had stolen money from the government, submitted to homosexual advances, been doubled by the opposition, committed adultery. The test was called the "flutter." But Brewster fondly referred to it as "the heart attack machine."

To Brewster, the heart attack machine was the ordeal of brotherhood. He believed that those who went through it were cold in their minds, trained to observe and report but never to judge. They looked for flaws in humanity and were never surprised to find them; the polygraph had taught Chase so much about himself—taught him that guilt can be read on human skin with a meter.

Releasing the straps, Tabitha smiled. "Jonathan, Brewster's always so glad to see you. He tells me in bed that you're absolutely the best in the company. The best he's ever seen. In bed—what is the significance of that, do you suppose?"

Chase grinned back, somewhat enigmatically.

"Why are you so good at the work, Jon?" Tabitha asked. "Do you know?"

"People trust me."

"Do they? Wouldn't you think that word would get around?"

"Oh, I think it has, Tabitha. You notice the old man only leaves us alone together for the test? Probably has the room bugged just in case."

Five minutes later, Chase entered Brewster's office wondering at the strangeness of this world where all personal secrets were known. The truth along with the gossip and the lies.

"Okay, break it to me gently," said Chase as the doors to Brewster's office shut behind them.

"You did good things on the last one by the way," Brewster grunted, studying Chase as he found a chair. "A little spooky—the way you walk right in on the customers, but I like that."

His number two agent wore large horn-rimmed eyeglasses, had dirty-blond hair that covered his forehead and the tops of his ears, was broad-shouldered but slim, and very handsome. His eyes were a warm blue and he had the kind of weather-beaten face that suggested years of outdoor activity. Chase almost had the look of an old-time matinee idol, but there was a certain quirkiness, a wistfulness, a rueful irony to his face that left a different kind of emotional trademark. An almost dandified alienation. This, Brewster guessed, was what had endeared his number two man to all those serious dark-haired women in Paris and Milan.

Also, it was evident to Brewster from the day he met Chase in Korea that he was the finest natural spy he had ever encountered. There was no easy explanation for this talent. Perhaps the first reason for his excellence was his truculent refusal to believe in anybody's innocence. Chase treated all men and women as enemy agents at all times; they could be used, paid, praised. They could even be loved. But they could never be trusted. What might seem paranoia in another man was shrewd intuition in Chase.

"Ever hear of these people?" Brewster asked, handing over a letter in a transparent plastic sleeve. "That went directly through the mail to Langley."

Chase looked at the piece of paper. It was an eight-by-ten-inch piece of typing paper with the words "The Rope of Lies is Always Too Short" centered in the middle of the page. At the bottom it was signed "ZD."

Chase nodded. In recent years, his world had grown crowded with an ever-expanding and esoteric vocabulary of acronyms. He'd come to accept them as part of the forbidden atmosphere. Somehow the mumbo jumbo made the whole process seem more serious. More connected to some invisible power.

"Zero Directorate. We only recently became aware of their activities."

"There's nothing in the files on them. Is Langley just accepting they exist on good faith?"

"Not at all. They exist all right and they're pros all the way. This is a group of serious mercenaries out for hire by any individual or government that will employ them."

"How long have they been around?"

"Not long. Two years, maybe."

"Never heard of them."

Chase handed the letter back to Brewster. "They're reportedly responsible for the theft of those military maps of Hanoi from the Pentagon last month. A well-protected Mafia don was murdered about a year ago in Cuba. Zero Directorate supposedly supplied the hit man for that job. They recently blackmailed a French politician for thirty million francs. The Deuxième got wind of it and passed the information on to us. Apparently they have no loyalty to any one nation. Their primary motive is greed, and they can be quite ruthless."

Chase looked pensive. "Where are they based?"

"We don't know. Despite all the intelligence we've gathered on them thus far, neither we nor the CIA have any clues as to who they are or where they make their home."

"Sounds like we should get rid of that intelligence, and then begin over again and concentrate."

Brewster had been listening intently. "Concentrate on what?"

"What it is they're *really* after."

"Well, for one, they seem to have an uncanny ability to infiltrate law enforcement and intelligence organizations."

"Such as?"

"KGB, Mossad, MI6. And CIA."

"CIA?"

"So far they've got three," Brewster said.

"Together?"

"No, a month apart each time, one in Jordan, one in Cairo, one in Sicily. They worked them over the weekend, then left the corpses in hotel rooms. All three had been drugged. In each case, a reel of film recording what the man had spilled turned up within the week." Brewster let out a long sigh.

"Turned up where?"

"On the previews reel at the premiere for a film called *The Wild Bunch* in Los Angeles. On the nightly news show of Radiotelevisione Italiana. Projected on a stone wall in Tahrir Square. And there's more, Number Two."

"Oh?"

"They got Number One."

"Tom Hibbert? I can't say that's a pleasant surprise, sir." Tom Hibbert and Chase had gained their promotions at the same time: when Hibbert had become Number One, Chase had moved desks in the vault, and gone to Number Two. Thus, he and Hibbert had known each other very well, and it had been an easy and enduring friendship.

"On a train out of Paris. Hard to say how they did it: looks like it might have been a honey trap. We found traces of the drugs in what was left of him."

"What kind of drugs?"

"Some kind of supertranquilizer, but masked with other drugs given before the victims are killed."

"Did they film Tom?"

"Nah. He pulled the plug before they could."

"What are the other films like?" Chase asked.

"Everything the victim knows. Everything. Not only about the Company, but about themselves. It's stream of consciousness; they go on and on, overjoyed at the opportunity to confess everything. Luckily no one understood them in Italy and Cairo, but all of Grauman's Chinese Theatre had to sign a gag order after the show."

"They don't ask for a ransom?"

"They don't communicate with us in any way. They just take our people, flush out their brains, kill them, and make the film public. We don't know what we're dealing with or why they're doing this. What do they want? What's next?" To emphasize his point, Brewster smacked a ballpoint pen on his desk.

"Maybe all they want is information."

"That's what we thought in the beginning. But they don't seem to be doing anything with the information. They have the names of dozens of assets. Not one of them has been bothered. We're still running them, hoping these people will come after them so we can get one of them and give him a dose of his own medicine."

"Why me on this one, Chief?" Chase took off his glasses and made a motion to clean them on his shirt.

"Why you? I'll tell you why. Because when I read the files I thought maybe you'd gone to the other side. I didn't think that anybody but you could think something like this up, let alone bring it off."

Chase recognized Brewster's fear of his going to the other side as a side effect of the high level of training he'd received. He took it as a compliment. Gradually, as his powers had grown, Chase knew he'd become feared throughout the intelligence community. Some even thought he operated outside the apparatus; in fact, he was implanted so deeply within it as to be more or less detached from its rules.

"You can stop worrying. It isn't me." Chase grinned.

"I know. It's worse than that. It's somebody just like you. And he's working for the bad guys."

"What makes you think it'll happen again?"

"If it stops now, what's the point of it?"

"If it doesn't stop, we'll have to shut up shop."

"We will? Why?"

"You know why. Our whole stock-in-trade is secrets. But what happens to the market if you can't keep a secret, if you never know which one of your people is going to be grabbed next and given a shot of something that makes him want to tell everything he knows?"

"Go on."

"Maybe the plan is to make us obsolete. Espionage agencies, I mean."

"Right."

"Maybe they're doing the Lord's work. If they gave every member of the human race a shot of this stuff every day, they'd solve the problems of the world."

"That's right. There'd be a fresh corpse in every bedroom. And what if they move on from spies? What if they start going after elected officials? What then, Number Two? You know and I know that these guys with their huge brains and their huge ideas could never survive the probe. Hell, even their egos are too small to hold up the world, only just big enough to let everything slide."

"Hmm."

"And this is a particularly bad time."

"Why's that?"

"The militarization of American society, Chase. What Eisenhower called, back in sixty-one, the military-industrial complex. What I think of as a bunch of professional soldiers with nothing to do but try to promulgate their authority and influence. Professional soldiers with no time for us: their hazy, muddled-thinking soft civilian counterparts. Secure in the knowledge that in this era of potential holocaust there's just no room for the indecisive or the undecided. That the protection of the nation is directly related to the hugeness and effectiveness of its strike force."

"I'm familiar with the phrase, sir."

In truth, it made Chase think of generals like the ones in *Fail-Safe* and *Seven Days in May*. It made him think of a warm autumn evening a year before the shooting of John F. Kennedy when the president preempted regular television programming to give advance notice of the possible erasure of the world. Chase had been walking down K Street when the neon was just coming on. People

were walking around in the usual way. Never had ordinary gestures—buying a newspaper, putting the key in the lock, shoving
a quarter across the counter at the luncheonette—seemed so sub-
missive, so humiliated. Even if a more precise hour were fixed
for the great dissolution, the hand would continue in automaton
fashion to shove the coin across the counter.

"Well, it's a bad time for secrets to be at risk, Number Two.
With the defense contractors getting the lion's share of the federal
budget, the best scientific minds are being persuaded to devote
their time to developing more and more elaborate missiles, satellites, and other technologies that make more war."

"You're speculating that the frequency of wars is going to increase then, sir?"

"That supply will begin to dictate demand, yes."

Brewster did not explain this statement. He was famous for
his impulsive pronouncements. As Chase himself would say years
later, when he knew him better than anyone alive, the old man
decided everything between his pelvis and his collarbone. Chase
meant this as a compliment: anyone could be an intellectual.

"Going back to the Zero Directorate situation, sir. I think we
should forget about the *what, who,* and *how,* then. The only real
question is *why?*"

"I agree. But how do we answer it?"

"That's obvious."

"It is? Explain it to me anyway."

"Only the kidnapper knows the answer to your questions."

"So?"

"So kidnap the kidnapper."

◆

Brewster handed over an eight-by-ten-inch glossy, this time of
Number One's charred corpse. "He'd been working on the case,

knew they'd turn on the cameras. Looks like he chose the honorable way out. To think we used to make fun of him carrying around that damn grenade. He even left us a clue. One word in invisible ink. Inside a copy of *The Ambassadors:* Lazarus."

"Our Lazarus?"

"Fits the bill, doesn't it?"

"So Tom had seen some connection between Lazarus and this Zero Directorate, who were, presumably, his killers. Interesting."

Lazarus was the cryptonym by which Number One, Brewster, Chase, and two or three British agents knew an operative of the Russian intelligence service—they called it that, never the "Soviet intelligence service" or "the KGB," because in Brewster's opinion there was no such thing as the Soviet Union, only the Russian empire operating under an assumed name.

For the past year and a half Brewster and Chase and a very small group of people from MI6 had been paying close attention to Lazarus. He came to their attention after the assassination or kidnapping of half a dozen British agents in Europe and Africa. On the surface, these were senseless operations. The victims were doing the Russians no harm, and even if the opposite had been true, it is seldom good practice for an intelligence service to kill an enemy it knows, because the victim will only be replaced by one that it does not know and must therefore identify and neutralize at great expense in time, manpower, and money.

It was the very pointlessness of the actions that aroused Brewster's curiosity; if there was no apparent purpose to an act, it followed that there must be a hidden purpose. In order to discover what Russian intelligence's secret motive was, he set up a team to watch Lazarus, putting Agent Number One in charge of this operation. Brewster trusted Number One absolutely because, after leading a rifle platoon in Korea, he had concentrated in Russian at Harvard and later learned Arabic while working for I-Division in the Middle East. Number One had a flair for dangerous operations, and because he spoke Russian he was credited with understanding the Eastern mind. With the help of a Division computer expert, he targeted the British missions in Europe whose intelligence officers were most likely to be hit next.

The computer expert, an elderly woman whose specialty was the laws of probability, predicted that the next killing would take place in a neutral country—possibly Austria, but more probably Switzerland because it provided a larger number of escape routes. Within a month another Englishman was shot to death as he waited in the Parc Mon-Repos in Geneva for contact. As in all previous cases, the assassins used a silenced Czech-made 7.65 mm Skorpion machine pistol, firing all twenty rounds from the magazine into the target's back from a range of about one meter.

Number One's agents, posing as German tourists, were witnesses to the assassination. Using a Super 8 camera concealed in a baby carriage, they recorded the killing on tape, then followed the murderers home to a safe house across the French frontier in Annemasse. This led the American team to the terrorists' support group—loosely affiliated with the radical French organization Praxis—and, in due course, to Lazarus himself.

From Division file data the computer expert established that Lazarus's false-true Russian intelligence name—that is, the one he used inside his own headquarters in Moscow—was Anatoly Evdokiya. He spoke fluent Arabic and English and was an expert in small arms, explosives, and small-scale guerrilla operations.

"The strange thing about the operation," Brewster had noted at the time, "is that all of Lazarus's shooters and all the supporting cast are bourgeois European leftists and students. Why exactly are they killing the British? They're harmless these days."

"We think Lazarus is going to turn his networks loose," Number One had told Brewster.

"What do you mean, turn them loose?"

Number One handed over a large brown envelope. Brewster peeked inside, examining the contents without removing them. The envelope contained an eight-by-ten-inch X-ray print of a full-length silhouette of an adult male. Black images of hundreds of small rectangles were scattered all over the torso and legs.

"Who took this?"

"We did, in Milan, while he was waiting for his bags. Those are two-ounce gold ingots, two hundred and twenty of them, sewn into his coat and pants. The photo-analysts think he's also carrying a lot of cash in that money belt—more than a million dollars."

"And you think he's going to give all this loot to somebody?"

"To his agents. And then he's going to wish them luck and say goodbye."

"Why?"

"Think about it."

Brewster saw Number One's point. Lazarus's mission had been to create an asylum full of lunatics, and then unlock the doors and let them go. He was going to give them twenty-eight pounds of gold and a million dollars in currency, tell them they could kill anyone they wanted to kill, and say goodbye. Lazarus had never had any intention of controlling the monster he created. He wanted these terrorists out of control, acting according to no discernible plan—and, above all, disconnected from himself. When the slaughter began, he would deny that he knew anything about the terrorists.

Brewster okayed the grab with MI6 and Lazarus was now residing in a box—a portable cell, really—in the basement of the British Embassy in Brussels.

Chase shifted in his chair, asking Brewster with his eyes what his mind already knew. "So I'm going to Brussels?"

"You got it, Chase."

"You realize, sir, that if Tom was right, it started in back in Switzerland? It didn't have the first thing to do with the KGB. Lazarus was out there planting the seeds for this ZD organization."

Brewster gazed at Chase for several seconds in great seriousness—taking a quiet moment of pride in his creation. Then he threw back his head and laughed.

"I was right, by golly," Brewster said. "I knew you'd have your head screwed on straight for this one. Now go talk to Frankie, Number Two."

2

Francesca Farmer—assistant to the Armorer, and second-in-command of G Branch—was known to all and sundry within I-Division headquarters as Frankie. An odd nickname for the elegant, tall, and very efficient and liberated young lady with a taste for cocktail dresses and thigh-high boots.

After a slightly shaky start, Chase and Frankie had become close friends and what she liked to call "occasional lovers." He knew Brewster was sending him to Miss Farmer to turn him into a walking listening sabotage device for the mission because Chase didn't like to use guns. It was natural, then, for him to spend some time with G Branch, the experts of "gee-whiz" technology. In the past, he had often found himself bored by the earnest young men who inhabited the workshops and testing areas of G Branch, but the times were changing. Within a week of her arrival, Frankie had become the target of many seductive attempts by unmarried officers of all ages. Chase had noticed her, and heard the reports. Word was the colder side of Frankie's personality was uppermost in her off-duty hours. Throughout this period, Jonathan Chase remained professionally distant. Frankie was a desirable girl, but, like many of the women working within the security services these days, she remained friendly yet at pains to make it plain that she was her own woman. Only later was Chase to learn that she had done a year in the field before taking the two-year technical course which provided her with promotion to executive status in G Branch.

At forty-eight hours' notice, Frankie's team had put together a set of what she called "personalized matching luggage." This consisted of a leather suitcase together with a similarly designed, steel-strengthened briefcase. Both items contained cunningly devised compartments, secret and well-nigh undetectable, built to house a whole range of electronic sound-stealing equipment, some sabotage gear, and a few useful survival items. These included a highly sophisticated bugging and listening device; a VL22H countersurveillance receiver; a pen alarm, set to a frequency which linked it to a long-range modification of the CIA 900 Alert System. If triggered, the pen alarm would provide Chase with instant signal communications to headquarters. The pen also contained micro facilities so that it operated as a homer; therefore, when activated, it allowed headquarters to keep track of their man in the field—a personal alarm system in the breast pocket.

As a backup, there was a small ultrasonic transmitter, while, among the sabotage material, Chase was to carry an exact replica of his own Dunhill cigarette lighter—the facsimile having special properties of its own. There was also a so-called security blanket flashlight, which generated a high-intensity beam strong enough to disorient any victim caught in its burst of light; and—almost as an afterthought—Frankie made him sign for a pair of TH70 Nitefinder goggles.

Briefing finished, Frankie Farmer made it clear that if Chase was free, she was available until the following morning.

After having an early dinner—at Clyde's in Friendship Heights—the couple had gone back to Frankie's apartment building.

"Like to come in and see my gadgets?" she asked. Chase could not see the smile in the darkness of the car, but knew it was there.

Inside, Frankie's hand stabbed at some buttons and the lights dimmed and the room became bathed in a soft red glow which came from the baseboards. The large, circular, smoked glass table which formed a focal point at the center of the room seemed to sink into the carpet, and from it there came the sound of splashing water as it gleamed with light to become a small pond with a fountain playing at its center. Chase sniffed the air. A musky scent had risen around him, while the sound of piano music gently rose in volume. The scent and music began to claw at his senses. Then he took a step back, his eyes moving to the wall on his right. The wall had started to open up, and from behind it, a large, high water bed slid soundlessly into the room—above it a mirrored canopy hanging from crimson silk ropes.

Francesca Farmer had disappeared. For a second, Chase was disoriented, his back to the wall, head and eyes moving over the extraordinary sight. Then he saw her, behind the fountain, a small light dim but growing to illuminate her as she stood naked but for a thin, translucent nightdress; her hair undone and falling to her waist—hair and the thin material moving and blowing as though caught in a silent zephyr.

Chase caught hold of her, pulled her close. She slid her hands to his shoulders, gently pushing him away.

"What's it like to kill somebody? They say you've had to kill a lot of people during your time in the Division."

"Then they shouldn't talk so much. The need-to-know system operates in the Division. You, of all people, should know better than to ask questions like that."

"But I do need to know. After all, I deal with some of the

important 'gee-whiz' stuff. You must also know what that covers—secret death—undetectable. People die in this business. I should know about the end product."

"While it's happening, you don't think much about it," Chase answered flatly. "It's a reflex. You do it and you don't hesitate. If you're wise, and want to go on living, you don't think about it afterward either. There's nothing to tell, Frankie. I know it sounds bloodless and inhuman, but I try not to remember. That way I remain detached from its reality."

They made love with a disturbing wildness, as though time was running out for both of them. The draining of their bodies left the agile Frankie exhausted. She fell asleep almost immediately after their last long and tender kiss. Chase, however, stayed wide awake, thinking back to Korea and the long association with Brewster that had started all those years ago.

1953. The 38th Parallel. Brewster had been CIA then. It was a back-and-forth stalemate time in the war. In a small village on the Pusan Perimeter, the North Koreans had set up headquarters. The CIA's objective had been to enter the main communications house and capture a list of major Northern sympathizers in Taejon. Brewster had worked out a plan to have a full company of Marines stage a charge on the building with no one seeking cover, almost a kamikaze attack. This, Brewster hoped, would be fast enough to deny the time for record burning or anything else. The Marines gave him a company. But when he approached the captain in command of the unit, the captain just nodded to a tarpaulin-covered pile in which two Marines sat, their .30 M1 Garands cradled in their arms.

"What's that?" were the first words Chase ever heard come out of Brewster's mouth.

"Your records," the captain said. "Take your records and get your ass out of here. We've done our job."

Brewster had started to say something, but instead turned and walked into the tarpaulin. After twenty minutes of leafing through heavy parchment with Chinese lettering, Brewster nodded his respects to the Marine captain.

"I will make a report expressing CIA gratitude."

"You do that." Brewster then glanced at the farmhouse. Its dried mud walls were free of bullet pockmarks.

"How'd you go in? With bayonets?"

The captain pushed up his helmet with his right hand and scratched the hair over his temple. "Yes and No."

"What do you mean?"

"We got this guy. He does these things."

"What things?

"Like the farmhouse. He does them."

"What?"

"He goes in and kills the people. We use him for single-man assaults on positions, nighttime work. He, uh, just produces, that's all. It's a lot easier than running up casualty lists. Funny too, 'cause he kinda looks like a Poindexter."

"Ah?"

"You know, a brain. Like a librarian or something."

"How does he do it?"

The captain shrugged. "I don't know. I never asked him."

"He should get the Congressional Medal of Honor for this."

"For what?"

"For getting these damn records by himself. For killing . . . how many men?"

"I think it was eight in there."

"For this and for killing eight men."

"For that?"

"Certainly."

The captain shrugged his shoulders. "Chase does it all the time.

I don't know what's so special about this time. If we make a big deal now, he'll be transferred out. Anyway, he doesn't like medals."

"Where is he?"

The captain nodded. "Right there."

The fresh-faced Marine in clunky horn-rimmed spectacles looked up lazily at the big, bearded spook.

"What's your name?" Brewster asked.

"Who are you?"

"A major," Brewster answered. He wore the leaves on his shoulders for convenience. He saw Chase look at them.

"My name, sir, is Jonathan Barnaby Chase," the nineteen-year-old Marine said, starting to rise.

"Stay there. You get the records?"

"Yes, sir. Did I do anything wrong?"

"No. You thinking of making a career out of the Marines?"

"No, sir. My hitch is up in two months."

"What are you going to do when you get out?"

"Go back to Yale and finish up there."

"Skull and Bones?"

"Yes, sir."

"Boarding school?"

"Groton, sir."

"Ever think of joining CIA?"

"What would I do?"

"That's not your worry. It's up to me to find out what you want to do and make it possible for you to do it. What do you want to do?"

"I want to live in privacy."

"That's all?"

"No."

"Then what? Tell me what's in your heart, son."

"I want to work against war. Without guns."

"Work for peace?"

"No, none of that bullshit. I want to be an enemy of war."

And so, over a couple of Korean beers—or *Maekju*—by the Yalu River, Chase had been recruited for intelligence work. He didn't hesitate. He understood that what Brewster was offering him was a lifetime of inviolable privacy.

Certainly they'd seen changes in each other in the fifteen years since then, but the changes were physical. Their minds were as they had always been. Brewster believed in intellect as a force in the world and understood that it could be used only in secret. Chase knew, because he had spent his life doing it, that it was possible to break open the human experience and find the dry truth hidden at its center. Their work had taught them both that the truth, once discovered, was usually of little use; men denied what they had done, forgot what they had believed, and made the same mistakes over and over again. Brewster and Chase were valuable because they had learned how to predict and use the mistakes of others.

On Chase's last day as a Marine something went wrong. Just as MacArthur's X Corps rolled over the few defenders at Incheon and threatened to trap the main North Korean army, Chase's squad was encircled by a rogue battalion. Chase knew he'd be captured the moment it started. He knew they'd succeed. They never gave up. Chase knew that the North Koreans were not drugged or mad or gripped by a religious ecstasy. They fought as they did, caring nothing about dying, because it seemed obvious to them that dying was the natural consequence of charging an American machine-gun position. Their bravery was an alien form of intelligence, dazzling but incomprehensible.

There was a tremendous explosion above his head, a bloom of red flame and yellow smoke. Shrapnel rained down on his company. The Koreans had brought up a mortar. Three more shells burst in the branches, then the rounds began to walk up the hill toward their position as the Korean mortar crew shortened their range. Chase had been wounded in half a dozen places by the ricocheting shrapnel. Nausea flooded his body.

He took the scorched muzzle of a Bren Mk I light machine gun into his mouth and felt a horrifying pain, filled with flame and noise, inside his skull.

3

The Korean interrogator couldn't understand his name.

"Say your name!" he shouted.

"Jonathan Chase."

The interrogator drove a fist, surprisingly hard and sharp-knuckled, into Chase's naked stomach.

"Say your name!"

Chase had never for a moment been blessed with the illusion that he was dead. He had known, touching the muzzle of the Bren with his swollen tongue, that he had not pulled the trigger. He realized, at the moment in which he felt the pain of the blow, that a Korean soldier had crept up behind him and smashed a rifle butt against the back of his head. He had known in that instant, before he lost consciousness, that what was now happening to him was surely going to happen to him; if the Koreans had not wanted him for some reason or other, they would have shot him.

His captors had cleaned his wounds and given him rice and water. Now, even as they beat him and shouted at him, Chase could not suppress his admiration for them. They seemed to think well of him, too, in their way; the interrogator had told him, grunting out the English words in a matter-of-fact tone of voice, that he had killed twenty-eight Korean soldiers and wounded fifteen others with the Bren Mk I. The Koreans giggled; laughing at death seemed to be their way of displaying emotion.

The interrogator had got Chase's name, rank, and serial number written down in English when Colonel Zhao came into the picture. The Chinese colonel always wore a priest's cassock and a beret. He had a facial twitch; his cheek moved, causing the right eye to open like a caged owl's. Chase had never seen an Asian with such an affliction.

With the door closed and the lights reflecting from its polished white walls, the interrogation room looked like the inside of a dry skull. Chase, naked, was tied by his wrists to a ring in the wall. When the door opened, Chase closed his eyes. Zhao turned off the overhead lights. Only the table lamp, fitted with a brilliant photographic bulb, was burning. Colonel Zhao stood behind the lamp in the shadows. He removed a large hypodermic syringe from a leather case, and holding his hands in the light, filled it from an ampoule of yellow liquid. He laid the syringe on a white towel. Then he focused the lamp on Chase's face.

"You are no longer in Korea, Mr. Chase. This is An-Tung. Manchuria. A very unhealthy place," Zhao said in perfect English.

"You'll get nothing from me."

"Oh, but it's not information I want, you see. It's your services that I require."

The colonel put a chair in the center of the room, in front of the table, and untied Chase's hands. Chase sat with one flaccid leg wrapped around the other; his body shook and he wedged his hands between his crossed legs.

"I want you to understand your situation. It's possible for you to remain in this room indefinitely. Conditions will not change, except to get worse. No one will find you."

Chase stopped trying to control his shivering. "They'll find me," he said, "and when they do, you bastards..."

"No. You can forget about being rescued. It's not realistic. The war is over. Your people have better things to do."

The colonel's twitch became more active, and he placed a hand, ropy with age, over his cheek. With his other hand he tapped the glass barrel of the syringe.

"This needle is filled with the live bacteria of Hansen's disease."

Chase's eyes were fixed on the syringe.

"Hansen's disease is caused by the *Myobacterium leprae,* which is more usually called leprosy. It's a peculiar disease. The incubation period varies greatly. Sometimes the disease develops in a year or two after infection, but sometimes fifteen years can pass before any symptoms appear..."

Colonel Zhao called out a phrase in Chinese. A young woman entered, rummaged in a box and brought him an envelope filled with white powder. He turned his head away and snuffled heroin into his nostrils. In a moment his cheek quietened, and he composed himself.

"All that time, the germ works inside the body. It takes various forms. It causes madness, loss of sexual potency, loss of bowel control, and so on.

"I require your body alone, Mr. Chase. Its capacity to kill. This has nothing to do with your army. There's no question of your betraying them—I've no interest in them or their activities."

The colonel's twitch had stopped altogether. The heroin had had an effect and also, Chase saw, it was not the present that drove the man's nerves out of control, but a memory. He put his hands in the sleeves of his soutane and gazed at Chase.

"I'll tell you what I want. I want an American assassin."

A very old Korean entered the room. A black uniform with a yellow sash hung loosely over his skinny frame. A few white wisps of hair floated gently around his face. The skin was wrinkled like old parchment.

Colonel Zhao, almost deferentially, fell in behind the man.

"Jeong, this is Jonathan Chase, your new student."

Chase stared. "What's he going to teach me?"

"To kill," Zhao said. "To be an indestructible, unstoppable, nearly invisible killing machine."

"What's his line?"

"Murder," Zhao said calmly. "If he wanted, you would be dead now, before you could blink."

"So what do you need me for if you've got him?"

"His skin. Jeong can almost disappear but he's not invisible. Can you hear witnesses in your country or Europe saying they saw a yellow wisp of a man near every assassination we carry out? The Western cheap press would have a field day with such a phantom."

An American assassin. Set loose in his own country. Chase wondered if Colonel Zhao and his masters were really interested in results. Perhaps they were only interested in the idea, the style of the thing. Spending the end of the war in secret work on a secret weapon would be something to make themselves envied with. Were they actually naive enough to believe their brainwashing technique was so effective he'd really go through with it after his return?

This world of torture and secrets and secret assassins was a region of the mad, in which men such as these created distorted works out of the flesh of living persons and said—believed—that the result was just. It was like watching the inmates of an asylum daub an army of stick figures onto an enormous canvas, using buckets of blood for paint.

Chase played along with painful care.

For a week, Jeong only talked. There were no direct instructions on Chase's new trade. "I am supposed to teach you how to kill. This would be very simple if killing were simply walking up to your victim and striking him. But it's not always that way.

"Unfortunately, it takes many years to build an expert. And I do not have many years in which to train you. Once I was given a man from the KGB and told to train him in two weeks. I pleaded that this was not enough time; that he was not ready. They would not listen. And he lived but two weeks."

On the dirty floor of a Manchurian barn, Chase learned how to sit properly, to bow, to show respect, and to release an opponent in distress. The first two weeks were devoted to learning proper falls, the *katas,* or dance steps, and the means to unbalance an opponent. Once these basics were understood, Chase began the advanced training. He learned to choke an opponent, to lock his arms, to break his extremities.

"For a young man with instincts as quick as your own," Jeong explained, "you will see the kick coming as if it were suspended. All you must do is step back or to the side and watch your assailant lose his balance. Never allow yourself to be cornered. Instead keep moving forward to corner your man. At the same time, wait for him to attack. Defend yourself so surely that your one and only blow serves its purpose. Never square off with him within the length of his legs. Never allow him to grab you from the front. To do so is merely to wrestle with him, to create a sport with him. I will show you how to protect yourself against an attacker who grabs you from the rear, who clutches your neck, your arms. You will learn to bend at the knee, to use the fulcrum of your hip. These tactics must be automatic."

Chase came to understand profoundly that the ability to overpower an opponent did not belong to the young or the athletic but to those with secret knowledge. The skills he learned from Jeong gave him the confidence to relax and recognize danger. This power made him humble.

"When you learn the art of extending this power through your hands and through your feet, you will learn, too, to extend it through inanimate objects. In the hands of an expert, all things are deadly weapons." Jeong showed Chase how to make knives of paper and deadly darts of paper clips. How much more he could have shown Chase went unanswered. For Chase—using Jeong's expertise—killed him with his bare hands and fled the camp at three o'clock one morning.

Over the next few years, Jonathan Chase made his way through Mongolia, China, and India on foot the way a natural athlete plays a sport: he knew the game in his muscles and in his bloodstream. To drop cover was to lose; thought was a handicap, emotion a hazard. The time went quickly.

Jeong was dead; but Colonel Zhao lived on.

In Frankie Farmer's water bed, Chase turned on his side and tried to sleep. When at last blessed darkness swallowed his consciousness, he still did not rest. He dreamed, and his dreams were of a lost boy in the jungle.

He woke with a start. Light showed in a glimmer through the curtains. Turning to look at the TAG Heuer Monaco on the night table, Chase saw it was almost 5:45.

"Late to bed, early to rise." Frankie giggled, her hand moving under the sheets to add point to her humor.

Chase gazed down at her, breaking into a winning smile. She reached up, kissed him, and they began just where they had left off the night before, until the phone rang. His flight was in two hours.

"Damn," breathed Frankie. "Can't they ever leave you alone?"

–2–

Chase parked the '67 Triumph TR4 in a garage near the Grand Place, the magnificent square that is considered the centerpiece of Brussels. Bordered on all four sides by icons of Belgium's royal history, the Place is a dazzling display of ornamental gables, gilded facades, medieval banners, and gold-filigreed rooftop sculptures. The Gothic Town Hall, dating back to the early 1400s, remains intact; the other buildings, the neo-Gothic King's House and the Brewers' Guild House, date from the late 1600s. The Brussels aldermen continue to meet in the Town Hall, the exterior of which is decorated in part by fifteenth- and sixteenth-century insider's jokes. The sculptures include a group of drinking monks, a sleeping Moor and his harem, a heap of chairs resembling the medieval torture called *strappado,* and St. Michael slaying a female-breasted devil. Chase had once heard a story that the architect, Jan van Ruysbroeck, committed suicide by leaping from the belfry when he realized that it was off center and had an off-center entrance.

It was nearly two o'clock. Chase wore pin cord jeans in dark green, a light blue button-down under a navy herringbone sport coat, and a pair of well-worn loafers. He put on a pair of prescription Ray-Bans that would identify him to his contact, then walked southwest through the colorful and narrow cobblestoned streets to the intersection of Rue du Chêne and Rue de l'Étuve. There, surrounded by camera-snapping tourists, was the famous statue of the urinating boy known as Manneken-Pis. Although not the original statue, the current idol is an exact replica and is perhaps the most well-known symbol of Brussels. Chase didn't know what its origins were, but he knew that it dated from the early 1400s and was perhaps the effigy of a patriotic Belgian lad who sprinkled a hated Spanish sentry who had passed beneath his window. Another story was that he had saved the Town Hall from a small fire by extinguishing it using the only means available. Today, "Little Julian," as he is called, was dressed in a strange red cloak with a white fur collar. Louis XV began the tradition of presenting colorful costumes to the little boy and since then he has acquired hundreds of outfits.

"He must have a very large bladder to keep peeing like that," a female voice said in English, but with a thick European accent.

Chase glanced to his left and saw an attractive woman dressed in a close-fitting gray wool two-piece suit with green piping. She was also wearing Ray-Bans; she had strawberry-blond, short, curly hair and a light cream complexion; and her sensual lips were painted with light red lipstick. A toothpick was lodged at the corner of her mouth. She appeared to be around thirty, and she had the figure of a fashion model.

"I'm just glad this isn't considered a drinking fountain," Chase replied.

She removed the sunglasses to reveal bright blue eyes that sparkled in the sunlight. She held out her hand and said, "Marijke Van de Velde. Station B."

Chase took her hand, which felt smooth and warm. "Jonathan Chase."

"Come on," she said, gesturing with her head, "let's drop your things at the station house before we go to the embassy." Her English was good, but Chase could tell she wasn't terribly comfortable with it.

"*Parlez-vous Français?*" he asked.

"*Oui,*" she said, then switched back to English, "but my first language is Dutch, Flemish. You speak Dutch?"

"Not nearly as well as you speak English," he replied.

"Then let's stick to English, I need the practice."

She was not beautiful, but Chase found her very appealing. The short, curly hairstyle gave her a pixielike quality that most people would describe as cute, an adjective Chase tried to avoid. She was petite, but walked with confidence and grace, as if she were six feet tall.

She led him into a very narrow street off Petite Rue des Bouchers, near the famous folk puppet showcase Theatre Toone, and into a pastry shop. The smell of baked goods was overpowering.

"Care for a cream puff?" she asked.

He smiled and said, "Later, perhaps."

Marijke said something in Flemish to the woman behind the counter, then led Chase through a door, into a kitchen, where a large, sweating man was loading a tray of rolls into an oven. She went through another door to a staircase that led to a second-floor loft: the headquarters of Station B.

It was a comfortable one room/one bathroom flat that had been transformed into an office, just barely large enough for an operative and some equipment. In addition to the usual encryption machine, file cabinets, and copier, there was a sofa bed, a television, and kitchenette. It was decorated with a decidedly feminine touch, and there was an abundance of Belgian lace draped over the furniture.

"I don't live here, but the sofa bed is handy if I ever have to stay late," she said as they entered. "Have a seat anywhere. You want something to drink?"

"Coca-Cola with ice, please. Before we do anything, though, I have to check something."

Chase reached for the phone and removed from the inside pocket of his jacket his cigarette lighter. He pulled out a three-inch antenna from its base and flicked a tiny switch. He scanned the phone with the detector.

"I do that every morning, Mr. Chase," Marijke said. "With more sophisticated equipment."

"I doubt it could do much better than this little toy," Chase said, satisfied with the reading he got. The GSS 870V Bug Alert was always accurate. "Sorry, I had to check."

Chase stretched back in the large reclining leather armchair behind the desk. Right on cue, Marijke brought his Coke and a bottle of Orval beer for herself. She sat on the sofa bed and put her feet up. Chase noticed she wore no stockings.

He held up his glass and said, "Cheers." He took a sip of the ice cold liquid and was reminded of America in the summertime. "Well done."

"Thanks. I heard you were hard to impress."

"Quite the opposite. America is such a bore most of the time, we're really quite easy."

Marijke managed to keep the toothpick sticking out of her mouth as she drank her beer. Chase noticed how fit she really was. Her shapely, strong leg muscles could be traced past the beginning of her skirt. Her arms were also well toned. Although she was dressed a tad conservatively for the times—certainly hadn't heard of the Chelsea Look—the toothpick gave her an impish, mischievous quality. There was no mistaking that this woman was streetwise. She was a mature little Peter Pan with breasts, which also happened to be quite shapely.

"So tell me about our man at the embassy."

"Neville Scott? What do you want to know? He's a bore. Wears college ties. Smokes a pipe. Makes lots of awkward passes at the ladies."

"Is he a capable interrogator?"

"I'll let you decide."

✦

They were passing through the outlying streets of Brussels, past gray buildings, under rows of young plane trees prematurely pruned for winter so that they looked like cactus growing in the wrong country. As they went through the gates of the British Embassy and were at once on British territory, Marijke held out her left hand while she steered with her right. Chase returned the wallet containing false documentation to his jacket pocket. The emissary, a stony-faced middle-aged man who offered no name, whisked Marijke and Chase through security. The way had been prepared; the embassy personnel were deferential and inspected nothing.

Neville Scott wore a dove-gray billycock bowler hat like Winston Churchill's, and he left it on his head while he sipped Scotch whisky with Chase in his office. Scott had remarkable facial hair: thick flaxen eyebrows and a matching Hitlerian mustache. In these strange Belgian precincts, he was utterly at ease. His legs were crossed at the ankles, and his feet, encased in glossy oxfords, rested on the table. He seemed to want to look like a young minister of the Crown, lounging on the front bench at question time in Parliament, dealing jauntily with attacks from the opposition. In the peculiar English way of breaking the ice with a stranger, he asked Chase a series of rude personal questions.

"Whatever made you decide to work for that two-bit gangster Brewster?"

"Good health insurance."

"Don't you ever long for civilization, tucked away in Washington, munching on hamburgers and listening to hippies strum their guitars?"

Chase did not answer; he knew that this waggish interrogation must run its course. In Scott's mind, Chase saw, Britain was still an empire. He drank three glasses of whisky and talked about Berlin. He had been a famous young operative there in the postwar years. And he liked to deal with Germans—they were always on time and they liked to be trained.

Twenty minutes later, Chase was following the still-pontificating Brit down into the basement hold of the embassy, pleasantly surprised at the arrangements that had been made for his interrogation of Lazarus. The box in which the prisoner was confined was wired for sound and state-of-the-art closed-circuit television. Neville Scott sat Chase down in front of a row of monitors and switched it on. Lazarus's face, familiar to Chase because, courtesy of Number One, he had seen so many photographs of it, appeared immediately in full color. The eyes were dull, the face slack. He was seated in a metal chair, his wrists and ankles secured by heavy straps.

"Our interrogators have used sleeplessness, drugs, the polygraph, and endless relays of questioners. He has made no attempt to evade the questions. We've mostly been satisfied with his answers. Once a week we show him a documentary film about a mental hospital in Kiev. The hopelessly insane are confined there in conditions of unbelievable filth and squalor. The film shows them fight, copulate, defecate and smear themselves with feces. No one is ever released from this place. It seems to have *some* effect on him. It's a kind of brainwashing technique devised by academics..."

Chase listened to Scott reaffirm to himself the evidence his investigation had gathered. All the evidence, that is, that the Englishman saw fit to consider. Existing simultaneously with the evidence that confirmed Her Majesty's Servant's suspicions was a second body of evidence, like a planet identical to Earth on the other side of the sun, which just as conclusively demonstrated that his conclusions were incorrect. Chase could see what Neville Scott hadn't the equipment to see. It wasn't his fault; it was in the nature of the equipment.

"Is he drugged now?" Chase interrupted finally.

"He's hung over from all the drugs, but the effects have worn off," Scott replied. "He may be a little disoriented."

"Does he remember being drugged?"

"Yes, of course. But in theory he doesn't remember what he said to us under the influence."

"What did he spill?" Chase asked.

"It's all on film. We have an unedited copy for you. In brief, we've confirmed all the names and faces of Lazarus's network. Also details of the network's organization and training."

Neville Scott had a high-pitched boyish voice and now that he had abandoned his junior minister pose, he crackled like a school-boy with mischief and caginess. Scott waited alertly for Chase's next question. Knowing the right question to ask was a test of breeding; Chase had the impression that he would be admitted to some sort of club if he asked it.

Scott was the kind of spy, Chase could see, who did things primarily for the fun of it. The kind of spy who had come to look on his work, in the field at least, largely as sport. Lazarus provided an opportunity to match wits with the opposition. But Scott knew from the start he would win: he had physical control of the agent. All the opposition had, as far as Scott was concerned, was Lazarus and a bunch of deluded tramps who couldn't think for themselves to maintain decent security.

"Confirmed? That means we already knew all that. What else?"

"More confirmation. Lazarus did in fact come to Switzerland to turn those maniacs loose. Moscow has no channels to communicate with the rogues. Wouldn't want to if they could. They're cut off, on their own."

"On their own?"

"The Russians want total deniability." Chase looked toward Scott, but not at him, deliberately avoiding eye contact.

"I don't think we're dealing with the Russians. An independent group perhaps, calling themselves Zero Directorate. Second: there must have been, at some point, a hit list. Otherwise how do they make their choices?"

Scott blanched at the mention of Zero Directorate. Chase heard his heart beating in his ears. Of course it was possible. It was so brilliantly simple. Why hadn't he thought of it sooner?

"Lazarus insists that no such list exists. The whole operation was designed to be random, unpredictable, with no two actions resembling each other." Scott tilted his billycock bowler over his flaxen eyebrows and gave Chase a conspiratorial smile.

As Chase listened to Scott, it dawned on him: there was something wrong here. The British were too easily satisfied with the paltry results yielded by their superficial interrogation methods. They never went all the way to the bottom of a prisoner's mind because in their hearts they did not believe that any enemy was truly dangerous to them. But this was more than the usual sloppiness, this was more akin to a willful ignorance of motive. One could almost say a fear of discovery.

Chase looked across the monitor panel at Neville Scott and said, "I'd like to ask Lazarus a few simple questions before you ship him off. Without drugs."

Scott looked furious, but turned his hands palm upward in a gesture of generosity. "Be my guest."

2

After almost five years of inducing confessions from people like Lazarus, Jonathan Chase held certain basic principles. All spies are liars, it is their métier, and like ordinary liars they live in panic, knowing that the truth about themselves may be discovered at any moment—or worse, is already known by people who are too disgusted, or too clever, to confront them with it. A spy under questioning by the enemy is in a state surpassing dread because he knows that he must sooner or later tell the truth. His captors will use any means to get it out of him, and sooner or later he will spill what he knows because he cannot stand the pain, or because he is so exhausted that he will do anything for sleep, or because he wants to have the long-festering secret in his breast removed by his interrogator as a tumor on the lung is excised by a surgeon, permitting the patient to breathe freely with at least one lung. He is only valuable, and therefore alive, so long as he does not talk. The worst thing he can imagine is that the person who is asking him questions already knows the truth.

This was Lazarus's case. He may not have known what he had been asked or what he had answered while under the influence of drugs, but he knew that he had been under their influence. What had he done? What had he spilled? Why did he feel so guilty?

Chase did not share Brewster's faith in the polygraph; too many categories of human beings were immune to it. Africans, Asians, and psychopaths laughed at it. As a practical matter it only worked on people who came from cultures that controlled human behavior by instilling guilt and mandating supernatural punishment. It had no power over those who were not possessed of a Western conscience. Chase connected the polygraph to Lazarus because he was a Communist and probably also a vestigial Christian as nearly all Russians were, and therefore the creature of the two most implacably confessional faiths ever invented.

Chase attached Lazarus to the lie detector and put the machine where the prisoner could see the needles. The machine, autopens whispering over the graph paper without human intervention, would remind him of what he had to do in order to be saved. In terms of the sequence of questions, unlike Scott, or Scott's pretended methods, Chase did not believe in dancing around the point.

"When did you join the cell of terrorists called 'Zero Directorate'?"

Lazarus flinched at Chase's words. He was obviously wrestling with himself. His skin had a reddish shine, as though discontent had burned away its outer layers.

"There is no Zero Directorate."

Chase caused a grin to cover his face, as if he knew a joke too delicious to conceal. Chase went on speaking, as if prolonging the joke.

"What did you say? Look at the machine. It knows; the pens are going crazy. Do you think we don't know when you're lying? Do you think we don't remember what you told us when you were drugged? If you can't tell us the truth while you're conscious, I can't help you. Other drugs will be used. The questions will continue. How else can we know that you're sincere? How else can we help you? Answer me. Why is the cell called 'Zero Directorate'?"

"The Dark One," Lazarus croaked, barely able to speak; he had had nothing to drink for hours. Chase knew that a man who is trained to keep secrets can be counted upon, when at last he breaks his oath of silence, to tell everything he knows. He feels remorse, guilt, shame at being caught: he is an outcast; imprisonment is a relief. The spy will reveal the true names of his superiors and his agents; he will suggest ways to destroy his own networks.

He will bore his interrogators, who until the day before were his enemies, with the details of his thefts, betrayals, unauthorized murders, sexual vices. Lazarus had just reached that point. He understood that the man asking him questions already knew the answers.

"Which dark one?"

Lazarus twisted his neck down to the polygraph, the kilometers of tape covered with jagged peaks drawn by the automatic pen. He cleared his throat, long and convulsively.

"Give him water," Chase said.

He raised his colorless eyes from the polygraph, let them linger on Chase's face. Chase remembered a thousand interrogations and a thousand men with eyes like these. Men who suddenly sensed how close they were to a world they'd rather not consider, where only the iron force of alien authority vested in men like him could give them immunity against the nightmare fates of barbed wire and silhouetted guards and special windowless trains bound for the camps in the Komi Republic.

Half a life is better than none, the prisoner thinks. But he knows that this is a delusion. There is nothing waiting for him after the ordeal is over, not even half a life. This is his choice: if he does not yield he will die; and if he yields, he will die.

Chase realized, in that moment, that he had become the Russian's entire world.

"Don't you get it? Spies. Not countries. Not races. Spies. They were always the real target. He wants them to release all their secrets. To destroy the whole idea of espionage altogether. He would do it with or without the Directorate. He created the Directorate just to do what he would have done in any case."

"What spies?"

"His goal is to kill them all, all of them, like the Final Solution for spies."

Chase contemplated the meaning of the prisoner's words. "Who?"

The Russian's face went cold as he looked up at Chase.

"The Mirza."

✦

In the bathroom of the British Embassy Chase checked the place as well as possible, screening himself from any mirrors, examining walls and ceiling for any hint of the pinhole lens of a fiber-optic camera. When he was satisfied, he took off his canvas belt and opened the inner lining, which contained a miniature shortwave transmitter, the Winkelmann Model 300, complete with a tiny tape recorder, all held in place by Velcro straps.

Checking that the mini-cassette had been recording, he pressed stop on the battery-powered tape recorder and rewound. When it was done, he returned the recorder to its hiding place and put the tape inside the transmitter, which he set to the required frequency before that was also slipped back into the belt's lining.

He made a last check to be sure his finger could reach the concealed transmitter. Then he went back to join Marijke.

It was only when they left Station B that Chase pressed the transmit button. He was certain the range would be right as the sudden two-second squirt-transmission leaped silently and invisibly into the air, guided straight to the heart of the American Embassy.

Back at the Metropole, Chase was given a suite on the fifth floor. He unpacked his bag and removed an electric toothbrush. He snapped off the brush and unscrewed the bottom of the device. Chase let the scrambling device—a VL22H, which could be used on any telephone in the world and allowed only the legitimate receiving party to hear the caller en clair—fall into his palm. Eavesdroppers of any kind heard only sounds that were completely indecipherable, even if they tapped it with a compatible system, for each VL22H had to be individually programmed. It was standard I-Division practice for its three agents—on duty or leave—out of the country to carry one, and the access codes were altered daily.

Chase was not calling to report. Thanks to the Winkelmann Model 300, Brewster would have already heard a recording of the interrogation. Chase was making the call to see the result of the Division's analysis of his work with Lazarus.

Brewster came on the line straight away from his narrow brick residence on the quiet street near Washington Circle.

"Don't say anything, Chase, just listen. You have new instructions."

"Of course."

"We've decided to lead the enemy to the target of our choice."

"How exactly?"

"By removing every target except the one we want them to hit," Brewster replied.

"I understand the principle. But you're talking about a lot of people. CIA has stations, bases, and deep-cover operations in every country in the world."

"Obviously, and therein lies the rub. Without warning, we've issued a blanket order to clear all the embassies of CIA, break contact with every agent in the world, explaining nothing, creating unbearable curiosity. Then putting somebody out in the open—in the danger zone—and waiting for Zero Directorate to strike."

"You mean baiting the trap with real agents who know real secrets?"

"I mean baiting the trap with you."

"That would keep the tiger's attention on the goat until we can get in a shot."

"Do you remember Jim Proctor, Number Two?"

"Proctor?"

"You met him at Fisher's Island. My aide-de-camp."

"Sure."

"He's my institutional memory."

"And?"

"And he's quantified everything. He's figured out, off the books of course, which international agents in the field have the most to lose."

There was no need for Brewster to explain the underlying meaning of his words. If Jonathan Chase's memory was emptied by Zero Directorate like the others who had been kidnapped, the U.S. intelligence services could not continue to exist. In his role as I-Division watchdog, he simply knew too much.

"You mean the most secrets to spill, don't you, chief?"

"Exactly. Want to know where you land? Bronze medal."

"Only third?"

"Both Proctor and the supercomputers put two operatives in front of you: a Russian called Yuri Konstantinov and a British agent named Harriet Ashdown."

"If you're looking for ants, go find yourself a picnic."

"KGB and MI6. We need those two out of the way if the opposition is going to come after you."

"Last time I checked the British were still our allies, sir."

"Exceptional circumstances, Number Two."

"No matter who they are, what they do? No matter whether they're working against the U.S. or not?"

"We don't do politics, Chase. We keep the water clean."

"Pretty short-term way of thinking."

"We're in a short-term business."

"By killing them, I make myself the target."

"Correct."

"This is the place where I become the international mercenary of my trade?"

"Amoral and without motive beyond that of your government's gratification."

"Wonderful."

"Number Two, I need you to rediscover some of that old clinical objectivity of yours. And go to Frankfurt while you're at it."

Chase put down the phone and sat there feeling oddly detached. The scenario, as he understood it, had a dreamlike, nightmarish quality. He knew the devil incarnate in Brewster would promise the world for hard intelligence, and then give the source of the supply a very small plot of earth.

He unhooked the VL22H. Already he knew that his life was possibly forfeit for those other two spies. If there was no other way, then he would have to die. He also knew that he would go on to the bitter end, taking risks, but in the last resort . . . they would have to see.

It crossed his mind that he had nothing to go on when it came to the Zero Directorate but assumptions and the ramblings of a Russian. He began to run the shower, closed the door and started to strip. He could guess at the truth, seizing facts as a pack of hunting animals will rip mouthfuls of meat from a large beast they have surrounded in the dark. He could assume that everyone was an enemy and a liar. Or he could believe nothing, especially not a concrete fact. Concrete, Brewster was fond of saying, could be poured into any shape. He and his colleagues never knew anything for certain. Sometimes it felt like a weakness.

Naked, he went back into the main room for his Dunhill lighter, which he placed on the floor, under a couple of hand towels, just outside the shower. Then, after testing the water to check it was not too scalding for him to bear, Chase stepped under the spray, closed the sliding door, and began to soap himself, rubbing his body vigorously with a rough towel.

It was the nature of Chase's work that he never knew how matters were going to turn out. He began and ended in the dark and mostly did not mind it. But there was an overlay of efficiency in everything I-Division and the other American intelligence agencies did. He was almost convinced there was no more intelligent or unemotional group of people on earth. That, Chase thought now, was their principal weakness. Because their people were so bright, because their resources were so huge, they consistently tinkered with reality.

The Lazarus situation was a classic example of this tendency. They began with a vague suspicion: that Lazarus was a Russian agent arming terrorists in Western Europe. Tentative conclusion: he will soon go to ground. Obvious question: what is the true purpose of his assignment?

What they had at the beginning was a set of assumptions. It was proper to test those assumptions. After all, that was their job. But the testing process—calling up their own resources and those of friendly services all over the world—created an almost irresistible psychological force. They were experts in suspicion. They searched diligently for evidence that would confirm their suspicions. To transform a supposition into a fact was the sweetest reward a spy could know. Chase did it all the time, and usually he was right.

He was trained to regard all behavior as cover. At no time at Station B did he spontaneously believe anything Lazarus said to him or indicated to him through his overt personal conduct. But he had an instinctive feeling that all the indications that he was telling the truth were, just possibly, there.

The problem was: it was instinctive. There was no way to argue a feeling in cables and dispatches, or even in clandestine conversations with a case officer whose proper function is to discount the emotional reactions of his agent. Chase knew all too well that Brewster would be primarily interested in information that was stripped of the background noise created by the personality of the source.

It was like living in the future, Brewster had told him. From training onward, out there in the future, you learn two languages—one is heard with the ear, the other with the back of the neck.

In the end, his training brought him around to the conclusion that if the Zero Directorate existed, then Lazarus was, in fact, an agent.

And Neville Scott was his handler.

There was no other rational explanation for many of the things the Englishman did: the reluctance to let Chase anywhere near Lazarus, his shock at the mention of Zero Directorate, the mixture of self-revelation in unimportant matters and obsessive secrecy in others he used to confuse the matter at hand. In a conflict between instinct and what appears to be objective evidence the latter must always win.

In order to make any headway with Zero Directorate, Chase had to believe that Neville Scott was an enemy. Otherwise his activity, for all its surface of cleverness and technique, would be wasted. To keep his attentions on Lazarus would not be a return to objectivity, but a flight from it. Not to turn toward Neville Scott as the truly interesting party would be a turn away from a search for the truth. It was the only way to go to achieve operational results.

Concentrate on this: why, if the Zero Directorate wanted to provide an extremely sensitive operation with Lazarus as principal agent, would they send him to Milan with gold ingots sewn in his clothes? Why expose him—virtually confirm his identity—to such an array of enemies? Answer: because they knew Scott was leading the team that would nab him. Answer: they had people everywhere and weren't afraid to lose the grunts who did the kidnapping, the killing, and the filming, if they could protect assets like Lazarus and Scott. Thinking: Marijke worked with Scott at Station B.

Picturing Lazarus tied to that metal chair, Chase saw in his mind's eye all of the complex machinery that had produced this simple result.

Allowing the water to cool quickly, he stood under an almost ice-cold shower. The shock hit him, like a man walking from the warmth of his home into a blizzard. Thinking: perhaps civilization is going into a long night. Perhaps: history is one long prank designed to be played on this generation.

He turned off the water, shaking himself like a dog. He rubbed his face with the towel and reached out to open the sliding door. As he did so, Chase became suddenly alert, his extra intuitive senses clicking on like a guidance system. In a fraction of a second he could almost smell danger nearby, and before his hand touched the door handle the lights went out, leaving him disoriented for a second, and in that second his hand missed the handle, although he heard the door slide open a fraction and close again with a thud.

They are after me all right. I hear it here. He touched the back of his neck.

This time, in the darkness, he knew he was not alone. There was something in the shower with him, brushing his face, his body, and the sides of the shower.

They have people everywhere, he thought.

The panic all but transferred itself to Chase, who scrabbled for the door with one hand, whirling the towel about his face and body to ward off the unseen evil. When his fingers closed over the handle and pulled, the door opened.

A second later, the lights went on again. He was aware of his own reflection in the bathroom mirror, but could not see his adversary.

✦

The exodus had begun. The spies were leaving the embassies like pieces in some abstract, nihilistic game. The CIA had broken contact with every agent in Western Europe. Entire operations closing themselves down. Fragmenting. No orders from Langley. Whole networks vanishing in broad daylight with attaché cases full of coded address lists, transcripts of conferences on weaponry, data on the Communist penetration of foreign labor movements. These were men and women whose brains were maps. Who, under duress, could recapitulate underground fuel transport systems and the orbital patterns of satellites. On telephones across the continent exotic work names like *Crystal, Ariel, Orphan,* and *Sulphur* were worked into conversations about going to ground.

Making his way down the Rue de la Loi, Chase could almost feel it in the air: his fellow agents fading with willowy grace into the background chatter of diplomatic receptions or on the crowded bourgeois avenues. Trying not to panic and not doing the greatest job of it. The fact was, they'd all been marked. In a sense, he'd just taken them off the endangered species list. *Dodger, Tester, Cobweb:* these were the cryptonyms of famous men; Brewster had recruited and handled them all. To the unwitting, they were prime ministers and statesmen. In fact, they were aspects of Brewster. They had run every kind of operation in the book, from dangles to false flags, deceptions and even the odd honey trap. Their history was the history of the Cold War and now they were quietly disappearing.

People in disguise, agencies in disguise, nations in disguise.

Chase tried to picture it all in his mind, but the only way to untangle the mess was to take each strand of the human web and follow it through the myriad patterns from its source to its destination, adding up the information and silence from the chess players in Washington as one went along.

They'd left only him to cut the strings.

At Station B, Chase found Marijke wordlessly packing up shop. She said she had some coffee in the kitchenette. Her voice had begun to quaver. Chase made a quick decision about his order of questioning, deciding it would be best to show some very positive side before he tackled the really big problem: how well did she know Neville Scott and, particularly, how did his interactions with Lazarus strike her?

"You've got a car near here, Marijke?"

She had a car.

"I may well ask a favor of you—later."

"I hope so." She gave him a brave come-on smile.

"Okay. Before we get down to that, there are more important things." Chase fired the obvious questions at her—rapid shooting, pressing her for fast return answers, not giving her time to avoid anything or think about answers.

Had Scott ever talked to her about friends or colleagues in Brussels since they had first met? Of course. Had he done the same about friends or colleagues in Britain? Yes. Could she remember the number of people he had mentioned? She gave some names, obvious ones—people with whom they both worked at Station B. Did she have any memory of Scott mentioning Chase himself? That was quite possible, but Marijke could give no details.

Chase moved to recent events. Had anyone been with her before their rendezvous by the fountain that afternoon? No. Was there any way she could have been followed? Possibly. Had she spoken to anyone after dropping him at his hotel, mentioned that he was in Brussels, and meeting her again at eight? Only one person. "I canceled a dinner date with a girl, a colleague from another department. She used to be Neville's assistant, actually. We'd arranged to discuss some work over dinner."

This woman's name was Victoria Bailey, and Chase spent quite a long time getting facts about her. At last he lapsed into silence, stood up, and peered out the window.

"Is the interrogation over?" Marijke said.

"That wasn't an interrogation. One day, maybe, I'll show you an interrogation. Remember I said I may have to ask a favor?"

"Ask, and it will be given."

There was luggage at the hotel, Chase told her, and he had to go back to the embassy to check out Scott's office. Could she stay awake until about four in the morning, then drive to the hotel in her car, pay the bill, and meet him at the train station?

"Of course, Jonathan. I can even give you my key."

3

Neville Scott never believed or said or ate or drank or wore or displayed anything for any other purpose than to be admired by the best people. By this he meant conscientious objectors to capitalism and liberal democracy like himself who had been made rich by a system they despised. He loved the common people but lived in an imposing Mayfair house filled with the works of fashionable artists living and dead and owned a weather-beaten summer cottage in St. Ives, Cornwall. He played tennis on the Wimbledon courts, always using a Head Genesis racquet, and played golf in Scotland with Pine Eye II clubs. He owned two of the largest and most powerful German automobiles that British pounds sterling could buy, dressed in two-thousand-dollar suits tailored in Savile

Row, and loved to see Communist insurgents win wars of liberation. Now that the Vietnam War was in full swing he had the same sentimental admiration for Vietcong guerrillas as he had formerly had for Soviet dictators.

But he hated North Africa. It smelled of fish, the vast culture shock frightened him, he was suspicious of everyone he met, and it was hot. It was so hot that he was afraid the sweat would ruin the carefully applied makeup that enabled him to get to Morocco at all.

And he hated Jonathan Chase. If that psychotic boy scout—who looked so much like the actor Robert Redford in *Barefoot in the Park*—hadn't broken Lazarus, he wouldn't be here now groveling for his life.

At least Casablanca was a bit more Westernized than some other places Scott had been to for MI6. By far Morocco's largest city with a population of three million, it was the country's industrial center and port, and the most attractive tourist stop in western North Africa. As it was the place to go when Moroccans aspired to fame and fortune, Casablanca had all the trappings of a Western metropolis, with a hint of the decadent ambiance of southern European cities. Alongside the business suits, long legs, high heels, and designer sunglasses were the willowy robes of djellabas and burnooses of traditional Morocco.

Wearing a Turnbull and Asser suit much too heavy for the climate, Scott stepped out into the bright sunlight and donned his sunglasses. The heat was barely tolerable, and it was only midmorning. Frowning, he walked away from the Sheraton and went south on Rue Chaoui, ignoring the cluster of beggars, old and young, who reached out to people entering and exiting from the hotel.

He walked along what seemed to be a fairly modern street with Western architecture. The atmosphere completely changed two blocks away, when Scott entered the Central Market bazaar. Here he felt as if he'd walked into another century. As colorful and noisy as any Hollywood film depiction, the market was an overwhelming assault on the senses. Scott focused straight ahead, walking quickly through the mass of veils, fezzes, turbans, and fedoras. The visual display of the distinctive customs and clothing of local tribespeople who had come to buy and sell didn't excite him. He didn't want to buy fruits, vegetables, or spices.

Scott was drenched with sweat by the time he got all the way across the bazaar to its southeast corner where a dilapidated shanty was built against a larger stone building. A beggar, who seemed at least ninety years old, sat cross-legged on the dirt in front of the door, which was simply an open space in the wood covered by a cloth hanging from an eave. There was a bent metal dish next to the beggar. Scott knew he had to do something specific. He reached into his pocket and found ten dirhams in coins and dropped them into the tin. The old man mumbled something and gestured to the cloth. Scott turned to make sure no one was watching, then he ducked under the drape and went inside the shack.

It stank like a toilet. Scott was forced to take a handkerchief from his jacket pocket and hold it over his mouth. Other than the rancid smell, the room was empty. Scott immediately went to the stone wall and put his hand out to touch it. He felt the ridges along a crack, searching for a catch that couldn't be seen. He found it, then pushed it with the requisite force. The secret door slid open, revealing a passage lined in steel. Scott stepped through, and the door closed behind him.

At last! Air-conditioning! And hopefully his ticket out of this dreary place. If he could explain away the Chase situation, he might go on to the next phase of his life, which would resemble nothing of what he had left behind in England.

Scott knew, however, that the Mirza was capable of anything.

During the siege of Madrid, in the autumn and early winter of 1936, the Mirza—still in his teens—was, at one and the same time, an important agent for the Comintern, and the leader of the Fascist fifth column in Madrid. He lived both his roles fully, murdering efficiently to win the trust of those he was betraying.

Scott had heard the story years ago; it was a famous story in certain quarters of the secret world.

There was nothing, in all the stories he'd heard, to indicate the Mirza was anything but a skilled professional. When he was still in his twenties, he had saved a kingdom in the Near East by penetrating a revolutionary organization and turning it against itself, so that the terrorists murdered each other instead of their monarch. The king he saved was still his friend. Like all good intelligence officers, the Mirza had known how to form friendships and use the friends he made.

However, there were rumors of his having a weakness for the gadgetry of espionage. He equipped his agents with invisible ink, with luggage with secret compartments, with miniature radios, with codebooks that destroyed themselves when ampoules of acid concealed in their spines were crushed in the instant before capture. In his day, it was said, the Mirza had been a great field agent, a master smuggler. During the British mandate in Palestine, when he was a young officer in the Jewish Underground, he had carried a pistol through many checkpoints by taking it apart and taping the disassembled pieces to various parts of his body with flesh-colored tape to which he had glued body hair plucked from the thick mats of fur on his chest and back. Even when the British stripped him naked they did not discover the pistol. He used it to kill three people—two Arabs and a Sephardic Jew from London whom he suspected of being GRU, which was already, even then, trying to penetrate the future secret service of the unborn Jewish state.

An Arab dressed in fatigues appeared and gestured for Scott to follow him. It was unnerving, especially when the clank-clank of the man's boots on the metal floor echoed throughout the tunnel. The corridor took a right turn, and they went down eight steps to a wider, open area with a table, a supercomputer, banks of surveillance screens, and other sophisticated, high-tech equipment. Two more guards were waiting there.

"Spread your legs and arms," one of them said.

Scott did so while the other one ran a metal detector around his body.

"All right, he checks," said the second man. Scott's escort tapped his shoulder and led him around the table to a door. The guards pressed a button and released a lock. The escort pushed the door open and held it for Scott.

"The Mirza is waiting," he said.

The room was dark, long, and had a very low ceiling. The only illumination was provided by lamps hung over the five men and three women who sat at a conference table, each with a legal pad in front of them. One of them, Scott knew, would be Thinkingcap, the Mirza's right-hand man. There was no light hanging over the man at the head of the table, the one sitting in shadow.

The *Amirzad*. The Prince. The Mirza.

Scott had never met him face-to-face. Very few Zero Directorate agents had. The inner circle, those sitting around the table, were the only individuals so entitled. Nevertheless, it was still difficult to discern what the Mirza looked like. His silhouette disclosed that he was tall and broad-shouldered, but thin and fit. The face and hands were in shadow, but there was just enough illumination to reveal that he wore a beret and was dressed in dark military clothing. His face was further shielded by dark glasses that completely hid his eyes.

As the British spy walked into the room, conversation halted abruptly and everyone turned to look at him.

"Come in, Mr. Scott," the Mirza said. His voice was educated and smooth, and its deep timbre sounded vaguely British. If the man was indeed a Spanish Jew, he didn't sound like one anymore. "Sit down there at the end of the table. We have saved a seat for you."

Scott took the chair and swallowed. Now he was nervous as hell.

"It's good to meet you at last, Mr. Scott," the leader said. "We have been following your progress since the arrival of this American Chase with great interest. I congratulate you on your handling of Lazarus on behalf of Zero Directorate. It must not have been easy to find the courage to betray your country and hide one of our agents in plain sight."

The Mirza took a moment to extract a cigarette from a gun-metal case that he removed from the inside of his jacket. He kept his head straight, staring into Scott's eyes as he did so. The Mirza lit the cigarette with a gold-plated Rothman's lighter, took a deep drag, exhaled, and spoke again.

"Tell me, Mr. Scott," the Mirza said. "Do you know about the fuse on the bomb that was supposed to kill Adolf Hitler on July 20, 1944?"

Scott knew all about the bomb and the plot by German aristocrats to kill Hitler and end the war, but he shook his head no.

"This particular bomb had to be a time bomb, to allow the assassin time to get away," the Mirza said. "But it had to be silent, no ticking clock, because everything was very hushed in the presence of the Fuhrer. A special trigger was invented —a wire inside a glass capsule submerged in acid, inside a metal tube. When you crushed the tube with a pair of pliers, the glass capsule broke and the acid ate through the wire in a stated number of minutes, tripping the detonator. The technology was amazing for 1944. It made the conspirators feel very good. 'Look how much smarter we are than Hitler to have such a bomb,' they said to themselves. They were aristocrats, the flower of the German nobility, all vons and zus. The assassin, Colonel Count Klaus von Stauffenberg, smuggled the bomb into Hitler's presence in his briefcase. First, in the toilet, he broke the tube with his pliers, which wasn't easy because he only had one arm and one eye as a result of war wounds. He placed the briefcase at the target's feet, under the conference table, and left the room. Another man who knew nothing, suspected nothing, pushed the briefcase six inches across the floor because it was in his way. Because he did this, the briefcase with the bomb and its wonderful silent trigger was now in a different position—the leg of the table stood between Hitler and the bomb, so when it went off most of the force of the explosion was absorbed by the table leg. All that happened to Hitler was that his eardrums were broken and he suffered a little concussion. He thought the Teuton gods had saved him so that he could carry out his great destiny. His secret police tortured the bluebloods who had tried to kill him, then wrapped piano wire around their necks and hung them on meat hooks. His photographers made movies of them as they died, quite slowly, and Hitler watched these movies while maybe five million extra people, Jews mostly, died because he was still in charge and the war didn't end for another eleven months. What is the moral of the story, Mr. Scott?"

Scott eyed the Mirza anxiously. "Leave nothing to chance," he said.

"Unusually astute for an Englishman," the Mirza said. "When most people hear that story, they say there was something wrong with Stauffenberg's bomb. But there was nothing wrong with the bomb. It functioned perfectly. There was something wrong with the assassin. He was very brave, very daring. But he was a snob and he could not stop being a snob even to rid the world of a monster. He armed the bomb and excused himself. Not because he was afraid to die, but because Stauffenbergs don't die in the same room with scum like Hitler; it simply isn't done."

"Thank you, sir."

"Now, tell me about your progress. How long has the team trained together?" the Mirza asked.

Scott's pulse raced. Was this a trick question? He looked at his questioner. The Mirza was calm, casual. He was smiling now and searching Scott's face for reaction.

"More than a year."

"What is the age of those you've chosen?"

"Late twenties, early thirties."

"Too old. It is best to use teenagers or even children for this kind of work. Even twenty is too old."

Scott could feel the conversation turning toward something unpleasant. He felt the Mirza's eyes on him. His pause had been too long.

"But if they're older there's less chance they'll act on impulse."

"You guarantee results, is that what you're telling me?"

"No, sir. But there's no Stauffenberg factor."

The Mirza flicked a switch on the control panel in front of him and a bright photograph appeared on the back wall. It was a picture of two North Africans Neville Scott knew all too well.

He knows! Scott thought. My God, he knows!

"Mr. Scott, do you know these men on the screen behind me?"

Scott shook his head. "I've never seen them before."

"Never?"

"No, sir."

The Mirza flicked another switch on the control panel and the slide changed. This time it was a shot at an English pub, one that

Scott recognized. When he saw who was in the picture, his heart skipped a beat.

The two North African men were sitting with pints of lager talking to none other than himself.

"This photograph was taken in the Crown and Anchor public house near Aldershot. You know it well, don't you, Mr. Scott?"

Scott closed his eyes. It was all over.

"You hired these men, Zero Directorate employees, to make you a map of our private clinic in Marseille, did you not?"

"No—I—it's that I..." Scott was blubbering.

"Quiet!" The Mirza pushed another switch on the panel and the door behind Scott opened. One of the guards came in and stood behind him. Terribly frightened now, Scott glanced over his shoulder and back at the rest of the people at the table. They were all staring at him, expressionless.

"You were going to betray Zero Directorate, steal the specifications for some of our more sensitive installations, and make more money than we were paying you to mind Lazarus by selling them to some national intelligence service. You got greedy. Isn't that right, Mr. Scott?"

"No, sir. I mean yes, sir."

"You're a fool and an enemy of mankind, Mr. Scott. A disgusting hypocrite who has volunteered to believe and merchandise the lies both the Western powers and the Russian totalitarians have told the world about themselves, and are therefore an accessory to millions of political murders and other crimes against humanity. You are an intellectual slut, Mr. Scott. A clown, a whore, a sycophant. Six months ago you thought Brezhnev was the savior of the world because I told you so. This year you're wise to him because of what some kid in the American Embassy tells you. I could have you the same way I could have dumb girls in California—put my hand between your legs and tell you that I love you. You don't have a mind—you have a clitoris between your ears. You are an idealist, Mr. Scott. An idealist is a most dangerous thing. Idealists make brave agents, but they are bad intelligence officers. They cannot exist for long without the company of like minds; they have a need to speak their beliefs and to hear their beliefs spoken. You, Mr. Scott, wanted to talk and had no one to talk to. You tried to sell something you had no right to know. We did not tell you. How then did you know? You betrayed us, put us in danger."

The Mirza gave an imperceptible nod to the guard behind Scott.

The guard roughly grabbed Scott's hair with his left hand and pulled back his head.

"Where is this map, fool?"

"S...S...Switzerland!"

The Mirza nodded again and the second guard hurried from the room. Momentarily, Scott wondered if he'd been ordered to run all the way to Zurich for the map.

"Now, Mr. Scott, it is perhaps one of life's greater ironies that you will die in a two-thousand-dollar suit at the hands of a Bedouin who would have used the same method of execution in the year two thousand BC."

The guard produced a long, thin Gerber MK II combat knife in his right hand and with one smooth, swift stroke, slit Neville Scott's throat from ear to ear.

—3—

In espionage there wasn't usually any evidence of anything. Those who committed crimes in this world were not criminals, they were government servants. In the real world, a murderer will leave clues because his mind is clouded by passion or fear, because he lacks the money to obtain suitable weapons, because there is no place to hide. Usually he is alone—nobody has taught him the proper way to murder a man; nobody has gone over his plan for the crime, pointing out flaws, suggesting a better technique. The man who kills at the orders of an intelligence service has none of these practical or psychological problems: in committing a murder that in other circumstances would be regarded as the work of a psychopath, he has done his country a service and his country pays him, gets rid of the murder weapon, and folds him in its maternal embrace.

Chase had already proven to himself and to others that he was cold in his mind. Over the years, as more and more prankish operations were disapproved before they could begin, many thought that Chase was exercising a puritanical influence over Brewster's sunny nature, that he was systematically robbing the Division of its Ivy League élan. One disappointed officer tried to saddle him with the nickname "Mr. Freeze." It stuck.

Chase did not object to the nickname because the comic book it came from expressed so aptly the situation in which he perceived himself to be from the first day he opened a secret operational file until today.

He had let himself be recruited by Brewster all those years ago because he wanted to make the world a more peaceful place. Like Brewster and his colleagues in the Division, Chase believed in liberal democracy, fervently and unequivocally—but he also knew that to secure its future, you couldn't play, as Brewster liked to say, by Queensberry rules. If your enemies operated by low cunning, you'd better summon up some good old low cunning of your own. "We're the necessary evil," Brewster had told him. "But don't ever get cocky—the noun is *evil*. We're extra-legal. Unsupervised, unregulated. Sometimes *I* don't even feel safe knowing that we're around."

Chase had known fanatics and he found comfort in his chief's ambivalence. He had never felt he'd fully had the measure of Brewster's mind: the brilliance, the cynicism, but mostly the intense, almost bashful idealism, like sunlight spilling through the edge of drawn blinds.

Now, Chase realized, he would have to become cold in more than just his mind. A weapon to be used against the world. The opposite of what he'd wanted to be. He had to become that weapon in order to create a world in which such weapons would no longer be necessary.

Chase walked out of Frankfurt Central Station, under the bare elms along the River Main. Autumn chill, smelling of wet pavement and the river, went through his clothes and dried the sweat on his spine. He walked across the Mainbrücke Ost. There were two policemen on the bridge. Each carried a submachine gun under his cape. Chase walked by them and waited until he was in the shadows at the other end of the bridge before checking again to see that he was not being followed.

Near the old opera house, Chase went into a café, bought a *Brötchen,* and called his Frankfurt contact. When Ted McIntyre answered, Chase heard the click of the poor equipment the Germans used to tap McIntyre's phone. The volume of their speech faded and increased as the recording machine in the vault under the Romer pulled power out of the line.

"Ted? Stafford here."

They spoke English because McIntyre did not understand German easily; he was slightly deaf, and he learned Arabic as a young officer. The effort, McIntyre said, had been so great that it had destroyed his capacity to learn any other foreign tongue.

"I'm staying with Katya tonight," Chase said.

"Then you've got better things to do than come over for a drink," McIntyre said.

Chase smiled. McIntyre's tone of voice told him that he was proud of this quick-witted reply; he thought it made the conversation sound natural. McIntyre paused, sorting out with an almost audible effort the simple code they used on the telephone.

"Let's have lunch," he said at last. "Tomorrow, one o'clock at Zum Anker. I know you like the lobster there."

◆

Yuri Konstantinov came face to face with death at exactly 8:17 p.m. on a chilly October Thursday near his home in the heart of Frankfurt. In the last split second of his life, Konstantinov knew the arrival of death was his own fault. During the iceberg center of the Cold War, Konstantinov had instructed many novice spies, and his watchword was "Wear tradecraft like a good suit. If your tradecraft sticks out like a lion in a monkey run, it will kill you."

So, at the end, Konstantinov's tradecraft, or lack of it, killed him.

That evening, Konstantinov was clearly intent on getting

home in a hurry for dinner. At five minutes after seven o'clock his Opel emerged from the Russian Embassy's garage. Chase and McIntyre were waiting, in a grimy white package-delivery panel truck across the street, and McIntyre immediately radioed ahead to his confederate. The timing would be tight, but it should be manageable. Most important, it was still rush hour in the congested city.

McIntyre, who had spent years tailing Russians around Frankfurt, knew the city intimately. He drove, following the Opel at a discreet distance, only pulling up fairly close when the traffic was heavy enough to provide cover.

When the Opel turned left onto Kaufingerstrasse, it ran into a serious traffic jam. A large truck was jackknifed and stalled across all lanes of traffic, halting all cars in either direction. Truck horns blared, car horns honked repeatedly; there were loud shouts as frustrated drivers stuck their heads out their car windows to hurl epithets at the obstruction. But there was nothing to be done; the traffic was frozen.

The filthy white panel truck was stopped immediately ahead of Konstantinov's Opel, cars hemming them in on all sides. McIntyre's confederate had abandoned his eighteen-wheeler truck, taking the keys with him, on the pretense of searching for help. Traffic would not move for a good long while.

Chase, in jeans and a black windbreaker and wearing black leather gloves, crouched on the floor inside the truck and released the hinged trapdoor. There was enough clearance to the ground that he was able to drop to the pavement and belly under the panel truck and then under Konstantinov's Opel. In the extremely unlikely event that traffic somehow was able to move a few feet, the Opel could not, since it was blocked by the delivery truck.

Moving quickly, his heart racing, Chase slid under the Opel's chassis until he located the precise spot he was looking for.

Although the undercarriage was mostly one solid mass of molded steel, aluminum, and polyethylene, there was a small perforated area where the air-intake filter was located. Swiftly, he pressed an adhesive-backed aluminum-alloy filter panel over the vent, a specially designed, radio-controlled device McIntyre had been able to acquire from contacts in the private-security industry. Once Chase assured himself it was securely in place, he wriggled out from under the car and, still undetected, back under the panel truck, the hinged trapdoor still open. He lifted himself up and into the truck and shut the trapdoor behind him.

McIntyre's friend returned to his abandoned truck and got it moving just as police sirens began to sound. Traffic started moving a few minutes later, the blaring horns stopped, and the cursing came to an end. The Opel roared ahead, gunning its engine, passing the paneled delivery truck as it resumed its course down Kaufingerstrasse. Then it made its customary left turn, onto the quiet side street where Konstantinov lived.

It was then that Chase pressed the switch on the transmitter he had in his hand. As McIntyre maneuvered down the street after the Opel, they could see an immediate reaction. The car's cabin filled at once with thick white tear gas. The Opel veered crazily from one side to another before pulling over to the side of the deserted street; the driver had obviously been overcome. Both front and back doors of the large automobile were flung open as both driver and Konstantinov emerged, coughing and retching, hands pressed over their stinging eyes. The driver clutched a handgun uselessly at his side. McIntyre veered the truck over to the side of the road as well, and the two men jumped out. Chase fired a projectile at the driver, who toppled at once. The short-acting tranquilizer dart would knock him out for hours; the amnesiac effect of the narcotic would ensure that he had little or no recollection of the evening's events. Then Chase rushed over to Konstantinov, who had collapsed on the sidewalk, coughing and temporarily blinded. Meanwhile, McIntyre hoisted the driver back into the driver's seat of the Opel. Taking out a bottle of schnapps he had bought on the street, he spilled a good quantity into the chauffeur's mouth and over his uniform, leaving the half-filled bottle on the street beside him.

Chase looked around to confirm there was no one on the street who could see what they were doing; then he exhaled halfway and held his breath as the crosshairs of his silenced Browning settled upon the Russian's torso.

His concentration was unwavering as his finger caressed the trigger.

As Konstantinov's chest erupted in a spray of scarlet, a wisp of cordite seeped from the automatic's perforated cylinder.

✦

By temperament and by training, Chase knew how to remain impassive, but his heart was still thudding from what he'd done to the Russian. Konstantinov, like himself, was probably a pawn, lied to and manipulated, recruited to an assignment about which he was carefully kept in the dark until it was too late to turn back. In a way the Russian had been a victim, too. A victim of Zero Directorate as much as Chase and his people. If only he'd been able to question the man, find out everything he knew. But there was no time.

Chase slept on the train from Frankfurt, protected by three nuns and a schoolboy who shared his compartment. When he arrived in midafternoon, Strasbourg was bathed by the nickeled light of autumn sun. He stayed long enough to buy two hundred feet of nylon climbing rope, a dozen pitons and a mountaineering hammer, a good camera with a close-up lens, and a small, powerful floodlamp bulb. Then he collected a '68 Iso Rivolta from

Hertz under the name Jonathan Stafford, making certain that the trunk contained a set of tire chains.

There was little traffic on Route E-9, the road to Switzerland. The car was pushed toward the edge of the road by gusts of wind. At the Swiss frontier, Chase was required by the relaxed police to show nothing but the green insurance card for the rented Iso. He inquired at Jura, where the road forked, about the condition of the passes, and was advised to cross the Alps through the Splügen pass, since the higher Saint Gotthard and the Furka were closed.

There had been an early, heavy snowfall in the mountains, and he pulled off the road and attached the chains. It took him a long time to maneuver among the cars that had lost traction on the switchback road leading to the summit. At the top he got behind a Swiss postal bus, equipped with a snowplow and a sander, and followed it down the other side of the mountains into the valley of the Rhine.

It was ten o'clock when he reached Zurich. He drove through the dim streets, past the leaden Swiss architecture, until he found the hotel he was looking for. It stood in the Talstrasse, in a block whose rooftops led into the Bleicherweg.

After he had hooked up the VL22H to the telephone in his room, he walked along the street until he reached the stone town house that was the bank of Zurbriggen und Co. The bank had a mansard roof, with a steep pitch falling to the eaves but a flat top divided by three wide chimneys. The buildings on either side were twenty feet higher than the bank. Chase fixed the proportions and the distances in his mind and walked back along the lake shore to his hotel.

At precisely eleven o'clock his phone rang. "We've lost another one," Brewster said on the other end of the line, after he'd heard the little click that told him the VL22H was on.

"Harriet Ashdown?"

Chase felt something like hope rise in his throat. Realizing: he wanted to avoid the anguish of waking up the next day and knowing he'd left a sizable amount of blood on the carpet of an anonymous room somewhere.

"No. One of ours again."

"Where from?"

"Headquarters."

"Headquarters." Chase spoke the word without inflection, but this was a startling turn of events. The others had been kidnapped on foreign soil. But headquarters? That was a different kettle of fish.

"Who was it this time?" Chase asked.

"A man named Hillman, from Op Tech."

Chase's mental filing system clicked into operation. "I remember him. Tall guy from Rhode Island with a bald head. Loud laugh. Good head for detail. Wesleyan. What happened?"

"He went to the men's room at the movies Saturday night and didn't come back. We found the body this morning. This time there was no film reel."

"Then you don't know what he told them?"

"No, but that doesn't matter so much. We know what he knew."

"Which was what?"

"Advanced Russian military technology. Specialized in satellites."

Satellites? Where did they fit in?

"Doesn't sound like they hit a random target."

"Yes, Number Two, it's beginning to look like there's some method to their madness after all."

"Diversionary tactics?"

"Which would imply there is some kind of endgame."

Even as a boy in New Hampshire, before he went to Korea,

Chase had disliked games because they were mere parodies of reality. Afterward, as a spy, he despised them, a peculiarity that set him apart from nearly everyone in the intelligence community, a world populated by men who looked on the Cold War as a sort of Hasty Pudding Olympics between the combined track and field teams of Harvard, Princeton, and Yale and an awkward squad of European bookworms and Asiatic oafs.

"So what now?"

"Yuri wasn't a problem."

"I heard."

"I just hope it was worth it."

"Not for us to say."

"Ms. Van de Velde from Station B was helpful, sir. Got me into Neville Scott's office at the embassy. The guy's an amateur. Found a deposit slip for a box in Zurich."

"You there now?"

"You got it, sir."

"You realize it would be safer to commit sodomy at high noon in Alabama than break into a bank in Switzerland?"

"It's a test of skill."

"Let me hear a little more."

Chase described the roof of Zurbriggen und Co. and the adjoining buildings and the distances involved.

"What is the access to the roof?"

"I have a room on the highest floor of the hotel. There's access to the roof by the fire stairs. I can cross the adjoining roof without difficulty. The roof of the bank will give me some trouble."

"What kind of surface?"

"Copper sheathing."

"Slippery stuff, and you say it's snowing? Then a vertical climb of four meters to the top of the chimney? Very challenging."

"I know nothing about the alarm system, nothing about the

internal security. But they're an old-fashioned firm, and the Swiss have faith in locks. It's in their national character."

"All right, Jonathan. Keep it up."

"Is Ashdown still a priority, sir?"

"Proceed as planned."

"Right."

"And Jonathan?"

"Sir?"

"Remember to make it sloppy. We *want* them to find you."

✦

The headquarters of the eminent Swiss bank Zurbriggen und Co. was located on the Bahnhofstrasse in the southernmost part of the Lindenhof, just a few blocks from the Paradeplatz. Unlike the mock-Renaissance palazzo of Credit Suisse nearby, the Zurbriggen und Co. building was unassuming yet proud. It seemed to belong to a different place, a different era—to Paris in the time of Napoleon, when the French dared to dream of a world empire. It was famous for its genteel reputation, for managing the fortunes of generations of Switzerland's wealthiest families, its clients the oldest of old money. The name Zurbriggen und Co. called to mind its legendary mahogany-paneled partners' room, yet at the same time carried with it the scent of mystery. When one is dealing with Swiss banks, especially a private bank like Zurbriggen, rumor is sometimes the best one can hope for; but because the intelligence agencies in his country had once or twice utilized the private banking services of institutions like Zurbriggen, Chase had managed to learn that a minimum deposit of approximately five million dollars was required.

The Zurbriggen bank was a small enterprise—Herr Zurbriggen and a half-dozen employees, if that. If you wanted someone to hide your money and your belongings in Switzerland, Herr

Zurbriggen was your best friend. He took over control of the family business from his father in the early 1930s. It had not been a good time for the banks of Switzerland. There was the worldwide depression, the German panic, a currency crisis in Austria that was sending shock waves through Zurich. Many private banks were forced to merge with larger competitors to survive. Herr Zurbriggen managed to hang on by his fingernails. When Hitler came to power in Germany, Jewish money and valuables began to flow into the private banks of Zurich. Zurbriggen himself opened more than two hundred numbered accounts for German Jews. But in the late thirties, agents of the Gestapo came looking for all the Jewish money. It was rumored that Zurbriggen cooperated with the Gestapo in violation of Swiss banking laws and revealed the existence of the numbered accounts. He was hedging his bets and knew that the money deposited by a few Jews was nothing compared to the riches that awaited him from the plunder of Nazi Germany.

Pondering the great Swiss conspiracy of silence in such matters, Chase attached crampons to his boots. He put the camera in his chest pocket and draped a coil of rope over his shoulder. He ran up the stairs to the hotel roof; once in the open air, he spread his arms and took deep breaths one after the other, exhaling through his nose. Snowflakes gathered in his eyebrows.

He rappelled down the wall of the building and a second later was on the roof of the bank, running up the steep pitch of the gambrel, his weight thrown into the slope. Chase reached the top, swinging his arms for balance, and walked across the roof, leaving footprints behind him. At the base of the farthest chimney, he uncoiled a second rope and cast it toward the bottom; Chase heard the faint rattle of the grappling hook.

He tugged on the rope and walked up the bricks, his body nearly horizontal. He sat on the top for a moment with the snow drifting down around him before he adjusted the grappling hook, seized the rope, and dropped down the chimney.

There were six documents in Neville Scott's box. A deposit slip, a memorandum of identity, an explanation of the withdrawal code, a hastily drawn map of some kind of medical facility or complex labeled "Prince," a withdrawal slip with an address in Zurich written on the back, and a memcon (or memorandum of conversation).

Chase took four photographs of the first five, but pocketed the last. It had been filed by the MI6 station chief in Brussels and had a question mark in ink next to the name "Victoria Bailey." Chase knew that kind of thing could be a career-ender for anyone involved and wondered who'd had the foresight to spirit it away to Zurich.

Back on the roof, the moon's slanting light made it hard to see, but Chase scrutinized every patch of ground that was visible to him, dividing it up like a quadrate grid, to the point that his eyes began to ache.

Perhaps now that he had seen these items, the proverbial agents would come out of the woodwork for him. Russian or English, he guessed, who—like his own people—were frantically taking out anyone on the board perceived to pose too much of a risk.

Several hours later, when the agents still hadn't come, Chase allowed himself to—at least for the moment—accept that the operation was real. That his value within it was on the level. Against the backdrop of the rest of the mission—killing men and women just like himself—it felt good to be doing what in the espionage world passed for honest work.

He knew the feeling wouldn't last.

2

Harriet Ashdown arrived at a pleasant, unpretentious hotel in one of the many tributaries which flow off Zurich's Manessestrasse.

Ms. Ashdown, a lady in her late forties, had never stayed in this hotel before, though she knew the city backward. If the authorities had taken the trouble to check up on her, they would have discovered that she had been in Zurich many times over the years, and, on this occasion, had already lived in the city for the best part of a month, although they would have been hard put to seek out the different addresses she had used—apart from the five alternative names.

Harriet Ashdown was an English businesswoman, and it showed from her severe suit—navy with white piping—to the briefcase she seemed to guard with her honor. Certainly, it was later said, she would not let the bellboy take it with the two suitcases to her room.

From his vantage point in the bathroom of her suite, Chase coolly regarded the slightly built woman as she put her things away, the roundness of her hips and breasts offset by the tightly muscular frame; in her way, she was indeed quite beautiful. He knew what she was capable of—had seen her file: astonishing marksmanship, extraordinary strength and agility, swiftness and shrewdness of mind. She had been trained to kill, and nothing would deter her from doing so if she thought her life was in danger.

He moved the silenced pistol to his right hand, following her pacing figure with its muzzle. The sudden certainty of what he had to do filled him with loathing, self-disgust. Yet there was no other way. *Kill or be killed:* it was the awful shibboleth of an existence he hadn't really asked for. Nor did it mitigate the larger truth, the ultimate truth of his career: kill *and* be killed.

Another dumb, inanimate slug would shatter another skull, and another life would be stricken, erased, turned into the putrid animal matter from which it had been constituted. This was not progress; it was the very opposite. He cast his mind back to Konstantinov and the others, snuffed out, and for what? Some of the rage that filled him was displaced rage at himself, yes. But what of it? Harriet Ashdown would die—she would die at his hands, and that would be their one moment of true intimacy.

Stepping out into the light, Chase decided to crash his pistol against the top of her head; the blow would be carefully calculated neither to kill her nor seriously cripple her. When she'd regained consciousness, he'd tell her to disappear for a few weeks.

But immediately, he knew something was wrong. *She'd known he was there.*

Before he could react, the Englishwoman had propelled herself with all her coiled force toward Chase's gun hand. She wanted his automatic—it would change everything. At the last fraction of a second, Chase dodged her outstretched arms. She seized his jacket instead, and hammered her knee toward his groin. As he torqued his pelvis back defensively, she flexed her wrist into a slap block, and sent the Browning flying through the air.

Both took a few steps back.

Her right arm was extended straight down, and held a small knife; it had been boot-holstered, and he had not even seen her draw it. If he lunged forward, her posture made it clear, she would peel his arm with her blade: an effective counter. And straight from the manual.

She was well trained, which, oddly, reassured him. He choreographed the next ten seconds in his head, preparing a counter-response to her probable actions. The fact that she was well trained was her weakness. He knew what she would do because he knew what she had been taught.

Suddenly, he fell forward, grabbing her extended arm; she raised her knife hand, as he had predicted, and he delivered a crushing blow to its wrist. The median nerve was vulnerable about an inch from the heel of her hand; his precisely directed blow caused her knife hand to open involuntarily.

Now he grabbed the Browning from the floor—yet, at the same moment, her other hand shot out toward his shoulder. She dug her thumb deep into his trapezius muscle, jolting the nerves that ran beneath and temporarily paralyzing his arm and shoulder. A bolt of agony shot through the area. Her fighting stance was awesome, a triumph of training over instinct. Now he swept his foot toward her right knee, causing intense pain and destabilizing her footing. She toppled backward as he transferred the gun to his other hand.

On her back, she inhaled and exhaled heavily for a few moments, catching her breath. "Let me tell you something," she said, looking up at Chase. "I was once like you. A weapon. Aimed and discharged by someone else. I thought I had autonomous intelligence, made my own decisions. The truth was otherwise: I was a weapon in the hands of another."

A shudder ran down Chase's spine. He had no choice but do what he should have done in the first place. It was kill or be killed after all. He had no choice but to eliminate her; sentiment and wishful thinking, and her own accomplished line of blather, had distracted him from that one essential truth.

Chase squeezed the trigger of the silenced pistol.

◆

Chase positioned himself by a phone booth just off the hotel lobby to make sure he hadn't picked up a tail. As five minutes stretched into ten and then fifteen, people came and went in seemingly random procession. Yet not everything was random. Thirty feet to his left, a man in a caftanlike shirt was reading a newspaper. But whatever he was interested in, it wasn't the words in front of him. Chase took a closer look and felt a pang. This man was not unlike some of the British agents he'd seen at the embassy in Brussels. The powerful neck straining at the collar, the dead eyes—this man was a professional killer, a gun for hire. Chase's scalp began to crawl.

Seated diagonally opposite, another man was reading a travel guide to Zurich. He was dressed like a businessman, bespectacled, in a light gray suit. Chase looked more closely: his lips were moving. Nor was he reading out loud, for when his eyes darted off, he continued speaking. He was communicating—the microphone could have been in his tie or lapel—to a confederate, somebody with an earpiece.

He continued to scan the hotel lobby, alert to further anomalies. The businessman was now apparently napping, his chin resting on his chest, suggesting a postprandial siesta. Only the occasional movement of his mouth—murmured communications, if only to keep boredom at bay—betrayed the illusion.

The two figures he'd identified were clearly not American; that much was plain from their attire and posture. Conclusion: an expert British tag team, people who knew the terrain and could act quickly.

But for God's sake, why the dragnet?

Conclusive evidence was impossible, but his mind kept returning to the notion that these were Harriet Ashdown's minders, her tactical team. And in some calculating part of his mind, a clockwork mechanism spooled with a hard, icy clarity: just as he had been sent to eliminate Harriet Ashdown, she had had been sent to eliminate *him*. Perhaps, even, by lying in wait defensively for his attack.

The realization did little to calm Chase's nerves, for he knew how often traps caught those who set them. To get to the next phase of this operation, his principal weapon would have to be his own composure. He thus had to steer clear of the pitfalls of anxiety and overconfidence. One could lead to paralysis, the other to stupidity.

He took the stairs to the roof.

It was a six-story building with a flat roof, one of the new concrete additions to the ancient city, bare of tiles or balconies or arched outer walls that might have offered him exit. He would have to go out by a door.

He walked to the end of the concrete passage and found a trapdoor to the roof, and an iron ladder. The night was calm, with pale stars and a wash of light from the streetlamps six stories below. He began crawling when he neared the edge of the roof on the south side, to avoid presenting a silhouette against the skyline in case they chanced to look upward.

One.

He was in the doorway almost directly opposite, his back against the wall and his head turned to watch the street; from there he could see the main entrance of the hotel and the windows along the whole of its length. He was in the uniform of a hotel employee.

Chase crawled to the east parapet, straightening up in the cover of the elevator tower. Body awareness was increasing, helping him to prepare for survival. He crouched low again, the sharpness of the loose flint burning against his palms as he dropped onto his hands and toes, reaching the parapet.

Two.

It took Chase five minutes to make him out, because he was in deep shadow and standing absolutely still; it was the blinking of his eyes that signaled his presence, covering and exposing the faint glow of the corneas. Chase couldn't tell what he was wearing, but the color of his clothes was neutral, midway between dark and light. From his position he would be able to see that narrow flank of the building and the back entrance.

Chase moved on, crossing the corners of the roof and once kicking a flattened tin can and dropping immediately into a crouch clear of the roofline. Sometimes he heard voices below, the light fluting tones of vacationing couples; the chambermaids had left many of the windows open along the north side of the building. It took Chase half an hour to locate the three other men: one at the end of a narrow street leading toward the Manessestrasse; one in the shadow of a bus shelter on the west side; one almost lost in the darkness of an alley where the lamp on the wall had gone out.

Total of five. Plus the two in the lobby. At least seven, possibly more.

We must make no sign, and leave no shadow. Those were the rules set up by men in Washington, planning their operations in the civilized comfort of their offices, unaware that a beleaguered little ferret like Chase would very much like to wait for daylight and try for the safety of an open street rather than crouch here with the knowledge that he must go down in the dark and make an end of it one way or another.

Finally, he moved from the north parapet, straightening up and keeping close to the elevator tower, stepping over the low radio aerial that crisscrossed the roof, going down through the trapdoor and shutting it quietly.

On his way down to the lobby, he passed two chambermaids; one of the women asked him something and he made a gesture that could have meant anything, going down to the next flight of stairs before she could try to stop him. On the ground floor he turned left, because it was on the west side of the building that he might stand a chance. From the roof he'd seen that one man was posted on each side, with a fifth placed so that he could cover the main doors and the side entrance together. On the north side there was a small park, an open space with no cover; on the west side there was only one man posted, and he was at the end of the alley where the lamp had gone out. He was the man Chase would have to go for, and try to put down before he could signal the others.

At the end of the passage there was a narrow door, half-blocked by a maid's pile of linen, and Chase stopped in front of it to loosen his collar and pull his shoelaces tight; then he opened it and went into the street.

The figure in the alley straightened up as he heard Chase and faced his way. The man was in silhouette now: from the roof Chase hadn't been able to see beyond him along the alley, but now there were three lamps visible and beyond them an open square in the dim of the distance; it wasn't a cul-de-sac and the way was open. If Chase turned to the left or right along the street he would move closer to a second man, with this one at his back. He had to cross the street here and make straight for the one in the alley, and the man must see him coming and feel confident, with the knowledge that time and strength and expertise were all on his side, together with the element of surprise—because Chase didn't look at him as he neared. Then the man might not call or whistle or radio the others; he'd want to take Chase alone for pride's sake.

He mustn't signal them, this one in the alley. That was Chase's only chance.

Chase walked across the street with his head lowered, stepping onto the pavement, moving straight toward the man with no indication that he knew the man was there.

They drew their weapons at the same time.

"You're overmatched, Chase," the man said. He was blunt, with pudgy features and black smudges under his eyes. "No British lard-asses like the ones in the lobby this time. See, this time they cared enough to send the very best." His voice had the twang of the Appalachian backcountry, and although he was trying to sound conversational, the tension showed.

The American accent was something Chase wasn't prepared for. It was beyond a surprise; the shock was deep, stunning, taking his breath away.

But he put on a bland smile. "Let me make you a very reasonable proposition: you walk away, or I kill you."

The American agent snorted. "Think you're lookin' at number thirty-four? In your dreams, buddy."

"What are you talking about?"

"That would make me number thirty-four." When Chase did not reply, the southerner added, "You've done thirty-three people, right? I'm talking sanctioned, in-field killings."

Chase's face went stiff. The number—which was never a source of pride and increasingly a source of anguish—was accurate. But it was also a count that few people knew.

Chase saw the muscles of his adversary's neck flex, saw he intended to pull the trigger.

"You really want to kill me, don't you?" Chase said, almost with amusement. It was not a question.

"Shit, no," the southerner said with heavy sarcasm. "This is just foreplay as far as I'm concerned."

"So what did they tell you? About me?"

The southerner inhaled and exhaled for a few moments. "You've gone rogue. You've betrayed the agency."

"Bullshit."

"Bullshit's what you are. Double-crossed everything and everybody you could. Sold out the agency, sold out your country."

"Is that right? Did they say why I went bad?"

"You snapped, or maybe you were always a piece of shit. Don't matter. Every day you live is a day our lives are in danger."

"That's what they told you?"

"It's the *truth*," he spat.

"They had me kill Konstantinov and Ashdown as part of a manipulation. And one of the people being manipulated is me. What a directive means and what a directive signifies are two different things."

"More lies."

"The whole point was to draw the opposition to me. But then your people got cold feet and thought I might spill too much. So now they're manipulating you in order to get me out of the picture."

"Jesus, this is making my head spin."

"I don't mean to confuse you. Only to make you think."

"Comes to the same thing," he said. "But *why?* Why would they turn the tables on you like that?"

"You think I haven't been asking myself that?"

"You're a legend to us regular field agents, especially the younger ones. You've got no idea, Chase. No idea how *demoralizing* it was when they told us who the target was. They'd never do that on a whim."

"Most people lie to save themselves, or better themselves. That's not the kind of lie that bothers me. The kind of lie that bothers me is the 'noble' lie. The lie spread for higher purposes. The sacrifice of small men for larger ends. The liars who lie in the interest of the greater good."

"You're losing me."

"They're using us both as fodder for what they believe to be a noble purpose. A noble purpose that might strike someone else as an administrative convenience."

"Lookit, I've read your profile. Well, you're right, now that you say it. Something about the story doesn't make sense. Either you aren't as good as you're supposed to be or you're not as bad as they say you are."

"I see," Chase said. "Then you have a decision to make."

"But our directive..."

"It's my life, of course. I have an interest. But it's yours, too. A lesson I learned the hard way."

The southerner looked confused. He glanced at his watch and said, "Go. Me and my guys on the roof, we'll watch those Englishmen for you."

Chase felt a wave of nausea welling from his gut, and a sense, too, of emptiness as he sprinted down the darkened alley. Whom could he trust? Which sides had taken arms against him?

Which side was he on?

At this point he could only say: his own. Could he expect allies? Did he deserve them? The CIA man, who did not know how fast betrayal traveled, had almost believed he was guilty; would Chase have done anything different in his place?

A chill ran down his spine as Chase realized: Brewster's worst predictions had come true. He had finally left the reservation.

TWO

TWO

–1–

Where *was* the Zero Directorate? The interrogative rose in Chase's head as he hailed a taxi the following evening outside his dimly lit pension in the disreputable Seebach neighborhood. It was a part of Zurich he was wholly unfamiliar with. The sidewalks were tight with people, more Asian and Arab than European, for Seebach seemed to be a strange cultural meeting place. Garish banners overhung the street; on ground level modern shopfronts squeezed together, yet above them there could still be seen old ramshackle buildings dating back to the 1890s or even '80s. Neon and paper signs hung drunkenly at angles, sprouting out to catch the eye, while the omnipresent Chinese restaurants added an amalgam of smells. A murky part of the world, indeed.

Gone to ground in this old quarter of the city, Chase knew he had the sole advantage of action over reaction: he alone knew his next move; the organization would have to respond to what he did. And if they could condition his actions, make him act according to a curtailed number of options in reaction to their own actions, that edge would be lost.

As far as his own people went, Chase knew he was alone: the only sane man in the asylum. If he described what he knew he would destroy any chance he might have of being believed. Reality was poison. Too many people, over too many years, had failed to see the truth to be able to recognize it now.

The taxi bowled steadily south, down the Bahnhofstrasse. Snow was neatly piled off the main pavements, and the trees bowed under its weight, some decorated with long icicles festooning the branches. Near the Wohn Museum, with its sharp tower fingering the sky, one particular tree seemed to crouch like a white-cowled monk clutching a glittering dagger. The address Chase had found and memorized in Neville Scott's Swiss deposit box overlooked the Bruno Webers Weinrebenpark, at the southeasterly end of the Uraniastrasse. It was a part of the city Chase didn't know. The park itself was a long, landscaped strip running between the houses.

There were signs that in summer it would be an idyllic spot with trees, rock gardens, and paths. Now, from the fresh snow of recent days, there rose shapes and figures: abstract masses, pieces so delicate you would imagine they could only be carved from wood.

The cab pulled up almost opposite a life-sized work in which a man and woman entwined in an embrace from which only the warmth of spring could rend them apart. Around the park the buildings were mainly old, with occasional pieces of modernity looking like new buffer states bridging gaps in living history. For no logical reason, Chase had imagined 143 Dianastrasse would be a new and shining apartment house. Instead, he found the address to be a house four stories high, with shuttered windows and fresh green paint, decorated by blossoms of snow hanging like window-box flowers and frosted along the scrollwork and gutters.

Two curved, half-timbered gables divided the house, which had a single entrance, glass-paneled and unlocked. Just inside the door, a row of metal mailboxes signified who lived where: the cards, slid into tiny frames, each telling a small tale about the occupants. The hallway and stairs were bare of carpet. Shining wood spoke back with the smell of good polish, mingled now with cooking fragrances.

Slipping the buttons on his winter coat, Chase began to make his way silently up the stairs. At each landing he noted two doors, to left and right, solid and well-built, with bell pushes, and the twins of the framed cards on the mailboxes set below them.

At the third turning of the stairs, the name "Victoria Bailey" was elegantly engraved on a business card under the bell for 3A. Chase pressed Victoria Bailey's bell hard and long, then stood away from the small spy hole visible in the door's center panel. From the inside came the rattle of a chain; then the door opened, and there she was, dressed in a long silk robe fastened loosely with a tie belt.

Victoria Bailey had a complexion which, if catching, would put all the makeup firms out of business, and thick white-blond hair so heavy it seemed to fall straight back into place. If all this was not enough, she was slender, sexy, and had lips built for one purpose. Her eyes were large, blue with violet flecks, oval, like her face, and set off by exceptionally long, curled lashes. They were eyes, Chase thought, that could be the undoing of a man, or, conversely, the making of him. His own eyes flicked down to the full firm curve of her breasts under the robe.

"Miss B..."

Chase saw her lips move as though trying to get out words of inquiry. In that fraction he realized something was wrong with this girl. Her cheeks were drained white, one hand trembled on the door. Deep in the violet-flecked eyes was the unmistakable flicker of fear.

Intuition, Jeong had taught Chase, is something you learn through experience: you are not born with it like an extra sense.

Loudly Chase said, "It's only me from over the sea," at the same time sticking one foot forward, the side of his shoe against the door. "Glad I came?"

As he spoke, Chase grabbed Victoria Bailey by the shoulder with his left hand, spinning her, pulling her onto the landing. The right hand had already gone for his Dunhill lighter. In less than two seconds, Miss Bailey was against the wall near 3B, while Chase had sidestepped into the apartment, the lighter out and ready.

There were two of them. A small runt with a thin, pockmarked face was to Chase's left, flat against the inside wall, where he had been covering Miss Bailey with a small revolver which looked like a Charter Arms Undercover .38 Special. At the far side of the room—there was no hallway—a large man with oversized hands and the face of a failed boxer stood poised beside a handsome chrome and leather chair-and-sofa suite. His distinguishing marks included a nose which looked like a very advanced carbuncle. He carried no visible weapon.

Chase turned away, having made his identification of the second man. The face was known well enough to him—unpleasant features, with bright darting eyes. What, he wondered to himself, was Alfredo Fiorino doing in Zurich? Chase knew him only because, some years ago, there had been a suggestion that the KGB—posing as an American government agency—had used him to do a particularly nasty piece of work in Texas. Men like Fiorino were not nickel-and-dime hoods, but contract killers who came at Cartier prices. Chase had no doubt that Fiorino was charging the Zero Directorate a usurious rate of interest.

The runt's gun came up to Chase's left, and Fiorino began to move.

Chase went for the gun. The large Dunhill lighter seemed to move only fractionally in Chase's hand as it clipped down with force onto the runt's wrist.

The revolver spun away, and there was a yelp of pain above the sharp crack of bone.

Keeping the lighter pointing toward Fiorino, Chase used his left arm to spin the runt in front of him like a shield. At the same time, Chase brought up his knee hard. The little gunman crumpled, his good hand flailing ineffectually to protect his groin. He squeaked in French like a pig and squirmed at Chase's feet.

Fiorino was undeterred by the lighter. He didn't know the Dunhill could, at this range, blow away a high percentage of a human being. Chase stepped over the body of the runt, kicking back with his right heel. Raising the lighter, arm outstretched, Chase shouted at his adversary: "Stop or you're a dead man."

Fiorino did not do as he was told. Instead, he suggested in Italian that Chase should commit incest with his female parent.

Chase hardly saw him swerve. The man was better than he had estimated and very fast. As he feinted, Chase moved to follow him with the lighter. Only then did he feel the sharp, unnatural pain in his right shoulder. For a second, the blossom of agony took Chase off balance. His arms dropped, and Fiorino's foot came up. Chase realized that you cannot be right about people all the time. This was a live one, the real thing—a killer, trained, accurate, and experienced. Together with this knowledge, Chase was conscious of three things going on simultaneously: the pain in his shoulder; the lighter being taken from his hand by the kick; and, from behind him, the whimpering of the runt, decreasing in volume as he made his escape down the stairs.

Fiorino was closing fast, one shoulder dropped, the body sideways.

Chase took a quick step back and to his right, against the wall. As he moved, he spotted what had caused the pain in his shoulder.

Embedded in the door's lintel was an eight-inch knife with a horn grip and a blade curving away toward the point. It was a skinning knife, like those used to great effect by the Lapps when separating the carcass of a reindeer from its hide. Grabbing upward, Chase's fingers closed around the grip. His shoulder now felt numb with pain. He crabbed quickly to one side, the knife firmly in his right hand, blade upward, thumb and forefinger to the front of the grip in the fighting hold. Always, they taught, use the thrust position, never hold the knife with the thumb on the back. Never defend with a knife; always attack.

Chase turned, square on, toward Fiorino, knees bending, one foot forward for balance in the classic knife-fighting posture.

"What was it you said about my mother?" Chase growled back in Italian.

Fiorino, showing stained teeth. "Now we see, Mr. Chase," he said in broken English.

They circled one another, Chase kicking away a small stand chair, giving the pair a wider fighting arena. Fiorino produced a second knife and began to toss it from hand to hand, light on his feet, moving all the time, tightening the circle. It was a well-known confusion tactic: keep your man guessing and lure him in close, then strike. Come on, Chase thought, come on in; closer; come to me. Fiorino was doing just that, oblivious to the danger of winding the spiral too tightly. Chase kept his eyes locked with those of the big man, his senses tuned to the enemy knife as it glinted, arcing from hand to hand, the grip slapping the palm with a firm thump on each exchange.

The end came suddenly and fast.

Fiorino inched nearer to Chase, continuing to toss the knife between his hands.

Chase stepped in abruptly, his right leg lunging out in a fencing thrust, the foot midway between his antagonist's feet. At the same moment, Chase tossed his knife from right to left. Then he made a subtle twist of his wrist, as though to return the knife to his right hand.

The moment was there. Chase saw the big man's eyes move slightly in the direction the knife should be traveling. There was a split second when Fiorino was uncertain. Chase's left hand rose two inches, then flashed out and down. There was the ringing clash of steel against steel.

Fiorino had been in the act of tossing his knife between hands. Chase's blade caught the weapon in midair, smashing it to the floor.

In an automatic reflex, the big man ducked toward the floor, his hand reaching after his knife.

Chase's knife drove upward.

The big man straightened up very quickly, making a grunting noise. His hand went to his cheek, which Chase had opened up into an ugly red canyon from ear to jawline.

Another fast upward strike from Chase, and the knife slit the protective hand. This time, Fiorino gave a roar of mingled pain and anger.

The big man's eyes went wide with disbelief as Chase moved in again. The knife flicked up again twice, leaving a jagged slash on the other cheek and removing an earlobe.

Fiorino had obviously had enough. He stumbled to one side and made for the door, breath rasping. Chase considered the man had more intelligence than he had first thought.

The pain returned to Chase's shoulder, and with it a sensation of giddiness. Chase had no intention of following the would-be assailant, whose stumbling, falling footsteps could be heard on the wooden stairs.

"Mr. . . . ?" Victoria Bailey had come back into the room. "What shall I do? Call the police, or . . . ?"

She looked frightened. Her face was drained of color. There

was something else: her hair was red now—in a Vidal Sassoon bob—quite red.

For a moment, something about the change of hair color, the blond wig, struck like a bell in Chase's memory. Then it was gone.

"No. No, we don't want the police, Ms. Bailey." He sank into the nearest chair. "Close the door, put the chain on, and take a look out the window."

Everything seemed to withdraw around him. Surprisingly, he thought vaguely, Victoria Bailey did as he asked. You did not normally give orders to girls like Victoria Bailey.

"Weren't you a blond a minute ago, Ms. Bailey?"

"Just a wig. Neville suggested I wear it for a few days. Just in case."

"Just in case what?"

"He didn't specify. He had a business trip to take and told me to wear it 'til he got back."

"Ah. See anything out there?" Chase's own voice sounded far away.

"There's a car leaving. Cars parked. I can't see any people ..."

The room tilted, then came back into normal focus.

"Your shoulder."

He could smell her beside him.

"Just tell me what happened, Ms. Bailey. It's important. How did they get in? What did they do? What did they want?"

"Your shoulder."

He looked at it. The thick material of his Barbour jacket had saved him from serious injury. Even so, the knife had razored through the epaulet, and blood seeped up through the clot leaving a dark, wet stain.

"Tell me what happened," Chase repeated.

"You're wounded. I have to look at it."

They compromised. Chase stripped to the waist. A nasty gash

ran diagonally across the shoulder. The knife had cut to the depth of around half an inch in the fleshy parts.

Victoria Bailey, with disinfectant, tape, hot water, and gauze, cleaned and dressed the wound, telling her story at the same time. Outwardly she was calm, though Chase noticed how her hands shook slightly as she recounted what had happened.

The pair of killers had arrived only a couple of minutes before he himself rang the doorbell. "I was running a little late," she made a vague gesture, indicating the silky robe. "Stupid. I didn't have the chain on and just thought it was my dinner date. Didn't even look through the spy hole."

The intruders had simply forced their way in, pushing her back into the room and telling her what to do. They also described in some detail what they would do to her, if she did not carry out instructions.

"Well, thanks for tipping me off at the door," Chase said, easing his now taped and dressed shoulder.

Victoria Bailey gave a little pout. "I didn't mean to tip you off. I was just plain frightened."

"You only acted frightened," Chase smiled at her. "I can tell when people are really frightened."

"I'm still frightened. Scared stiff if you really want to know. What about you? The way you operate? American Secret Service? CIA?"

"Technically, yes. A kind of intelligence officer. But lately they've had me playing the role of international gangster." He paused, ready to begin the important questions, but Victoria moved across the room to retrieve the Dunhill, which she nervously handed back to him.

"Why don't you have a proper gun?"

"I've always thought someone might take it away from me and shove it down my throat."

"Will they come back? Am I likely to be attacked again?" She spoke with an English public school accent, but—perhaps because she was nervous—other intonations were audible to Chase. Australian? he wondered.

"Look," Chase said, spreading his hands. "For some reason a couple of hoodlums were after you. Or, more likely, me. But there's no reason I can think of they would know I was coming here. So why don't you begin by telling me about your relationship to Neville Scott."

"It's quite simple really. I was his assistant at the embassy. Nothing more, nothing less."

"And he warned you to wear a wig, a disguise. Why?"

Victoria Bailey disappeared into another room and returned with a manila envelope, sealed with Scotch tape. She handed it over to Chase.

"Here," she said. "Skim this. It'll be quicker."

Chase, throwing back his head and holding the papers at arm's length, read through the file. It was an MI6 digest of the very case he was on—the agents Zero Directorate had drugged, flushed, filmed, and murdered—badly typed on drugstore foolscap. When he had finished reading, Chase switched on Ms. Bailey's record player. The song "Green Tambourine" by the Lemon Pipers blasted out of the speakers.

"Lazarus's boss?"

"Yes, the number two man, Thinkingcap, as Lazarus called him. Very good, very slippery. He got away, with two others: an old Finn and a Frenchwoman."

"Scott didn't tell me."

"We, MI6 I mean—I'm just a glorified secretary—thought we could deal with him before you Americans knew he was gone, and then it was too late to tell you. He's never been heard of since."

"That could mean he's been sleeping and someone has woken him."

"One of the things this fellow Tom Hibbert, your Number One, was working on before they tried to give him the treatment was Lazarus's link to the ZD. Hibbert was a very good man. Just a week or two before they got to him, he made Thinkingcap."

"Made him?"

"Identified him. Got him cold. True name Rami Walid Kamel Hamdallah, born in Jordan of Palestinian parents. He went to Berkeley under a scholarship set up by good-hearted citizens for deserving young Palestinians. Got a PhD in chemistry with honors. Brilliant student. When this mythical 'Mirza' character picked him up, he was working for Kelch und Kuhns, AG, a research laboratory in Munich. He specialized in pharmacodynamics, which is the experimental study of the action and fate of drugs in animals. What works with animals, of course, usually works with people."

Applied research in drugs? Chase was very interested now. He didn't speak, waiting for her to continue as long as she would on her own, before asking specific questions.

Victoria Bailey closed her eyes and concentrated. Chase understood: Bailey was no doubt an MI6 analyst, a glorified secretary, as she'd put it. That meant she dealt with hundreds of cases at any given moment; the details of the Lazarus case were stored somewhere in her memory, but it would take a moment to search them out.

"He now works in his old specialty, running a drug research laboratory in Marseille, where he is very highly regarded. He married a French woman whose surname, DuBourdieu, he adopted, along with the forename Marcel. There's nothing unusual among Europeans in a man adopting a wife's name if it is a better one than his own, and clearly it is more advantageous to have a Gallic name in Marseille than an Arab one. Before he met his wife Hamdallah's appearance had been altered by plastic surgery, eliminating the more pronounced Semitic facial features. In Western clothes, with Western manners, accompanied by a French wife, he could pass for a Mediterranean Frenchman. According to his identity card he is thirty-six years old, born in Damascus, formerly the center of French civilization in the Middle East, so he could very well have had one French parent. Monsieur and Madame DuBourdieu, who have no children, attend a Calvinist church, and are active in one of Marseille's patriotic organizations. He has marched in medieval costume in parades there."

"You're sure of all that?" Chase walked to the window and looked down at the street. It looked bleak and a little sinister, the white frozen sculptures throwing shadows onto the layer of frost on the ground. Two small fur bundles scuffed their way along the pavement opposite. There were several cars parked along the street. Two of them would have been ideal for surveillance: the angle at which they were parked gave good sight lines to the front door. Chase thought he could detect movement in one of them but decided to put it out of mind until the time came.

"Ninety-nine percent sure. I realize it seems impossible, knowing the French police, but it seems to be the case. The man is a born deceiver. He met his wife on a beach in Yugoslavia one August, took her skiing in February, and reentered France as her husband in April. We think she has no knowledge whatsoever of his other life. He has a mistress, a Frenchwoman who was an auxiliary of Lazarus's team, living in the countryside near Marseille. He never goes to the house where she lives. They meet every second Thursday in the same small hotel *pour faire l'amour,* always in the same room. This cuckoo-clock adultery seems to be part of the cover. The innkeepers are quite fond of them; they're like a married couple. They play Scrabble afterward and always stay for dinner. They drink no alcohol. This is what we found under the floor of the bathroom of her house in the country while they were having their biweekly orgasm."

Victoria handed Chase an enlarged photograph of a cache of arms and ammunition and some other supplies, including apparatus for intravenous administration of fluids.

"Do you have a car near here, Ms. Bailey?"

Victoria nodded.

"Do me a favor then? Pack a bag? A little bit of everything."

"Why?"

"Ms. Bailey, your boss Neville Scott was a double agent. He was mixed up with these Zero Directorate characters. In a pretty substantial way. It seems clear he's fingered you."

"Bloody hell."

"You do have an awful lot of information on them in that ginger lid of yours."

"Where will we go?"

"When people are trying to kill you, it's best to spend as much time as possible in heavily trafficked public places. To dinner, of course."

When she left the room Chase set up the VL22H and called Washington. Brewster came on the line straight away, then hesitated a split second.

Chase knew the ensuing conversation would be uncomfortable for the old man. Brewster could lie, blithely and easily, when the need dictated, but Chase knew his old friend and mentor found lying to him distasteful. In short, no matter what his orders, Brewster would tell Chase the truth, consequences be damned. That in mind, Chase kept his questions simple.

"I want to know what the hell CIA was doing following me last night. I really hope you have a good explanation, or at least a convincing lie."

"Terminate orders are in effect."

"Yours?"

Chase realized he was glad he was having the conversation with Brewster on the phone. It would be a shame to end their tacit friendship with some sort of crass Mexican standoff, he and Brewster pointing guns at each other at the edge of some remote Langley adjacent parking lot, the shadow of an outlying patriotic monument looming over them like a Jungian symbol.

"Heavens, no! Jim Proctor and the DNI, Charles Vanlandingham, made the decision. They cut me out of the loop, Chase. They knew I'd give them hell."

It occurred to Chase that Brewster might be one step removed from a terminate order himself, could in fact be in the crosshairs of a lethal attack at the very moment. Against the dictates of his training, he felt his attitude toward his mentor softening.

"I've just taken out the only two field operatives in the world with deeper memories of official secrets than mine. The whole point of doing that was to lure the Zero Directorate *in,* to put them on my trail."

"True," said Brewster. "And yet—"

"There's always time for 'and yets,' " Chase said.

"Proctor is a number-cruncher. He decided you were potentially a variable we wouldn't be able to control. Something about the probability matrix. That outcome optimization means erasing any variables."

"A 'variable' who happens to have given fifteen years of his life to his country," Chase shot back. "Funny thing about guys like Proctor—the loftier the language, the lower the deed."

"I keep telling them you're the best we've ever had. But as I told you, they cut me out. The decision was reached at the consortium level, not at my desk."

A chill ran through Chase hearing the bureaucratese that told him Brewster was already distancing himself from the operation.

It all sounded like an homage, and homage, he knew, was a key element in the ritual of separation. In the world of espionage, it was akin to a eulogy.

"You know the rules, Chase. Everyone cleans up their own litter box. Everyone in the intelligence community has received rumors and reports about Zero Directorate now, and they're all running scared. Can't make their minds up what to do."

"Because they have no clue what's really going on."

"Look, you can still succeed with this mission. That's what I would do. Forget everything I just told you and go for it. They'll maybe send some more cowboys from Langley, but that won't be a problem for you."

"What about you?"

Brewster paused again, for an even longer period of time. Chase assumed the conversation was being taped, and wondered what the analysts would make of it.

"Considering that I know more about Jonathan Chase than the rest of the agency combined, your current status as a priority target provides a strange form of job security."

"Happy to be of service."

"Very good. And if I was still your commanding officer, I might recommend that you proceed south to Marseille." Now there was anxiety in Brewster's voice. The two men had found their old rhythm. The active components of the various tasks at hand could now be addressed. "The schematic you sent this morning, Jonathan, the one from the safety deposit box. We've located it. It's a drug research facility outside the city called 'Prince Industries.' In the meantime, trust nobody. Don't get seen."

"Understood. Zero Directorate's number two man, the one doing the kidnappings—Thinkingcap—seems to be camped out there. And I'm with the Bailey girl now. I'm taking her with me. She's dead here otherwise. What's the form on her from Tabitha?"

"We haven't got it all, but her sympathies are with the people she worked for, not Scott. Guess he treated her like a lech. Seems clean enough. Treat her with care, though. Don't let her get behind you. I'd say leave her with an embassy on the way, but we've more or less closed them all down as per your request. So stall her as much as you can on your destination. You really don't know who are your friends and who your enemies. I don't think she's part of the game, though she could be bait. We'll give you full strength once we've got it. Lock your door; keep your back to the wall."

Speed was essential, Chase knew, but his main thought at the moment was what he should do about Victoria Bailey. She was there, an unknown quantity, yet he felt she could be used somehow.

As though by some act of clairvoyance, Ms. Bailey entered the room, suitcase in hand. She had changed into a red and black woolen jacket with a black fur collar and hem with a matching skirt, black gloves, and heels. The jacket was fastened with three toggles.

"I'm ready if you are."

"We won't be able to leave until late morning. That was a business chum who's going to call back tomorrow and I really can't miss the chance of hearing from him."

Adjusting one of the straps of her suitcase, Victoria seemed to take the itinerary in stride. "I was hoping for a lie-in tomorrow anyway." Could he detect an invitation in her voice?

"We'll get you checked in at my pension. There's a decent Italian restaurant a few blocks away."

2

All things considered—Chase thought—Victoria Bailey showed that she was an uncommonly cool lady. After an evening out on the Limmat Quai, where Victoria had displayed her prowess on the dance floor—all sinuous legs, sultry come-ons, and brusque refusals—Chase had swallowed a couple of Benzedrine tablets and sat up all night, ready for anything.

The next morning he showered and shaved after his phone call with Brewster confirming her cleanliness, and now he worked out a plan to deal with Victoria as he dressed. He then placed his case, and briefcase, near the door, and went quickly downstairs where he settled both his own and Victoria's accounts with his brand new company Master Charge card, returning with equal speed to the second floor, going straight to her room.

Her bag stood next to the door, which she opened with his knock. She wore a collarless military-style cardigan—pleated patch pockets and epaulets—with tartan skirt and black and white ankle boots. He gently pushed her back into the room, although she did open her mouth to protest, saying she was ready to leave, but his face was set in a serious mask that made her ask, "Jonathan, what is it?"

"The kind of people we're up against are about as exciting as tarantulas, and lethal as sidewinders. I hope what's going to happen now isn't going to be too nasty for you, Ms. Bailey. I have no other option, and I have to be very careful. I promise you this is no game. You're to do everything I say, and do it very slowly. No disrespect is intended but just turn around—right around, like a model—with your hands on your head."

Initially, he was looking for two things, the makeshift weapon or the more cunningly concealed. She wore a small cameo brooch, holding together the neck of her shirt. He made her unpin the brooch and throw it gently onto the bed, where her shoulder bag lay. The brooch was followed by her shoes. He kept the cameo—it looked safe, but technicians could do nasty things with brooch pins. The shoes were clean—he knew every possible permutation with shoes—as was her belt.

He apologized for the indignity, but her clothes and person were the first priorities. If she carried nothing suspicious he could deal with the luggage later, making sure it was kept out of harm's way until they stopped somewhere, so he emptied the shoulder bag onto the bed. The usual junk spilled out onto the white quilt—checkbook, credit card, cash, tissues, comb, small bottle of pills, a small scent spray, lipstick, and a gold compact, plus a dozen or so other miscellaneous items, thrust into the bag out of habit or sentiment.

He kept the comb, some book matches, a small sewing kit from the Plaza Athénée, the scent spray, lipstick, and compact. Comb, book matches, and sewing kit were immediately adaptable weapons for close-quarter work. The spray, lipstick, and compact needed closer attention. In his time he had known scent sprays to contain liquids more deadly than even the most repellent scent; lipsticks to house razor-sharp curved blades, propellant of one kind of another, even hypodermic syringes; and powder compacts to conceal miniature radios, or worse.

She was more embarrassed than angry about having to strip. Her body was the color of rich cream, smooth and regular, with a freckle or two here and there. It was the sort of body that men dreamed of finding alive and wriggling in their beds.

He would have given much to examine the body in detail, but now was not the time, so Chase went through the skirt and shirt, making doubly sure there was nothing inserted in linings or stitching. When he was satisfied, he apologized again, told her to get dressed and then call down to the concierge. She was to use the exact words—that the luggage was ready in her room and in Mr. Chase's. It was to be taken straight to Mr. Chase's car.

Victoria did as she was told, and as she put down the receiver, gave a little shake of the head. "I'll do exactly as I'm told, Jonathan. You're obviously just being professional. I'm not a fool. I like you. I'll do anything, within reason." Her voice shook slightly, as though the whole experience had unnerved her.

On the tenth floor, Victoria and Chase, briefcase in hand, sauntered toward the elevator. Large leafy plants decorated the elevator alcove. Chase, his back now to the plants, pressed the Down button.

Chase smiled at Victoria. "Here we go, then. Heading south."

"Wagons roll—" Victoria's words were cut short as the lights went out, and they were both thrown to one side. The elevator lurched, then began to drop down the shaft at a sickening speed.

Victoria opened her mouth in a scream, but there was no noise, only her face contorting in terror. Chase, seeing her dimly in the gloom, did not know if the sound was blotted out by the terrible crash and banging as the elevator plummeted, swaying and smashing against the sides of the shaft.

In those seconds, though, Chase seemed to hear her—a horrible diminishing shriek of terror, as if he stood apart, still at the top of the elevator shaft. It was a strange experience, in which half of his mind remained detached. "Hold on!" Chase's yell was drowned by the cacophonic crash of metal and wood, combined with a rushing wind-like noise and pressure on his ears. When the car had started its fall, he had his palm loosely on one of the hand rails which ran along three sides of the car. Pure reflex tightened his grip at the first jolt, before the long drop began.

A picture of the car, splintered and shattered out of all recognition at the bottom of the shaft, flashed in and out of his mind.

From the tenth floor, with increasing speed, they went past

the ninth...eighth...seventh...unaware of their position in the shaft, only knowing the final horror would soon be on them.

Then, with a series of shaking bangs, as the sides rattled against the metal runners, it happened.

Two metal cables ran down the length of the shaft, their use unaffected by the loss of power. These thick hawser-like ropes were threaded loosely through the claw safety brakes under the car itself. The very action of the car overspeeding on a downward path caused the hawsers to tighten, exerting pressure inward with the result that two of the claws were activated, one on either side at the front of the elevator car.

In the first few seconds of the downward plunge, one of these last-chance automatic devices, on the right of the car, had been sheared off by the buffeting of metal against metal. The left-hand cable held, slowly pressing inward. At last, as they streaked past the sixth floor, the safety brake clicked, and the claw automatically shot outward. Like a human hand desperately grasping for a last hold, the metal brake hit one of the ratchets in the guide rail, broke loose, hit a second, then a third.

Inside the car, there was a series of reverberating jarring bumps. The whole platform tilted to the right, and each jolt seemed to slow the downward rush. Then, to the sound of tearing wood and metal, the car tipped completely to the right. Chase and Victoria, both trying to keep a grip on the handrail, were conscious of part of the roof being torn away, of the ripping as they slowed, then of the final bone-shuddering stop which broke the forward section of the floor loose.

Victoria Bailey lost her grip.

Still gripping hard to the handrail, he lunged outward, just managing to grasp her insecurely by the wrist.

"Hang on! Try to get some kind of hold." Chase thought he was speaking calmly, until he heard the echo in his distraught voice. He leaned forward at full stretch, allowing his hand to loosen its grip for a second, then tightened on Victoria's wrist.

The whole car creaked under them, its floor sagging downward like a piece of cardboard, so that almost the entire length of the shaft below became visible. Slowly, giving her encouragement, goading her into trying to get her other hand onto his arm, Chase began to pull Victoria back into the car.

Although she was not heavily built, Victoria Bailey felt like a ton weight. Inch by inch, he hauled her back into the car. Together they balanced precariously, almost on tiptoe, clinging to the handrail.

How long the car could stay as it was, precariously jammed in the shaft, was impossible to tell. Chase was sure of only one thing: unless some of their weight was removed, their chances diminished with every minute that passed.

"How are they going to . . . ?" Victoria began, in a small voice.

"I don't know if they can." Chase looked down. Miraculously, he saw that his briefcase was still with them, trapped behind his feet. Moving gently, pausing after each shift in position, he reached down for the case.

Balancing the briefcase at an angle against the handrail, Chase sprang the tumbler locks. Carefully he delved into the hidden compartments for a bag he always made certain to pack. Diminutive in size, the bag was just large enough to carry a handful of objects considered a spy's stock-in-trade: gloves, a length of rope, lock picks, assorted tools, and grappling hooks.

The hooks would take immense weight. In the packed closed position, each of them was about seven inches long, roughly three inches wide, and a slim couple of inches in thickness. It was necessary to go through a three-part unlocking sequence to unspring one of them, which then shot out to form a circle of some eight claws, all running from a steel securing base.

With the gloves on, tools and picklocks hanging from a large thong and clip on his belt, and the rope coiled over one arm, Chase closed the case. He passed it to Victoria, telling her to hang on to it at all costs, then secured the nylon rope to the grappling hook. He leaned forward, one hand still on the handrail, to peer down through the ripped and broken floor. The sides of the shaft were plainly visible, together with the crisscross of metal girders.

Taking the bulk of slack on the rope and coiling it into his left hand, Chase dropped the grappling hook through the gaping mouth which formed the forward end of the floor. It took three or four swings on the rope before the claw clamped into place around one of the strengthening girders, some five feet below the car. Gently Chase paid the rope out, trying to gauge the exact length that would take him clear of the car and past the grappling hook.

It would have to be a straight drop, so that the hook would not become dislodged; but if it worked, he would then be able to use the elevator slide rails, and their cross girders, to climb back toward the car.

Slowly, he allowed himself to slide forward, feeling the car move, shuddering, as his weight shifted. It was now or never. Then, as he neared the final gap, the whole car began to vibrate. There followed a rasping noise, as though the metal holding it in place would give way at any moment. Suddenly he was clear and falling, trying to control the drop, keeping his body straight and as near to the side of the shaft as he dared. Metallic vibrations from the car seemed to surround him, and the fall went on forever, until the sudden jerk on the rope cut into his back, arms, and legs. As Chase feared, the weight of his fall pulled the nylon tight; then the tension released, and he felt himself rising again like a yo-yo. It only needed too much of a backward spring on the rope for the grapple to become unhooked.

Winded, and not quite believing it, Chase found himself hanging, swinging hard against the concrete and girdered wall. The rope cut deeper. Chase felt his muscles howling in protest, while his wrists and hands struggled to hang on.

The small, enclosed world gradually swung into focus; dirty concrete; girders, with traces of rust, oil, and, below, the dark cavern that seemed to descend to hell itself.

His feet were firmly against the wall now, and Chase was able to look upward. The car was jammed across the shaft, but for how long was anyone's guess. Already the upper section of the woodwork had developed a long crack. It was only a matter of time before the crack would widen, then split and give way. The car would then drop heavily on its side.

He took a deep breath and called up to Victoria. "Be up for you in a minute." Kicking out from the wall, he allowed his hands to slide on the rope, bringing his feet within touching distance of the nearest girder. As the bottoms of his tennis shoes slammed into the metal, Chase hauled on the rope, grabbing for support from the big oily guide rail.

The latticework of girders was reasonably easy to negotiate, and Chase climbed it with speed, keeping the rope firmly around himself, until he reached the grappling hook. There he paused for breath, the car rattling in the breeze that came up the shaft's tunnel. Vaguely, among the creaking metallic noises, he thought he could hear other sounds—shouting and steady hammering. The sagging floor of the car was some five feet from his head. Unhooking the grapple, he climbed higher, finally finding a suitable place among the girders to refix the hook: this time less than a foot below the car. Turning his body so that he could lean back against the wall, Chase once more shouted to Victoria, giving orders in a voice designed to command immediate obedience.

"I'm going to throw the rope in. Tie the briefcase on, then let it down slowly. But don't lose the rope. Keep hold of it until I tell you."

By this time he had pulled in all the slack of the rope, which had snaked down the shaft almost out of sight. Hanging on to the girders with one hand, Chase coiled several feet of rope around the other. Then, with a cry of "Ready?"—and an answering affirmative from Victoria—he aimed the balled rope at the flapping mouth which was the open floor of the car.

The ball of rope went straight as an arrow. For a second or two he saw that the length now protruding from the opening in the car was sliding back. Then it stopped, and Victoria's voice came filtering down with a "Got it." About a minute later the briefcase, tied now to the end of the rope, descended slowly toward him.

Victoria paid out the rope until Chase shouted for her to stop. Precariously he reached forward, took the case, and balancing it on the girder, untied the knot. He attached one of the metal fastenings on the briefcase to the large clip on his belt. Then he shouted to Victoria to haul in the rope and get a tight hold on it. "Wrap it around your wrists and shoulders if you want," he called to her. "Then just slide out. It's around thirty feet down to the next floor and set of doors. If we can make that, we'll have a secure ledge, and I'll try to open the damned things. Come on when you're ready."

She came quickly. Too quickly. Chase saw her legs emerge, and the rope dropped past him. Then he felt the blow as the side of her shoulder hit him.

He was conscious of the grapple taking the strain and of the car shifting just above his head. But by that time his balance had gone, and he was suddenly scrabbling for the swinging rope in front of him

His hands wrapped around the nylon, and they were both swinging gently, one above the other, bouncing off the walls of the shaft.

"We're going down one at a time," he called, short of breath. "Just straight rope-climbing stuff to the ledge of the next floor. The rope'll just about make it."

Victoria's voice came back, breathless and excited. "I only hope it'll hold our weight."

"It'll do that, all right. Just remember not to let go."

"You really think I'd forget?" she shouted back, starting to move, hand over hand, the rope wrapped around her ankles as she went.

Chase followed Victoria's lead, trying to imitate her rhythm on the rope in order to reduce the swing. He had been bruised and battered enough from bumping against the girders. Finally he saw below him that Victoria had made it, saw her standing on the narrow ledge, both hands still tight on the rope, her feet spread out and body leaning forward.

She was calling something up to him.

"There's someone on the other side of the doors," he heard her shout.

Chase pointed downward as he tied a new knot on the girder. They'd have to continue down this way several more levels to avoid potential hostiles.

Doggedly, they made a more or less silent descent the rest of the way, and eventually exited the shaft at the service side of the mezzanine level.

"No lights," Chase whispered. "Here, take my hand."

He felt her hand clasp his palm—it was remarkably cool for one who had just escaped death—as they negotiated their way past boilers and maintenance ephemera, then into a corridor punctuated with doors that stood out clearly in their hotel white.

A final door—SORTIE DE SECOURS visible in red overhead—opened with a push-bar safety lock, and the cool of the morning hit them as they emerged onto a metal platform—a black square studded with holes—from which you could almost reach out and touch the other buildings. To the right, narrow and swaying steps zigzagged down.

"How do we get out? At the bottom, I mean," Victoria asked. Chase looked down, seeing nothing but a tiny court-yard—square, surrounded by the backs of buildings.

The sound of heavy feet thudding echoed toward them from the other side of the door.

"Go, just go." He did not raise his voice. "Just get down and leave the doors open for me. There's a racing green Iso Rivolta parked opposite. Make for the Chinese restaurant and watch for me. If I arrive in a hurry, with both hands in view, run straight to the car. If my right hand's in my pocket and I'm taking my time, lose yourself for half an hour, then come back and wait. Same signals at half-hour intervals. Now, move!"

She seemed to hesitate for a second, then went down the metal stairs, which seemed to shake precariously as her speed increased, while Chase swiveled toward the exit, drawing his gun, holding it low against the hip.

The thudding of feet grew louder, and when he thought the distance right, Chase pulled back sharply, opening the door.

He did it the textbook way, leaving just enough time to be certain his targets were not friendly policemen—who were liable to be unfriendly if they thought he was some criminal intruder.

By no stretch of the imagination were these men police: unless Zurich's finest had taken to using Colt .45 automatics without warning.

The men slithered to a halt as soon as he showed himself. Oddly, they had put the lights on in the corridor, so they could be seen quite clearly—although Chase was aware that he was an equally good target, even turned sideways.

There were two of them—well-muscled trained hoods, one

moving fast behind the other, each hogging a different side of the narrow corridor.

It was the one ahead, to Chase's right, who fired, the .45 sounding like a bomb in the confines of the corridor. A huge piece of the doorjamb disintegrated, leaving a large hole and sending splinters flying. The second shot passed between Chase and the jamb. He felt the crack of the bullet as it cut the air near his head, but by this time he had also fired — low, to miss or do damage to feet and legs.

He squeezed the trigger twice, one shot to each wall, heard a yelp of pain and a shout, then turned about and hurtled down the stairs glancing below to see there was no sign of Victoria.

He thought there was another shout from above him as he reached the first door. Chase went through it as though trying to beat all existing records, slammed it after him and barreled down the passage to the street door. Seconds later he was in the street itself, turning left again, both hands in sight.

—2—

Paranoia was nothing new in Chase's life. You couldn't let it get in the way of work or spoil your leisure hours. The trick, as he was told as a trainee by what he then regarded as wise old instructors, was to avoid getting into situations from which there was no escape. You always cased the joint before you went in, always sat with your back to the wall, always made sure there was a back door. The majority of his classmates took this advice to heart and were not much good to themselves or anyone else thereafter. Sometimes getting out the back door involved breaking somebody's neck in a dark stairway.

Actually, the trick was to find a way to turn the threat back on the threatener. He had committed himself to an action, so it was jujitsu time: you used your attacker's energy to destroy him. This meant getting close to the adversary, and that meant overcoming the instinct to get as far away from the person trying to destroy you as you could, as quickly as you could. However, in operations the question was not, How do I get myself out of this? It was, What can I do to the other fellow next? One must always be the aggressor, never the defender. Always the joker, never the butt. Always the carefree American boy who was never suspected of guile until too late. Your opponent might have had more hair on his knuckles than you had on your entire body, but you had the inestimable advantage of his belief that you were going to be no trouble merely because you were less hairy than he was.

They settled in the car and Chase asked Victoria to fasten her seat belt, telling her there would be fast driving up ahead. He started the engine and waited, both for the traffic to clear and to be certain there was space free of pedestrians, and vehicles, behind him. When things seemed right, he slid the Rivolta into reverse, spun the wheel, banged at the accelerator and brake, slewing the car backward into a skid, bringing the rear around in a half circle, then roaring off, cutting between a peeping VW bus and a large truck—much to the wrath of the drivers. Sure enough, through the mirror he could see a Renault behind them in trouble and taken by surprise. He increased speed as soon as they were through the restricted zone, and began to take the bends and winds of the lakeside road at expert, if dangerous, speed. At the French frontier he told the guards that he thought they were being followed by brigands, making much of his spare passport—the diplomatic one always carried against emergencies.

The gendarmes were suitably impressed, called him Formidable, bowed to the lady and promised to question the occupants of the Renault with vigor.

"Do you always drive like that?" Victoria hummed. "I suppose you must. Fast-cars and fast-women kind of fellow. Action man."

Chase didn't comment. He concentrated on the driving, allowing Victoria to slip into idle chatter about the countryside.

Near Lyons were lines of trees, bent by the shimmering autumn sun as the spinnakers of a sailing squadron are tilted by the wind. Nearer were the villages, cubes of earthy masonry with their blind walls turned toward the road. Victoria said she imagined twisted dwarfs in their streets, and widows in black, and a corrupt priest, also in black, commanding the parents of beautiful virgins to marry them to the humpbacked sons of rich fathers.

Chase tried to make her see in the bleached sky and landscape and the severe peasant architecture the colors and forms in the painting of Picasso and Juan Gris. Victoria shot him a surprised look, but said she preferred ghosts and monsters. Wrapped round her head she wore a scarf of the same changing blue shades as her elongated eyes; as it grew warmer she took it off, and knotted one end to her necklace. With the windows open, her hair and the silk, red and blue, flew behind them like pennants.

There were some problems—particularly when she wished to use the restrooms—but they managed it twice during the afternoon, by stopping at service areas with Chase positioning the car so that he had full view of any pay telephones, and of the restroom doors. His own bladder had to be kept under control, but just before they started on the long, awesome mountain route that would take them through Monaco to Marseille, they rested together at a roadside café and had food.

It was here that Chase took the chance of leaving Victoria Bailey alone. The place was filled with workmen and a few pallid whores; the girls sat at the tables by the window, talking about shops and movies with the kindness and generosity they have for one another. Chase was reminded of Brewster; like him, the girls were aging too quickly, and they placed the same value on people who knew the things that they had learned. They understood one another's fatigue.

When he returned from the bathroom, Victoria looked as though butter would melt, though she seemed surprised when he popped a couple of Benzedrine tablets with his coffee.

"I was wondering...," Victoria began.

"Yes?"

"I was wondering what the sleeping arrangements are going to be when we stop for the night. I mean, you obviously—for any number of reasons—can't let me out of your sight..."

"You sleep in the car. I drive. There'll be no stopping at hotels. Not yet."

"Very Chinese," Victoria muttered.

"The sooner we get to Marseille the sooner I can release you. We've got someone waiting there to take charge of things."

Victoria gazed into Chase's face, her vivid eyes unblinking. He said nothing. She stared at him for a moment.

"Jonathan, we hardly know each other, but you have to understand that, for me, this is a kind of adventure—something I've only read about in books. This could be routine for you, but it's so abnormal for me, it's exciting."

"We'd better get back to the car," Chase said flatly. Inside, he knew Victoria Bailey was either going through a form of transference, like a hostage starting to identify with her captor, or trying to establish a rapport in order to lull him into complacency. To increase chances of survival he had to remain detached; and that was not an easy option with a young woman as attractive as Victoria.

Victoria gave a sigh of exasperation, but Chase stopped her with a movement of his hand.

"Into the car," he ordered.

They made exceptional time on the long run down through the twisting Pyrenees, through Nice, so that just before seven-thirty in the evening they were cruising at speed along the A8, having skirted Aix-en-Provence, now heading southwest. Within the hour they would turn further south onto the A50, which would lead them to Marseille. The day had been warm, even high among the mountains, and Victoria proved not to be insensible to the rugged and incredible grandeur of the terrain through which they passed. Chase drove with care and relentless concentration, cursing the situation in which he found himself. So beautiful was the day, so impressive the scenery, that, had things been different, the ever-changing landscape, combined with Victoria, would have made this a memorable vacation indeed. His eyes searched the road ahead, scanning the traffic, their signals, then swiftly crossing the instruments to check speed, fuel consumption, and temperature.

"Remember the silver Renault, Jonathan?" said Victoria, in an almost teasing voice. "Well, I think it's behind us, moving up fast."

Chase cursed.

"The plates are the same," from Victoria. "I remember them from Zurich. But I think the occupants have changed."

Chase glanced into the mirror. Sure enough, a silver Renault was coming up fast, about half a mile behind them. From the mirror he couldn't make out the passengers. "Let them have their day," he said, then touched the brakes and pulled into the far lane, watching from his offside wing mirror.

He was conscious of a tension between the two of them, like game that sensed the hunter. Fear suddenly seemed to flood the interior of the car, almost tangible, a scent of danger. The road ahead was empty, ribbon straight, with grassland curving upward toward outcrops of rock and the inevitable pine and fir, abundant and thick. Chase's eyes flicked to the wing mirror again, and he glimpsed the hard, screwed-up concentration on the face of the Renault's driver.

The red dropping ball of the sun was behind them, so the silver car was using the old fighter pilot tactic — coming out of the sun. As the Rivolta swung for a second, the crimson fire filled the wing mirror. The next moment, Chase was depressing the accelerator, feeling the proximity of death. The Rivolta responded as only that machine can, a surge of power, effortlessly pushing them forward. But he was a fraction late. The Renault was already almost abreast of them and going flat out.

He heard Victoria shout, and felt a blast of air as her window was opened. Somehow he realized that Victoria had shouted for them to get down, while lowering her window. He heard Victoria shout, "They're going to shoot," and the distinctive barrel of a pump-action sawn-off Winchester showed, for a split second, from the rear window of the Renault.

Then came the two blasts, one sharp and from behind his right shoulder, filling the car with a film of gray mist bearing the unmistakable smell of cordite. The other was louder, but farther away, almost drowned by the ending noise, the rush of wind into the car, and the ringing in his own ears. The Iso Rivolta bucked to the right, as though some giant metal boot-tip had struck the rear with force: the push was accompanied by a rending, clattering noise, like stones hitting them. Then another bang to his right. He saw the silver car to their left, almost abreast of them, a haze of smoke being whipped from the rear where someone crouched at the window. The Winchester's barrel was trained on them.

"Down, Victoria!" he shouted, his voice rising to a scream. There was a lurching sensation, then a grinding as the sides of the two cars grated together, then drifted apart, followed by another crack from the Rivolta.

They must have been touching 120 mph, and Chase knew he had almost lost control of the car as it veered and snaked across the road. He pumped the brakes, watched the road now, touched the brakes twice more and felt the speed bleed off as the front wheels mounted the grass verge.

There was a sliding sensation, then a rocking bump as they stopped. "Out!" Chase yelled. "Out! On the far side! Use the car for cover!"

When he reached the relative safety of the car's side, he saw Victoria crouched behind the trunk, her tartan skirt hitched up to show a stocking top and part of a black garter belt. The skirt had hooked itself into a neat, soft leather holster, on the inside of her thigh, and she held a large Beretta 951 pistol very professionally, in a two-handed grip, pointing across the trunk.

Over the long snout of the Rivolta, Chase saw the truth. He had no time to go into the whys and wherefores of Victoria Bailey's professional actions, her gun, or how he had missed finding it. The silver Renault was streaking toward them, up the slow lane, moving in the wrong direction, regardless of two other careening cars and a lorry, all three of which waved and screeched over the wide road to avoid collision.

"The tires," Chase said coolly. "Go for the tires."

"You go for the tires," Victoria snapped, angry at being given instructions suddenly. Clearly she had her own ideas about stopping the car, which was now almost on top of them.

In the fraction of time before she opened fire, a host of things crossed Chase's mind. The Renault had originally contained a two-man team. When the hit had come, there were three of them: one in the back with the Winchester, the driver, and a backup who seemed to be using a high-powered revolver. Somehow the shotgun-wielding killer had disappeared, but the one in the passenger seat now had the Winchester. The driver's side window was open, and in a fanatical act of lunacy, the passenger seemed to be leaning across the driver, to fire the Winchester as they came rapidly closer to the Iso, which was slewed like a beached whale, just off the hard shoulder of the road.

Victoria looked straight over the Guttersnipe sight on the Beretta. She was on target now: aiming not at the tires but at the gas tank, for the Beretta was loaded with those most horrific projectiles, prefragmented bullets—each containing hundreds of number 12 shot suspended in liquid Teflon. The effect of an impact from just one of these appalling little bullets was devastating, for the projectile would penetrate skin, bone, tissue, or metal before almost literally exploding the mass of tiny steel balls. They would cut a man in half at a few paces, take out a leg or an arm, and certainly ignite fuel in a vehicle's tank.

Victoria began to take up the pressure on the trigger, and, as the rear of the Renault came fully into the triangle of her sights, she squeezed hard. Several things happened quickly. The nearside front tire crossed the great divide in a terrible burning and shredding of rubber—the car began to slew inward, toppling slightly, looking as though it would cartwheel straight into the Iso, but the driver struggled with wheel and brakes, and the silver car just about stayed in line, hopelessly doomed, but running fast and straight toward the hard shoulder.

This all happened in a millisecond, for, as the tire disintegrated, so the two slugs from the Beretta scorched through the bodywork into the gas tank.

Almost in slow motion, the Renault seemed to continue on its squealing, tippling way. The effect of the slugs appeared to take minutes, but it happened just as the car had passed the rear of the Rivolta—a long, thin sheet of flame, like natural gas being burned off, hissing from the rear of the car. There was even time to notice that the flame was tinged with blue before the whole rear end of the Renault became a rumbling, irregular, boiling, growing crimson ball. The car now began its cartwheel, and was, in fact, a burning, twisted wreck—a hundred yards or so to the rear of the Iso—by the time the noise reached them: a great hiss and *whump,* followed by a screaming of rubber and metal as the vehicle went through its spectacular death throes.

Neither of them moved for a second. Then Chase reacted. Two or three cars were approaching the scene, and he was in no mood to be involved with the police at this stage.

"Chase! The driver!"

Chase twisted around in time to see the driver of the Renault hobbling away down the road. As he ran he was obviously reaching for a weapon, but Victoria already had hers out, and she fired the Beretta three times in rapid succession. With a scream, the driver tumbled to the ground, but he had managed to wrest his weapon from its holster, and he fired back. His aim was off; bullets spit into the ground near them. Victoria fired again hitting their enemy in the chest.

He flew backward, sprawled on the ground, dead.

Chase reached toward him, flipping the prone body over, rummaging through the man's pockets for identification.

He pulled out a wallet. He was not surprised to find one; the pursuer had probably been given no notice by Zero Directorate, and thus no time to rid himself of identifying documents.

The detritus of bureaucracy, in this case, was straightforward. Documents could be forged, but Chase was an expert at recognizing fake documents, and this was not one of them. There was no doubt. He examined it carefully in the blood-orange twilight, turning it over, locating the requisite fibers and irreproducible markings.

"What is it?" Victoria asked. He handed it to her; she saw at once.

"Oh, my *God!*" she said, her voice hushed.

The pursuer had been no mere Zero Directorate rent-a-cop. He was a U.S. citizen, employed by the Zurich station of the CIA.

As they rushed back to the car, Chase weighed his options. He knew there were only two choices now as far as Brewster went: retreat or confrontation, and he preferred confrontation, the only option that had a chance of eliciting spontaneous revelation, forcing unplanned truths.

"What kind of shape are we in?" he called out to Victoria, a few paces ahead of him.

"Dented, a lot of holes in the bodywork, but the wheels seem okay." Victoria was at the other side of the car now. She unhitched her skirt from the garter belt, showing a fragment of black lace as she did so. "There's a very nasty scrape down this side. Stem to stern."

Chase looked at her, asking if she was okay. "Shaken, but undamaged, I think."

"In!" Chase commanded crisply. "Into the car," as he dived toward the driving seat, conscious of at least one car, containing people in checked shirts, floppy hats, and the usual impediments of tourists, drawing up cautiously to the rear of the burning wreckage.

He twisted the key, almost viciously, in the ignition. The engine throbbed into life immediately, and, without ceremony, he knocked off the main brake with his left hand, slid into drive, and smoothly gunned it back onto the motorway.

The traffic remained sparse, giving Chase the opportunity to run through checks on the car's engine and handling. There was no loss of fuel, oil, or hydraulic pressure; he went steadily up the steps, through the gears and back again. Brakes appeared unaffected. The cruise control went in and came out normally, while whatever damage had been done to the body did not appear to have affected either suspension or handling. After five minutes he was satisfied the car was relatively undamaged. There was, he did not doubt, a good deal of penetration from the couple of Winchester blasts. The car, with its damage, would now be a sitting target for the French police, who, like the forces of most Western countries, were not enamored of shootouts between cars on their highways—particularly when one of the vehicles, and its occupants, ends up incinerated.

There was need to reach a telephone quite quickly, alert Brewster and get him to call the French dogs off. Something else nagged at his mind. Victoria Bailey swam, an image, into his head—the lush thigh and the Beretta being expertly handled.

Chase was deeply disturbed. All but one tiny doubt had told him that Victoria Bailey was absolutely trustworthy, just who she said she was: the helpless assistant of a British double agent named Neville Scott, a woman he had come to think of as intelligent, fun-loving, and clearly excellent at her job.

Set against what he had just seen, Victoria appeared suddenly to have feet of melting wax.

"I think you'd better let me have the armory, Ms. Bailey," Chase said quietly, hardly turning his head.

"Oh, no, Jonathan. No, Jonathan. No," she sang, quite prettily.

"I don't like MI6 secretaries roving around with guns, especially in the current climate, and within this car. How in heaven's name did I miss it anyway?"

"Because, while you're obviously a pro, I'm a better pro."

He recalled her flirtatious manner at the roadside café after he'd returned from the bathroom. "So, I suppose I now pay for the error of leaving you alone for two minutes. Are you going to tell me it's pointing at the back of my head?"

"Actually it's pointing toward my own left knee, back where it belongs. Not the most comfortable place to have a weapon." She paused. "Well, not that kind of weapon anyway."

A sign came up indicating a picnic area, ahead and to their right. Chase slowed, pulling off the road, down a track through dense fir trees and into a clearing. Rustic tables and benches stood in the center of the clearing. There was not a picnicker in sight.

To one side—praise heaven—a neat, clean, and unvandalized telephone booth awaited them.

Chase brought the car to a halt in the shade of the trees, turning it so that they could make a quick exit if necessary. He cut the engine, clicked off his seat belt, and turned to face Victoria, holding out his right hand, palm upward. "The gun, Ms. Bailey. I have to make a couple of important calls, and I'm in enough danger already. Just give me the gun."

Victoria smiled at him, a gentle, fond smile. "You'd have to take it from me, Jonathan, and that might not be as easy as you imagine. Look, I used that weapon to help you. Brewster's given me orders. I am to cooperate—to assist—and I can assure you that, had he instructed otherwise, you would have known it within a very short time of my joining you in the car."

"*Brewster's* ordered you?" Chase felt lost. And angry.

"He's my boss. I take orders from him, and ..."

"You're Number Three."

"You *are* quick."

Chase shrugged, took the keys out of the ignition, grabbed Victoria's arm, and climbed from the car.

"Let's just double-check that, shall we?"

After retrieving the VL22H from the trunk, they went over to the telephone booth, and Chase made the slightly more complex attachments needed for pay phones. He dialed the operator, placing a call to I-Division's number in Washington.

"Number Two?"

"Speaking."

"Where are you?"

"France."

"Ah."

"I have someone with me claiming to be the new Number Three. Can you confirm or deny, please?"

"I see. So, the lovely Victoria has broken her cover with you, then?"

"There was a firefight on the A50 to Marseille with some more cowboys from Langley. Where are they finding these guys, boss? It's like amateur hour around here."

"Jonathan..."

"What are they calling it over there, sir? A full 'sterilization'? Is that the phrase? Removing the splinters, mopping up?"

"Jonathan..."

"Why so many lies, old man?"

"This is a *huge* job, Jonathan. I thought you needed help. I wanted to tell you earlier, but I was also curious to see how long her cover would hold up against you."

"Testing me?"

"Testing *her,* by golly."

"Shouldn't we all be working together on this?"

"Well, I just taught you an important lesson, didn't I?"

"And what's that, sir?"

"Don't trust anyone."

A scrim of red momentarily suffused Chase's vision: which was the greater insult, he wondered—being treated like a fool, or being sacrificed as a pawn?

"Maybe you should have given me the benefit of all this worldly wisdom a few days ago."

"I thought about it. But I know you, Chase: you would have said no. You wouldn't have listened. You work alone. That's your thing. You're too busy romancing the eternal verities. I respect your instincts, Jonathan. They're the best instincts in the business, except, maybe, for hers."

"So we're partners now?"

"That's the idea, Number Two. Remember our original idea?"

"Which one?"

"About you being the bait?"

"Yes, I do. And oddly enough, I don't see any alternative now but to run to them with open arms. Like fishing with dynamite."

"Put Number Three on, would you?"

Chase passed the receiver to Victoria, mulling over Brewster's last words.

In his role as I-Division watchdog, Chase simply knew too much about U.S. intelligence. If his memory was drained like the others, there could be no going back to what had existed before; something new would have to be created to take the CIA's place—something that would recapture the energy, the sheer audacity, and patriotism it had in its youth. But Brewster and Chase had believed for a long time that a way must be found for American espionage to start over again. The Cold War, to the informed individual, was over. Marxism-Leninism-Stalinism had collapsed under the weight of its own pathology. The old secret alliances against the Russian Communists, built up over half a century by the CIA and men like Brewster, had outlived their usefulness. A new world was in the making. A new intelligence service was required to study it, to understand it, to discover America's real enemies and to help her real friends.

The three great ideologies of their lifetime had been capitalism, communism, and anti-Americanism. Communism had been defeated but the other two remained, and in the years ahead—it seemed clear to Chase—the United States would be faced with far more powerful and intelligent adversaries than totalitarian Russia and China had ever been, people who were possessed of a far stronger reason than the Communists had ever had for hating her: she had defeated them utterly in war, compelling their unconditional surrender, and then lifted them up and healed them and given them back their nationhood and their place in history. How could such magnanimity ever be forgiven? How could people laboring under such an unbearable moral debt ever be trusted? However right they were about this, they knew that there was no point in struggling against conventional wisdom. In its great, early days under Dulles, the CIA, manned by the flower of American youth, had been something almost entirely new in history, a secret intelligence service that was dedicated to doing good in the world by stealth. "If we said that out loud we'd be laughed out of town," Brewster had told Chase soon after he took him into his confidence. "But by George, I know it can be done!"

Now the question was: could Number Three be trusted to agree with their more or less radical scenario?

Victoria held out the telephone receiver so they could both hear Brewster. "Analysis has come back on everything MI6 found in the floor of Thinkingcap's girlfriend's house. The handguns are nine-millimeter Jerichos, made by Israeli Military Industries. The clips are loaded with unmodified production rounds. Very interesting that they'd choose Israeli equipment, but as you know, these weapons are available over the counter in the U.S. The serial numbers have been defaced with acid."

He continued, "There was a device. A device used to force fluids through the skin. They use it on children because it doesn't hurt as much as a needle. The tube attaches to a small container of compressed air."

"So that's how they got Hillman in the toilet," Chase interjected.

"We also found a bag of white powder. An agent gave a small dose to his poodle, and judging by the way the dog behaved, I think it may be the stuff we're looking for."

"Jesus, boss. We have all this evidence and they still wanted me out?"

"Neither Proctor nor the DNI know anything about this."

"One question," Victoria said. "If his habits, as DuBourdieu, are as regular as the file made them out to be, how does he account for the absences necessitated by the kidnappings?"

Clearly Brewster had been waiting for this question. "Under the law, and because of his seniority, good burgher DuBourdieu is entitled to seven weeks' vacation a year. For sentimental reasons, presumably, he and his wife take a week at Megève for skiing in

February and four weeks in Yugoslavia on the beach in August. Madame is entitled to only five weeks. As a good wife, however, she insists that he take all the time he is entitled to. That leaves him with two weeks', or ten days', extra vacation time all to himself. When the Mirza wants him to snatch a spy, he takes off Friday and a Monday, which gives him four days in which to operate."

"Our guys have all disappeared for four days—back on Tuesday morning," Chase said.

Victoria jumped in, "So he's only got a few days' vacation left this year and it's November already. If we want him to get to the person we have in mind, we'd better dangle the bait pretty soon."

"I told you she was good, Chase."

"Yeah, yeah."

"So who do you guys have in mind?"

2

For years Jonathan Chase had nurtured the habit of taking catnaps and being able to control his sleep—even under stress. He had also acquired the knack of feeding problems into the computer of his mind, allowing the subconscious to work away while he slept. Usually he woke with a clear mind, sometimes with a new slant on difficulties, inevitably refreshed.

After the exceptionally long and hard drive from Zurich, Chase felt natural fatigue, although his mind was active with a maze of conflicting puzzles.

At the Marseille safe house, an apartment on the sixth floor of an old building behind the Palais de Justice known only to agents of I-Division, Chase ate the food that had been left in the refrigerator for him and Victoria, took a shower, and sat down at a portable typewriter. He worked steadily on his report listening to the late traffic moving on the quays along the Vieux-Port. He wrote nothing about Victoria. He burned his notes and the type-writer ribbon and flushed the ashes down the toilet. Then, placing the typed report inside the pillowcase, he went to bed and slept for several hours. He dreamed that Victoria, standing with the light behind her in a room in Madrid where he had slept with an-other girl, told him she had given birth; his mind knew he had no child, and he ended the dream.

He seemed to have been asleep for only a few minutes when the tapping broke through to his consciousness. His eyes snapped open. The tapping continued—soft double raps at the door. Noiselessly, Chase slipped the Dunhill flamethrower lighter from under his pillow and crossed the room. The tapping was insistent. The double rap, then a long pause followed by another double rap.

Keeping to the left of the door, his back against the wall, Chase whispered, "Who's there?"

"Victoria. It's Victoria, Jonathan. I have to talk with you. Please. Please let me in."

Chase glanced at the illuminated dial of his TAG Heuer. It was four-thirty in the morning, that unsettling hour when the mind is far from its sharpest, when babies are more apt to start the last stages of their journey into the world, and when death often stalks most easily into the geriatric wards of hospitals. Psychologically, Victoria couldn't have chosen a better moment.

"Hang on," Chase whispered, recrossing the room to shrug himself into a white cotton T-shirt and return the Dunhill under his pillow.

When he opened the door, Chase quickly decided she had come unarmed. There were very few places she could manage to hide anything in the outfit she wore: an opalescent white negligee hanging loose over a sheer, clinging matching nightdress. She would have been enough to make any man drop his guard, with her pale and freckled body quite visible through the soft material, and the dazzling contrast of color underlined by the red shimmer of hair, and the eyes pleading with a hint of sadness. Chase allowed her into the room, locked the door, and stood back. Well, he thought, his gaze quickly traveling down her body, she is either an ultra-professional or a very natural redhead.

Sex was still a vital factor in covert operations—not so much for blackmail anymore, as it had been in years past, but for more subtle pressures, like trust, entrapment, and misdirection. As long as he remembered that, Chase could turn this situation to his own advantage.

Chase went over to the bedside table, picked up his cigarette case, and offered one to Victoria, who shook her head. Chase didn't smoke either.

"Look, Victoria. Our business breeds odd friends; and sometimes strange enemies. I don't want to become your enemy. But you need friends."

Victoria nodded, face set, masklike. "Then let me tell you the full story, Mr. Chase, so that you can set the record straight. After that, I think we'd both better try to work together on this."

"What's your real name?"

"My name is Verena Rautavaara. My father was Finnish. His name was Berg Rautavaara. You know the name?"

"Famous SS officer. Rare for being Finnish. Brave. Ruthless. A wanted war criminal."

She nodded. "I didn't know about that part until I was around twelve." She spoke very softly, but with a conviction Chase felt was genuine. "When my father left Finland he took several of his brother officers and some enlisted men with him. In those days, as you know, there were a fair assortment of camp followers. On the day he left Lapland, my father proposed to a young widow. Good birth, had large holdings of land—forest mainly—in Lapland. My mother was part Lapp. She accepted and volunteered to go with him, so becoming a kind of camp follower herself. She went through horrors you'd hardly believe." She shook her head, as though still not crediting her own mother's actions. Rautavaara had married on the day after leaving Finland, and his wife stayed near him until the collapse of the Third Reich. Together they had escaped.

"My first home was in Paraguay," she told Chase. "I knew nothing of course. It wasn't until later I realized that I spoke four languages from the beginning—Finnish, Spanish, German, and English. We lived in a compound in the jungle. Quite comfortable really, but the memories of my father are not pleasant."

"Tell me," Chase said. Little by little he coaxed it out of her. It was, in fact, an old tale. Rautavaara had been autocratic, drunken, brutal, and sadistic.

"I was ten years old before we escaped—my mother and I. To me it was a kind of game: dressed up as an Indian child. We got away by canoe, and then with the help of some Guarani, made it to Asuncion. My mother was a very unhappy lady. I don't know how it was managed, but she got passports for both of us. Swedish passports and some kind of grant. We were flown to Stockholm, where we stayed for six months. Every day my mother would go to the Finnish Embassy, and eventually we were granted our Finnish passports. Mother spent the first year in Helsinki getting a divorce and compensation for her lost land. We lived in Helsinki and I got my first taste of schooling. That's about it."

"It?" Chase repeated, raising his eyebrows.

"Well, the rest was predictable enough."

It was while she was at school that Verena began to learn the facts about her father. "By the age of fourteen I knew it all, and was horrified, disgusted that my own father had left his country to become part of the SS. I suppose it was an obsession—a complex. By the time I was fifteen, I knew what had to be done as far as my life went."

Chase had heard many confessions in his day. After years of experience you develop a sense about them. He would have put money on Verena/Victoria's being a true story, if only because it came out fast, with the minimum of detail. People operating under a deep cover often give you too much.

"Revenge?" he asked.

"A kind of revenge. No, that's the wrong word. My father had nothing to do with what Himmler called The Final Solution—the end of the Jewish problem—but he was associated, he was a wanted criminal. I began to identify with the race that lost six million souls in the gas chambers and the camps. Many people have told me I overreacted. I wanted to do something concrete."

"You became a Jew?"

"I went to Israel on my twentieth birthday. My mother died two years later. The last time I saw her was the day I left Helsinki. Within six months I began the first steps of conversion. Now I'm as Jewish as any Gentile-born person can be. In Israel they tried everything in the book to put me off—but I stuck it out—even military service. It was that which finally clinched it." Her smile was one of pride this time. "Harel himself sent for me, interviewed me. I couldn't believe it when they told me who he was—Isser Harel, the head of Mossad. He arranged everything. I was an Israeli citizen already. Now I went for special training, for Mossad. I had a new name..."

"So you're on loan to us from Mossad, then?"

"I've been done with Mossad since sixty-seven. Harel put in a good word for me with Brewster."

"And the revenge part, Verena? You had atoned, but what about the revenge?"

"Revenge?" Her eyes opened wide. Then she frowned, anxiety crossing her face. "Jonathan, you do believe me, don't you?"

In the couple of seconds which passed before he replied, Chase's mind ran through the facts. Either Verena Rautavaara was the best deception artist he had ever met or, as he had earlier considered, completely honest.

"There's no point in your lying to me, when all the facts can be proven in a very short space of time. My instincts tell me to believe you. We can run traces, even from here, certainly from Washington. Brewster already says you're Number Three." He smiled at her, his mind sending signals to his body. "I believe you, Verena Rautavaara. You were straight Mossad, now you're with us, and you've only left one thing out — the question of vengeance. I can't believe you simply want to atone for your father's actions. You either want him in the bag or dead. Which is it?"

She gave a provocative little shrug. "It doesn't really matter, does it? Whichever way it goes, Berg Rautavaara will die." The musical voice altered for a second, steel hard, then back once more to its softness and small laugh. "I'm sorry, Jonathan. I shouldn't have tried to play games with you. Maybe I'm not the professional I thought. I was naive enough to imagine I could con you, Jonathan. Lure you."

"Lure? Into what web?" Chase, 99 percent sure of Verena's motives and claims, still kept that tiny single percent of wariness in reserve.

"Not a web, exactly." She put out a hand, fingers resting in Chase's palm. "To be honest, I wanted to be sure you'd be on my side."

Chase let go of her hand, placing his own fingers lightly on her shoulders. "We're in the business of trust; and we both need it from someone, because I'm not happy with this setup any more than you are. First things first, though, I have to ask you this, simply because I suspect it. Do you believe your father's somehow mixed up with Zero Directorate?"

She did not pause to think. "Completely sure."

"How do you know?"

"Back in Israel the computers, and people on the ground, began analysis immediately after the first Lazarus incident. They always look at the old names—the former party members, the SS, and those who'd escaped from Germany."

"Back in Brussels, Lazarus did mention a Finn."

"There were several names. My father was high on the list. You'll have to take my word for the rest, but Mossad has evidence that he is tied in very closely. He's here somewhere, Jonathan—new name, perhaps a new face, the whole business of a new identity. He's spry and tough enough, even at his age. I know he's in on it."

"A game bird." Chase gave a wry smile.

"And game is in season. My dear father's well in season. Mother used to say that he saw himself as a new Fuhrer, a Nazi Moses, there to lead his children back to their promised land. The world's in such a mess that the young or the pliable will lap up any half-baked ideology. You only have to look at your own country...the flower children blowing in the breeze."

Chase bridled. "Which has yet to elect, or allow, a madman into power."

She gave a friendly pout. "We really do have to watch each other's backs, even if my theory doesn't hold."

Chase gave her his most charming smile, leaning close, his lips only inches from Verena's mouth. "You're quite right. Though I'd be much happier watching your front."

Her lips, in return, seemed to be examining his mouth. Then: "I don't frighten easily, Jonathan, but this Zero Directorate business has got me twitchy…" Her arms came up, winding around his neck, and their lips brushed, first in light caress. Chase's conscience nagged at him to take care. But the warnings were cauterized in the fires started by their lips, then fanned by the opening of their mouths and the conflagration as their tongues touched.

It seemed an eternity before their mouths unlocked, and Verena, panting, clung to Chase, her breath warm near his ear as she murmured endearments. Slowly, Chase drew her from the chair onto the bed where they lay close, body to body, then mouth to mouth once more, until together, as though at some inaudible signal, their hands groped for one another. She slipped her hands underneath his T-shirt so she could feel his chest. He did the same, running his fingers slowly around her firm breasts. They kissed some more, then he felt her hand exploring between his legs, encouraging his arousal.

Within a few moments they were both naked, their flesh burning against flesh, mouths devouring as though they contained some untapped ambrosia upon which they needed to slake their thirst. Verena squirmed under him as he alternated kissing her two breasts.

Then, keeping his left hand on one breast, he slid his right hand down to the mound between her legs. Verena moaned loudly. Her breath increased until her stomach tensed and she gasped.

"Take me now, Jonathan."

What began as a kind of lust or an act of need—two people alone and responding to a natural desire for comfort and trust—slowly became tender, gentle, even truly loving. Chase, still vaguely aware of the tiny remaining doubt in the back of his head, was quickly lost in this lovely creature, whose limbs and body seemed to respond to his own in an almost telepathic kind of way.

Only later, with Verena curled up like a child in Chase's arms under the covers, did they speak again of work. For them, the brief hours they had spent together had been a short retreat from the harsh reality of their profession. Now it was after eight in the morning. Another day, another scramble through the secret world.

"For the sake of this operation, then, we work together." Chase's mouth was unusually dry.

"Yes, and..."

"And I'll help you see SS-Oberführer Rautavaara in hell."

"Oh please, Jonathan, darling. Please." She looked up at him, her face puckered in a smile that spoke only of pleasure—no malice or horror, even though she was already pleading for the death of her father. Then the mood changed again: a serenity, the laugh in her eyes and at the corners of her mouth. "You know, this is the last thing I thought would happen..."

"Come on. You don't arrive in a man's room at four in the morning, dressed in practically nothing, without the thought crossing your mind."

"Oh," she laughed aloud, "the thought was there. It's just that I didn't really believe it would happen. I imagined you were much too professional, and I thought I was so determined and well trained that I could resist anything." Her voice went small. "I did go for you, the moment I saw you, but don't let it get to your head."

"It didn't." Chase laughed.

✦

When the breeze wakened Chase on the following morning, he noticed that Verena slept with her lips parted, so that she seemed to be smiling over the day she had just lived through. It was only a few seconds after he had covered her and touched her hair that he went to the window, looked out, and realized what it was that Marijke had said to him in Brussels.

All his life, Chase's unconscious had released images, and he had learned to trust this trick of his mind. He often knew what men had done before they confessed their acts to him. Brewster had likened him to a fortune-teller.

Chase knew that this gift, which grew stronger as he grew older, was only a kind of logic. His senses received everything, he forgot nothing. Experience and information joined in the brain to provide explanations.

Now, as he stood by the open window, he heard the plans being made for his capture. He saw the messages being passed, saw the look in the eyes of the conspirators, watched the tension flow out of their faces when the news of his imminent arrival in Marseille was brought to them. He wondered why it had taken him so long to realize the truth.

That damned blond wig.

—3—

The safe house near the Palais de Justice was converted into a command center: strewn with photographs, maps, papers, highlight pens, and magnifying glasses. The tension was almost palpable. They had arrived at the nerve center of the Zero Directorate. Chase shuffled the prints Brewster had sent him by diplomatic bag: many shots of Thinkingcap/DuBourdieu (hairy and well built) and his mistress, a scrawny blond with the hostile face of a political zealot. Also: an older dehydrated Nordic type who looked slightly familiar, and a number of contact prints showing exteriors of the target's apartment in town, his mistress's country house, and the cheap hotel used by the lovers.

"Brewster thinks he's dealing with some kind of mastermind. Would Thinkingcap have been able to design an operation like this start to finish? According to the old man it's so subtle nobody can figure out its purpose."

"I don't know if he could," Verena said. "Maybe he has good advice."

"A new case officer? This Mirza character, perhaps?"

A cordon of secrecy seemed to surround Prince Industries and the clinic. It was as if two or three sanitized accounts of the company's history had been doled out to medical and trade publications, published prominently, and then recycled endlessly. The result was that although much was written about the company, little was known.

They had more success in obtaining information about the clinic facility itself on the shores of Plage d'Argent designed by renowned architect Michel Charpentier. The building of this fortress had taken years and was accompanied by some voyeuristic speculation. Apparently, after a period of trying to suppress reporting on the building, DuBourdieu had shifted to trying to control the reporting. That he managed well. The clinic was described in tones of breathless astonishment, in "tours" published in magazines like *Casabella* and *Architectural Digest*.

Many of the articles were accompanied by photographs; a few even included rudimentary plans which, slightly more detailed than the ones Chase had found in Zurich, allowed them to note the approximate layout and purpose of many of the rooms. The modernist clinic was cut so deep into the cliff-side that much of it was underground. There were conference rooms, laboratories, convalescent rooms, even an indoor pool. The clinic's front lawn, Chase was careful to note, was directly on the shores of the small lake, with two boat docks. Deep under the front lawn was a giant concrete-and-steel parking garage.

Very little existed in the public record about the security at the Prince Industries clinic. All Chase could turn up was that the security system was, of course, redundant; there were hidden cameras everywhere.

"It would be a big help if we could get the building plans," Chase said after he and Verena had gone through the piles of articles photocopied from the local *bibliothèque*.

"Jonathan," she said, turning to him with anxiety in her eyes, "what do you intend to do?"

"I need to get inside. It's the seat of the organization, and the only way to blow it, and them, out of the water is to confront and witness."

"Witness?"

"Observe the members. See who they are, the ones whose names we don't know. Take photographs, get evidence. Shine daylight into darkness."

"But to try to enter on your own —"

"Will be difficult. But we may have a chance. One of the articles mentioned that the security is monitored locally."

"That doesn't really help us —"

"No doubt. But the point of vulnerability may be the link. How would the house be connected to a local monitoring station?"

"Optical fiber cable. Buried in the ground and connecting the two locations."

"Can fiber-optic lines be tapped?"

"Most people believe it's impossible."

"And you?"

"I *know* it's possible. We did it when I was with Mossad."

Chase spent the next hour conducting discreet surveillance of the clinic, using small but high-powered Zeiss binoculars, from the coastal land that adjoined it. The lakeside property occupied three acres. On the other side was a far more modest house on about half an acre.

The chainlink perimeter fence was eight feet high, with a stress-sensor line enmeshed throughout it. This ruled out climbing over the fence or attempting to cut through it. The bottom of the fence was buried in concrete, which made digging underneath difficult. In addition, the entire area was watched by surveillance cameras mounted on poles along the fence. Getting in this way had to be ruled out, too.

There was the lake. This seemed to Chase to present the best opportunity to infiltrate undetected. He returned to the rented PGO Hemera, hidden among the trees and far from the nearest road. As he drove down the access road he passed a small white van turning into the gates. It was painted with the words *La Belle Fleur,* no doubt a local florist.

Another possibility had just suggested itself.

There were errands to run, purchases to make, and far too little time remaining. Chase had no difficulty locating a sporting goods store specializing in mountain climbing. It was a well-stocked shop that catered to the diverse needs of hunters, which eliminated the need to make two other stops. But scuba-diving equipment had to be obtained at a separate dive shop. The chain-smoking Frenchman at the dive shop identified for him the location of an industrial safety products supply house, which serviced construction companies, telephone repairmen, window washers, and the like; there, he found precisely what he needed: a portable electric winch, battery operated and quiet, with a self-retracing lifeline—two hundred and twenty-five feet of steel cable, a controlled descent device, and a braking mechanism.

An elevator parts supply company had exactly what he needed, as did a military surplus warehouse, where an employee recommended a decent shooting range nearby. There he bought an old Beretta Serie 950 for cash from a young, grubby-looking man practicing with it.

By the time Chase returned to the safe house, Verena had purchased what she needed. After he explained what he'd seen on his visit, she asked, "Wouldn't it be much simpler for you to get in as a janitor or something?"

"I saw a florist drive in, actually. But I've thought it over and my calculation is that the florists are probably accompanied in, they do their work, and they're accompanied out. Even assuming

I could somehow enter with them, it would be next to impossible for me to disappear into the house without putting the whole place on alert. No, I've rented a boat; it's the only way to get up on shore."

"But then what? Surely he has the front lawn protected."

"No question. But from everything I can tell, it's the least secure entry point. Now, what have you learned about those cables?"

◆

The fourteen-foot aluminum fishing boat was powered by a quiet, forty-horsepower outboard motor. Chase moved quickly across the lake, buffeted gently by the swells. The sound was minimal, carried away from the clinic property by a prevailing wind. As soon as he saw the string of bright orange barrier floats that demarcated the protected waters before the clinic's dock and front lawn, he reduced speed and then cut the engine, which coughed and died. Theoretically he could have charged the line of floats, but he had to assume, even if he didn't know for sure, that Thinkingcap had some sort of security in place to detect the approach of intruder craft.

Even from here he could see the modernistic building, illuminated by floodlights, low-slung and hugging the hillside. Most of it was underground, making the structure appear more modest than it actually was. Chase dropped anchor, mindful of keeping the skiff in place as an escape option, if he was so fortunate as to be able to escape. He had told Verena, *assured* her, that his plan provided a way out, but it was not true; he wondered if she secretly suspected it but didn't care. Certainly *she* wouldn't need a way out.

Quickly, he began to assemble his equipment. Although he needed to travel as lightly as possible, he also had to provide for dozens of different obstacles that he simply could not foresee, which meant a range of equipment. It would be unfortunate to blow the entire operation for want of the right lock-pick set. His tactical vest was heavy with various weapons, neatly folded clothing, and other objects, all sealed in plastic.

He radioed Verena on the two-way communicator.

"How does it look?"

"Good. The eyes are open."

She had succeeded in penetrating the closed circuit TV surveillance feed through the fiber-optic line. "How far can the eyes see?" Chase asked.

"There are clear areas and areas that are not so clear."

"All right. I'll be back in touch after I've gone for a swim."

The lightweight black trousers and button-down he preferred for infiltrating the clinic were water-absorbent, so he wore a scuba wetsuit over them. He felt overheated, but the cold lake water would cool him down. Over the tac vest he now fastened his inflatable buoyancy compensator, which was already strapped to the tank, adjusted the quick-release buckles, adjusted the weight belt, donned his dive mask, put the second-stage regulator into his mouth. After a quick double-check of his equipment, he knelt on the side of the boat and plunged in, headfirst.

There was a splash, and he was floating on the surface of the lake. He looked around, oriented himself, and started deflating his vest. He sank slowly beneath the surface of the water, which was cold and crystalline. As he descended, he noticed that the water became steadily muddier. He stopped to equalize the air pressure, felt his ears pop. When he had reached a depth of about sixty feet, it was hard to see much farther than ten or twenty feet ahead. He would have to proceed carefully. Feeling weightless, he began swimming in the direction of the shore.

He listened for the distinctive, bass-toned moan of sonar, but he heard only silence—which was reassuring in one sense, nerve-racking in another: there *had* to be some sort of security system in place.

And then he saw it.

There, floating no more than ten feet ahead of him, swaying in the water like some marine predator. Netting.

But no mere netting. An underwater alarmed security barrier. Webbing with fiber-optic cables woven in, linked panels that formed alarm zones, sensors connected to electronic control units. This was an intrusion-detection system of unusual sophistication, used to protect marine installations.

The netting was rigged by a series of buoys and anchored to the lake bed by means of weights. Chase couldn't swim through it; nor could he cut or tear it without setting off the alarm. He deflated his buoyancy compensator until he was standing on the lake bed, then examined it.

He found that he was breathing shallowly, a reaction to fear, and this was causing him to feel unpleasantly short of breath, as if he could not fill his lungs. He closed his eyes for a moment, forced himself to be calm until his breathing became steady.

This is designed for boats, for underwater craft, he told himself. Not for divers, not swimmers.

He settled to his knees, inspected the sinkers that held the netting down. The lake floor was silt, soft muddy sediment that yielded as soon as he touched it. He pushed at the silt, then began digging with his fingers, his hands cupped like spades. A cloud arose all around him, turning the water opaque. Swiftly, and with remarkable ease, he had dug an elongated trench beneath the bottom of the mesh, through which he was able to half wriggle, half slither. As he passed by, the movement of the water rippled the sensor net. But that couldn't possibly be enough to set it off: the water in the lake was always moving.

He was on the other side now: in Thinkingcap's water. He listened again for the lowing of an active sonar system, but heard nothing.

He swam until he approached the pilings beneath the dock, mossy with algae. Maneuvering around to the far side of the dock, where he knew the boathouse was situated, he came closer and closer, the water increasingly shallow; now his feet touched the bottom. He deflated his vest completely, walking across the lake floor until his head emerged from the water and he was directly beneath the dock. He removed his mask, listened, peered around as far as he could see, and was satisfied there was no one in sight; then he unbuckled the buoyancy compensator and attached tank of air and hoses, placing the scuba gear securely on a broad support beam. There he hoped it would remain.

Then he grabbed the side of the dock and lifted himself up.

The boathouse blocked his view of the house; it also served to conceal him from anyone who happened to be looking out the front windows. The lawn was dark, the only illumination spilling onto the grass from the tall arched windows. Sitting on the edge of the dock, he took off the tactical vest, peeled off the wetsuit, and put the vest back on over his black shirt. One by one he removed the weapons and other instruments from the vest, pulled them out of their plastic bags and replaced them. He crawled the length of the dock and got to his feet in front of the boathouse. It was dark, seemingly empty. If he had miscalculated, he had the old Beretta handy. He pulled it out and gripped it as he walked toward the main expanse of lawn.

So far, so good. The security precautions would no doubt intensify as he approached the residence itself. From a pocket of the utility vest he took the Nitefinder goggles Frankie Farmer had given him.

He saw the beams at once.

The lawn was crisscrossed with them, motion-detection beam sensors. Anyone walking across the front lawn would break a beam and trigger the alarm.

But they went no lower than three feet, in order to keep from being set off by small animals.

Dogs?

It was possible. It was, in fact, likely that there were guard dogs as well, although Chase had not heard or seen any.

But as he dropped to his hands and knees, crawling under the level of the lowest beam, he heard something that made him freeze.

A low whine, a canine growl. He looked up, saw several dogs trotting across the lawn, their pace quickening. Not house pets: Dobermans. Bullet-headed, trained, vicious.

He felt his stomach tighten.

They galloped, stiff-legged, like horses, barking throatily, sharp teeth bared. Twenty yards off, he estimated, but gaining rapidly. From his vest he whipped out the Beretta 950 and attached the silencer. He aimed, heart thudding, and fired. Four short coughs, the first one wide of the mark, the remaining three hitting their targets. It was a silent business: two of the dogs sagged to the ground almost instantly, the largest one continuing on unsteadily for another few yards before wobbling and then crashing.

Chase was perspiring heavily, trembling involuntarily. Although he had prepared for the contingency, he had almost been caught unawares; a matter of seconds, and he would have been surrounded, powerful jaws at his throat. He lay flat on the dewy lawn, waiting. There might be other dogs, a second wave. The barking might have attracted the attention of the security guards. That was likely. But even highly trained dogs could have false alarms; if their barking stopped, attention would be turned elsewhere.

Thirty, forty-five seconds of silence. The black shirt and slacks enabled him to blend into the dark night. There were no other dogs in the vicinity; in any case, he could not afford to wait any longer. Built into the front lawn, as required by French building codes, would be several grates, ventilation for the underground parking garage immediately below. Chase resumed crawling across the lawn, moving to the left, careful to stay below the lower shaft of focused infrared light. He saw nothing. He crawled straight ahead another ten feet or so up the gradual slope toward the house, and then he felt it: the steel grille of a ventilation grate. He grabbed at the grating, prepared to unbolt if need be, but it loosened after a few tugs.

The opening was not large, maybe eighteen by twenty-four inches, but it was enough for him to enter. The only question was, how far down? The inner walls of the ventilation shaft were smooth concrete: nothing to grip on to, no handholds. He had hoped for an easier descent, though he had prepared for the situation he now found. He had learned over ten years of field operations to prepare for the worst; it was the only guarantor of success. The collar of the shaft into which the grate was seated was steel; at least that was something of a relief.

Peering through the Nitefinders into the shaft he satisfied himself that there were no laser sensor beams here. He finally removed the goggles, which had begun to chafe, and pocketed them.

Taking out the two-way radio, he radioed Verena. "I'm going in," he said. "Cue the effects."

2

As soon as he gave her the word, Verena pressed the button on the small transmitter, which instantly detonated the flares and flame-projector tubes Chase had wired. The projector tubes, which nestled among the leaves and low foliage just over the fence on Thinkingcap/DuBourdieu's property, immediately generated thick plumes of dense brush fire smoke, mushroom clouds of black smoke; the flares shot eight feet into the air, lasting only a few seconds. Chase had timed them to go off in sequence, simulating the effect of a wildly spreading forest fire. He had no interest in burning down trees in the South of France and there was no need to do so.

Working at top speed, Chase hooked the compact mechanical winch on to the steel collar at the head of the ventilation shaft. The double-locking snap hook at the end of the steel cable he connected to a carabiner, which hooked on the body harness sewn into the tactical vest.

Built into the portable winch was a controlled descent device with an auto-lock that gripped the rope as it was pulled through the spring-loaded reel, regulating the speed of the descent. It allowed him to lower himself down the shaft at a steady, metered rate.

As he lowered himself, he reached over and replaced the grate, shoving it up against the sturdy black casing of the winch, which would not be obtrusive at a distance. Then he resumed his descent down the dark, seemingly endless duct. In the distance he thought he could hear the warbling sirens of *les pompes incendies;* they had responded even more speedily than he had anticipated. As the line continued its metered payout, he reflected that he was about to enter the zone of heaviest surveillance. The mock brush fire would raise all sorts of alarms, diverting the resources of Thinkingcap's security complement. Attention would be riveted on the threat of an enveloping fire, a far more immediate concern than any theoretical intrusion. Any alarms Chase inadvertently set off would be attributed to the arrival of the *Sapeurs-Pompiers* on the property.

As the cable continued to spool out from the specially designed pulley far above, Chase marveled at the distance, the astonishing depth. When he saw the red end-of-travel indicator near the cable's end, he knew that he had descended almost two hundred twenty-five feet, the maximum length of the line. Finally the line jerked to a stop. He looked down; another five or six feet remained. He dropped down to the polished concrete floor, his crouch absorbing the impact of the fall. He left the line dangling in place, in case it was needed.

Chase found himself in a spacious parking garage whose floors were polished to the sheen of marble. There had to have been more than twenty vehicles here: antiques, collectors' cars—Duesenbergs, Rolls-Royces, Bentleys, classic Porsches. All Thinkingcap's, he was sure. At the far end was an elevator, which went to the main house directly above.

Depressing the talk button on the communicator, Chase asked quietly, "Everything okay?"

Verena's voice was faint but audible. "Fine. The last of the fire trucks has left. The flames and the smoke dissipated long before they arrived."

"Good. As soon as I'm in the house, I'm going to need you in close radio contact to guide me through the minefields."

Chase became conscious of movement in the shadows to his left, shifting between the rows of automobiles. He turned, saw a blue-jacketed guard with a gun pointed.

"*Arrêt!*"

Chase spun out of the guard's line of sight, then dropped to the floor. The gun fired, the explosion reverberant in the chasmlike bunker. A round hit the concrete inches from Chase's head, ricocheting, the spent cartridge clattering to the floor. Chase whipped out the Beretta, aimed with split-second timing, then fired. The guard attempted to dodge the bullet, but caught it in his chest.

He bellowed, body twisting; Chase fired again and the man was down.

Chase raced to the fallen man. The guard's eyes were wide, staring, his face contorted and frozen in pain. Clipped to the lapel of his blazer was a security pass. Chase took it, examined it carefully. The clinic's security system was structured in zones, he concluded, and controlled by means of a conditional-access system. The entrance to each separate zone would be equipped with a proximal scanner, much like the electric eyes of the doors at better supermarkets that opened automatically as you approached. The security pass, worn on the breast pocket of a shirt or blazer, was scanned and doors would not open for unauthorized persons. The system kept track of where everyone was at all times.

Chase knew that penetrating the clinic's security had to be more complex than simply stealing a guard's pass. Either there was a backup, state-of-the-art biometric scans for fingerprints—or codes would have to be entered by the person seeking entrance.

The elevator was his way in to the clinic, the *only* way. He raced toward it. He would have to move quickly now, for where there was one guard there would be others; the slain guard's failure to answer a routine, radioed question would raise alarms.

The elevator doors were brushed steel, with a call button and keypad mounted on the wall beside them. He pressed the button, but it did not light up. He pressed again, and again no response: a code had to be entered on the keypad in order to summon the elevator—probably a series of four numbers. Unless the sequence was entered, the call button did not function. The security badge he had taken from the guard and clipped to the front of his vest would do no good here.

He inspected the walls nearest the elevator, looking for concealed cameras. It was almost certain that there were in fact security cameras here, but Verena had managed to tap into the fiber-optic cables. If for some reason she had been unable to do that, or she had reason to believe that her ruse was not working, she would have radioed him already.

The elevator doors could, of course, be forced open by brute force and a crowbar, but that would be a mistake. Prying the doors open by ax or crowbar would break the elevator interlocks and stop the elevator from running; as long as any door on the shaft was open, the elevator would not run. That was a safety feature common to almost all elevators built in the last few years. And if the elevator did not run, Chase ran the risk of drawing the attention of security personnel. An effective covert entry required that tracks be covered.

For that reason he had brought a special tool called an interlock key, used by licensed elevator repairmen for emergency entry. It was six-inch length of stainless steel about half an inch wide, flat and hinged at the top. He inserted it at the top of the brushed-steel doors, and moved it to the right. Between three and six inches in, just inside the frame and atop the right door panel, was the mechanical interlock. The hinged key moved easily until it hit an obstruction: the protruding oblong of the interlock. The hinged flap of the key slid to the right, knocking the interlock to the right as well, and the doors slid smoothly open.

Cold air emerged from the dark, empty shaft. The elevator cab had been parked somewhere on an upper floor. Chase took out Frankie Farmer's "security blanket" flashlight and shone it onto the shaft, moving the small, bright circle of light from side to side. What he found was not encouraging. This was not a conventional residential elevator with a drum-and-winch system, nor was it traction-operated, with cables and counterweights. That meant he could not hope to use the cables to grab onto and pull himself up, using mountain-climbing techniques—there *were* no cables to grab. All there was inside the shaft was one large rail on the right side, along which the elevator was raised and lowered by hydraulic pressure. And that rail was slippery, highly lubricated; he could not grab it and pull himself up.

In the rear pockets of Chase's vest were small, lightweight magnetic gripper devices that were customarily used for bridge and tank inspections, as well as underwater examinations of ships' hulls and offshore oil rigs. He strapped one onto each boot, then onto both hands, and he began to climb, scaling the smooth steel wall slowly; releasing and repositioning hands, feet, moving upward pace by pace, release and reposition. It was arduous work and slow going. As he mounted the wall, he remembered the distance he had dropped to enter the garage: over two hundred and twenty-five feet, and that was from ground level, down the hill from the clinic. There would be at least one or two underground levels at which the elevator would stop, but he needed to go to the main level of the clinic.

At last he saw, by the beam of the flashlight, the first of the basement elevator landings. He was conscious at all times that the elevator might be called to the particular level, that it would descend quickly toward him; in such event, if he did not release the magnetic grippers quickly and flatten himself into the eighteen-inch clearance space, he would be killed instantly.

Now only ten feet or so remained before he reached the level marked *rez-de-chaussée,* where, inconveniently, the elevator car was stopped. Inconvenient, but not unexpected. Chase sidled over, shifting hands and feet one by one, until he was directly underneath the cab. Then, turning around methodically, he placed the hand grippers one by one, with a metallic clang, onto the lower edge of the steel-sided car. Now he hung from the car itself, his feet dangling into the empty expanse of the seemingly bottomless shaft. He looked down for a moment, which was a mistake: the drop was some two hundred and fifty feet to a concrete floor.

If anything went wrong, if the magnetic grippers somehow malfunctioned, that was it. He was not acrophobic, but neither was he immune to the fleeting sensation of terror. This was not a time to slow down, not when the elevator might be summoned at any moment. Moving as swiftly as he could manage, he began climbing up the side of the cab, sandwiched between the cab and the steel wall of the shaft with mere inches of wiggle room.

Reaching the top of the cab, he rested there for a moment, unfastening the grippers, jamming them back into the pockets of his vest. Then he swung over, grabbed the interlock at the top inside of the doors, and slid it to the left.

The doors opened.

And if someone's on the other side?

He hoped not. But he was prepared for that, too.

He was looking down at a dimly lit, elegantly furnished lobby of the International Style in what seemed to be the reception area of the clinic. He looked down, saw no one in the vicinity, then grabbed hold of the steel beam inside the door frame and swung himself down, landing on a burnished marble floor.

The lights went on, subdued lighting from several sconces along the wall, probably activated by the security guard's badge.

He was in.

Heart pounding from the exertion and from the tension, Chase sprang to his feet and turned back to the gaping elevator shaft. He approached, reaching carefully up for the interlock to close the doors, aware of the depth of the dark shaft. A fall would be fatal. Strangely, only now that he was out did he fully appreciate that.

The movement was almost imperceptible, a quick flickering of the lights in his peripheral vision. Chase pivoted, saw the guard almost on top of him, about to tackle him to the floor. When Chase slammed the guard with all his weight, the guard threw a lunging punch, which Chase blocked, grabbing the guard's right forearm while, at the same time, kicking the back of his knee with a Church's Chelsea boot. The guard groaned, sagged for only an instant, then immediately regained his balance as he reached for his gun.

A mistake not to have the Beretta at the ready. A mistake they both made. Chase took advantage of the Frenchman's momentary lapse and delivered a hard kick to the groin. The guard bellowed, knocked backward maybe a foot or two from the open elevator shaft. Still, he somehow managed to get his pistol out, aimed and prepared to fire. Chase lunged to the left, confusing the guard's aim, and then spun back toward his enemy, kicking the gun and sending it out of his hand.

"Bâtard!" The guard shouted as he leaped backward, arms extended, in an attempt to retrieve the gun; there was a look of almost indignant surprise on his face as he realized there was no floor beneath him, nothing to break his fall as he threw himself backward, his feet up in the air, higher than his head. The expression of surprise immediately became terror: arms flailing in the air in a vain attempt to clutch onto something, anything, his feet scrambling; he let out an enormous scream of horror, which echoed in the air shaft as he plunged quickly out of sight. The scream was long and sustained, gradually diminishing in volume as he fell away, ever more distant, then stopping abruptly as the body hit the bottom.

Sweat poured down Chase's face. He took several deep breaths, then stepped forward toward the shaft, reached up to the interlock, flicked it closed. The steel doors closed silently.

Now he needed to orient himself, to determine which direction to move in order to find the security control room. That was the first order of business. It would tell him where everything was. It was also Thinkingcap's eyes, and therefore needed to be shut down.

He pressed the talk button on the communicator. "I'm at the main level," he said softly.

"Thank God," came Verena's voice. Chase smiled; she was unlike any field backup he had ever worked with. Instead of being briskly professional, she was emotional, concerned.

"Which way to Control?"

"If you're facing the elevator, it's left. There's a long corridor running to either side...?"

"Check."

"Take the one to your left. When it ends, left again. There it widens out into some sort of laboratory. That looks like the most direct route."

The security pass he had taken from the guard had so far done him no good at all. It hadn't admitted him to the elevator, though it had switched on the lights. It seemed to be more for keeping track of its wearer than for penetrating security; it had to go. Chase unclipped it and placed it on the floor of the corridor, against the wall, as if it had been lost by the person to whom it had been issued.

✦

Verena put down the two-way radio when she heard the crunch of footsteps right outside the car. It was going too smoothly, she thought. The forest patrol would ask questions, and she'd have to be persuasive. Her job, after all, was to make sure Jonathan Chase got all the way to Thinkingcap.

She slid open the door of the car and let out a laugh when she saw the muzzle of the pistol pointed at her eyes.

"Let's go!" shouted the Frenchman in the blue blazer.

"Fool! You're going to regret this."

"Tapping into our security line? I don't think so. Hands down and no fucking around!"

She could only smile.

✦

Chase had reached the long, rectangular room that Verena had called a laboratory. It was a peculiar-looking chamber, lined with massive vats of welded sheet stainless steel. The kind, Chase knew, used for fractional crystallization and cold water extraction.

Yes, he thought, drugs are *certainly* being made here.

He was about to step into the lab for a closer look when he noticed a line of tiny black beads running up the wall in a vertical line between the vats. Every four feet or so another line of these minuscule black dots ran up one wall of the room. It almost looked ornamental, like part of the futuristic decor. Chase stood at the entrance of the lab without entering. The black dots began about eighteen inches from the floor and ended about six feet up. He was fairly sure he knew what they were, but in order to make certain, he took out the Nitefinders and put them on.

Now he could see row upon row of thin filaments strung across the width of the long room every few feet. What looked like glowing green strings were, he knew, laser beams; point-to-point sensors with columnated beams of light, invisible to the naked eye. But when the beams were broken by someone passing through an alarm would be set off.

The only way to traverse the room was by moving along the floor, staying below eighteen inches at all times. And there was no clean way to do it, either. He fastened the Nitefinders in place, he dropped to the floor and began sliding on his back, pushing off with his boots. The whole while he was looking up, making sure he did not cross the beam. The clothes he wore were slick enough to allow rapid, smooth movement.

He slid under a third, fourth, a fifth laser-beam. No beam was broken, no alarms triggered, not here.

Finally he slipped under the last beam. He paused, still on his back, and peered closely around to make sure there were no others. Satisfied, he sat up, then got carefully to his feet. Now he was not far from the control room; Verena would guide him in the right direction.

He depressed the talk button. "Where to now?"

No answer, so he spoke again, a fraction louder.

Again, no response, just staticky dead air.

"Verena, come in."

Nothing.

"Verena, come in. I need guidance."

Silence.

"Which way, damn it?"

Were the radios malfunctioning? He spoke again and received no response. Was there some signal jamming technology in place? Thinkingcap's people had to communicate. There was no way to jam all possible radio frequencies but the one you wanted to use yourself. That was an impossibility.

Then where was she?

He radioed again, and again. No answer, nothing.

She was gone.

He felt a cold dread come over him.

But he could not stop, he could not expend any time figuring out where she was or what happened to their communications. He had to move.

Chase didn't need radioed instructions to tell him where the kitchen was. He could smell food down the hall. A door slid open at the far end of the hall and a waiter came through, dressed in black pants and a white oxford, with a large, empty silver tray at his side.

Was there some sort of party going on?

That might explain the florist's van he'd seen.

Sticking his head into the hall that led to the kitchen, he heard laughter, bantering conversation, the metallic clink of pans and utensils. He stepped back into the gallery of vats, waited until he heard the sound of the kitchen's double doors swing open, then emerged stealthily. The same waiter was now holding aloft a large tray loaded with hors d'oeuvres.

Treading silently along the hallway, Chase stole up behind the waiter. He knew the man would be an easy mark, yet he could not afford noise, could not afford to attract attention. When he was just a few feet behind the man Chase lunged, clapping one hand over his mouth, crooking his elbow around the neck, forcing the man to the floor while, at the same time, grabbing the tray of food. The waiter tried to scream, his cry muffled behind Chase's hand. Chase set the tray down carefully and, with his free hand, squeezed hard at the nerve bundle under the man's jaw. The waiter slumped to the floor, unconscious.

Quickly dragging the body back into the gallery, he pushed the waiter into a seated position, hands folded, head down, as if grabbing a quick catnap. Then he ran back down the hall and grabbed the tray of food.

Move it, he told himself. At any moment another waiter could enter the hall and see his face, not recognize him. He knew the security control room was nearby, but where?

He turned into another hall, the door sliding automatically. No: this led directly to another room lined with beakers, tubes, and vials, which tonight was unused. He turned around, heading back in the direction of the kitchen, then retraced the path the waiter had taken. Another set of doors slid open to a corridor that he could see led to some kind of reception hall or auditorium, but another hall intersected before then, branching off to the right. *Perhaps.* He took the right, walked about fifty yards past empty hospital-style rooms, saw a door marked: *De sécurité. Le personnel autorisé.*

Chase stopped before it, took a deep breath to calm himself, then knocked on the door.

No answer. He noticed a small inset button on the doorjamb, which he pushed once.

In ten seconds, just when he was about to push the button again, a voice came over a speaker mounted on the wall outside the room. *"Oui?"*

"Salut. C'est la restauration—J'ai votre dîner," Chase said in singsong French.

A pause. *"Nous n'avons rien pour ne repas,"* the voice said suspiciously.

"Très bien, vous ne voulez pas tout, pas de problème. M. DuBourdieu a dit de veiller à son peuple qu'en a eu assez ce soir, mais je vais lui dire que tu n'en veux pas."

The door flew open. The man who stood there in the blue blazer was stocky, his hair dyed brown with an unfortunate orange tint. The name badge on his lapel said *Etienne*. *"Je vais prendre ça,"* the man said, reaching for the tray.

"Désolé, j'ai besoin du plateau—c'est une grande foule là-bas! Je vais mettre en place pour vous." Chase stepped forward into the security room; Etienne relaxed somewhat and let him through.

Chase looked around, saw that there was just one other guard there monitoring. The room was round, high-tech to the point of being futuristic, its walls smooth and unbroken by individual monitor screens, yet dozens of individual panels showed different views in and around the property.

"Nous avons magret de canard fumé, caviar, saumon fumé, filet de boeuf... Avez-vous une surface où je peux mettre les plats en place pour vous?"

"Mettez-partout," the man named Etienne said, turning his attention back to the images on the wall. Chase set down the tray gingerly on a bare area of console, then reached over to his left

ankle as if to scratch. He quickly pulled out the silenced Beretta and fired off two quick shots. Two sharp coughing sounds, and each of the security men was struck, one in the throat, one in the chest.

Now Chase rushed to the console that controlled the CCTV. The views of certain cameras could be enlarged, brought to the center. He located the cameras that represented views of the main reception hall.

The reception hall, where a cocktail party was taking place. *A Zero Directorate cocktail party?*

He pushed a button, quickly figuring out how to manipulate the images. By moving a small joystick, he was able to move a security camera, basically pan it from side to side, up or down, even move in for a close-up.

The reception hall was large—especially for a facility supposedly dedicated to pharmacological research. Around the white tablecloths, flowers, crystal, and bottles of wine were dozens of people—over a hundred. Faces. Familiar faces.

3

At one end of the room was a life-size bronze sculpture of Joan of Arc astride her horse, sword drawn and pointing straight up, leading her countrymen into the battle of Orléans. Strange but somehow fitting for the always enigmatic Zero Directorate.

Chase moved the joystick to zoom in on the guests, and what he saw stunned him, paralyzed him.

He did not recognize all the faces by far, but many of those whom he did recognize would be known to anyone who'd read a newspaper lately.

A prominent agent in the FBI.

An agent Chase knew from Britain's MI6.

Another from France's DGSE.

An important employee of the International Monetary Fund.

The assistant to the secretary general of the United Nations.

The democratically elected head of Nigeria.

The chiefs of the militaries and security services in another half-dozen third-world nations, from Argentina to Turkey.

Chase stared, jaw agape, gasping.

The CEOs of quite a few corporations, some of whom he recognized quickly, some vaguely familiar. All of them dressed in black tie, the women in formal evening gowns.

His eye was caught by a tall silver-haired man making his way to the bar.

Chase placed him immediately. Weather-beaten countenance, ramrod military bearing, well-groomed, iron-gray hair. The face was not that of an old man, the bone structure would last a long time yet. Berg Rautavaara was, as Chase would have guessed, a man blessed with ageless features—classic, still good-looking, but with eyes that held no twinkle of pleasure. At the moment they were turned on the French barman as though their owner was merely measuring the man for his coffin.

Chase waited until the old Finnish SS man, Verena's father, had picked up his drinks then followed him with the camera to his table.

So Verena had told the truth about his being mixed up with Zero Directorate after all.

Herr Rautavaara set the drinks down next to a spectacularly pale brunette in black leather pants, jacket, and peaked cap. Chase recognized her at once: the French assassin known as *La Flamme.*

It was said, along the bleak corridors in Washington, that La Flamme had been in Paris when the chargé d'affaires of the Persian Embassy was found on the top floor of an apartment house in the Place Pigalle with a steel knitting needle buried in his brain through the left eye.

It was rumored that La Flamme was in Buenos Aires when one of Brewster's people got on her track and was found the next day in the wreck of an elevator in the Hotel Conquistador with his spine driven upward into his skull.

Brewster had said that La Flamme was involved in the assassinations of General Batista, President Sri Phouma, and that she personally dispatched two gentlemen acquaintances of Eva Peron in the hope of receiving her favors in their place.

Unsettled, Chase turned his attention to another set of screens showing what looked like more laboratories. One of them caught his eye in particular—its walls were lined floor to ceiling with small vials of clear liquid. It gave the kind of infinite perspective one gets standing between two mirrors in a funhouse. The Droste Effect, Chase thought it was called.

Then something moved at the bottom corner of the screen.

Chase moved the joystick to zoom in and couldn't believe what he was seeing.

He recognized Thinkingcap immediately from Brewster's photos, his mistress as well. What didn't fit in this puzzle was *Marijke*.

Marijke, his contact in Brussels. Handcuffed to a cot, an intravenous tube running into her left wrist.

Thinkingcap had thrown his red-checkered Palestinian shawl aside, baring his face. He looked, Chase thought, like an extremely fit version of the disgruntled clerk who had never been given the promotions he knew he deserved. While his mistress tried to coax something from Marijke, Thinkingcap operated a movie camera.

There were three of his people in the room, but he ignored them. They stood idly by, shamefaced, with their weapons in their hands. Thinkingcap was peering through the camera lens at Marijke's smiling features.

So this is how they do it.

Thinkingcap slapped the Belgian girl's face. The French mistress put a comforting arm around Marijke's shoulders. Thinkingcap, with his kaffiyeh hanging down, took Marijke's blood pressure and listened to her heart through a stethoscope. He shined a flashlight into her right eye. The French woman rearranged her tangled hair for her with a few deft movements and gazed lovingly into her eyes.

Chase could take no more.

He opened the door a crack, it was clear. He raced down the empty corridor to the left, and when he reached a turning, stopped, trying to orient himself. The eastern end of the clinic was to the right; that was the direction in which he would have to go to rescue Marijke.

A well-dressed elderly man strode down the hall toward him, dress shoes clicking against the marble and echoing in the long hallway. He approached and passed with a curious stare, turning into a room farther down the hall.

Berg Rautavaara.

Chase followed the old man along the hall, his head down and deep in thought, walking silently, assuming a normal stride behind his prey as he headed for the restroom. When the old man went in, Chase followed.

Rautavaara entered a pristine white stall. Chase reached down and unsheathed the commando knife, which he had bound to his shin at the safe house. He waited until the old Finn was finished. When he stepped out of the stall, Chase grabbed hold of him and put the blade to his neck. He shoved him back in.

"Herr Rautavaara," Chase said. "Do you know who I am?"

Rautavaara's eyes were wide with fear. He nodded.

"What exactly are you planning? Tell me or I'll carve out your Adam's apple and flush it."

"The plans...they're in my pocket," the old man stammered.

"You get them," Chase said. "No tricks."

The old man reached into his trousers and pulled out a slip of notepaper. Chase took it and pocketed it.

"Thank you," Chase said. "Now you have to answer for Verena."

"Verena?" The old man coughed with laughter.

"Verena works with me! She's my partner," the old man cried. "She's the real Zero Directorate agent. She's one of the Commandants! I work for her. I swear! It was all her doing. I just followed orders."

For a flitting second, Chase experienced the strange sensation of a clammy hand running down his spine. The fact that his suspicions had been right—that he no longer knew who Verena truly was—created an unease Chase rarely felt. In that fraction of time, he even wondered if at long last he might have met his match.

Chase broke the old man's nose. "Tell the truth now!"

"I swear!" Rautavaara pleaded. "Verena! She brought me out of retirement. Lured me here with the operation. With Skypilot. Sounded too good to be true. I'm just her partner. She does all the dirty work. She...she likes it! Please, don't hurt me!"

"What about Mossad? Her conversion to Judaism?"

"Perverse, I know...but her idea. She...she likes to lie. She always has."

Chase made several lightning-quick calculations. Verena couldn't be more than thirty, maybe thirty-one at the most, which meant her formative years had in fact been spent in some hiding place with her father the Nazi. If this was so, then it was quite possible that she was some sort of neo-Fascist or Zero Directorate deep penetration agent, working first inside Mossad, then I-Division.

The ploy, Chase thought, dated back to the Garden of Eden, the oldest in the book. And he'd fallen for it.

The old man was starting to choke on his own blood.

"Why?"

"Why?"

"Why would she do it? Any of it?"

"Kennst du das Land wo die Zitronen bluhm?"

Chase blackened one of his eyes. "Don't give me quotes from Goethe!"

"What fragrance can be smelled through a mask?"

"I'm listening, Berg."

"She carries the curse of the witness. She does not live, she observes life."

"How do you know?"

"She saw . . . things . . . as a child. Things no child should see."

Chase slapped his face lightly.

The complexities were quicksand, sucking him deep. But this he knew—he had been bettered. She'd made him look like a fool, Brewster too. But that didn't matter now.

Nothing did.

Except revenge. It gave him pleasure to think the skills Brewster had taught him would be the weapons he'd use to destroy her.

"Perhaps Verena thought that you could carry her into the center of experience. Perhaps with you, she thought, she would see only the dark of her eyelids, she would smell, touch, hear—feel."

Jonathan Chase thought: *But who stood beside the bed in Marseille, looking down on her silken body and mine joined together? Who heard the groans and the whispers? Chase or Verena? The real Verena, the true?*

"Of course it's my fault. There were horrors everywhere . . . rape . . . torture . . . in Paraguay."

Chase blackened Rautavaara's other eye.

"You did it on purpose! To make her what she is today?"

"Yes."

Chase shook him.

"Life has no power over my daughter. She has been trained by experts not to live. Yet death itself does not interest her: it is the final act of life: only that. For Verena life is not enough."

Chase heard voices approaching. At least two men were on their way into the restrooms. He had run out of time.

Verena's father heard them and started to scream for help. Chase savagely sliced the man's neck, then stabbed him in the heart.

Chase spat on his face.

Rautavaara gasped, his eyes bulging, then fell to the floor. Chase wiped the knife clean on the man's clothes, then walked out of the stall just as two men stepped inside. One of them said something in Arabic and Chase grunted.

As soon as he was back in the corridor, Chase began to run. He heard shouts behind him, and the two men ran out of the bathroom in pursuit.

A big man appeared in front of him and shouted, *"Arrêt!"* Chase kicked, swinging his foot in the shape of a crescent moon. There was a discernible *crack* as he connected with the man's jaw. He screamed and fell to the ground. Chase leaped over him and kept running.

Chase cursed himself for letting his emotions take over. Going after Verena's father had wasted time he didn't have.

He had to get out, had to get to Marijke—but where was she? And how long would his ammunition last?

Thinkingcap's men pursued him; he fired at them, now aware of the need to conserve bullets. He was fairly sure he had another round in the chamber, maybe one in the magazine as well, but rather than stop for a second to check, he had to run, it was vital to *run*. He ran through the clinic, through silvery-gray corridors like the dusty wings of dead moths. Everywhere doors were half open.

Chase could hear screams at the end of the hall. *Could she be there?* he wondered.

He flung open the doors to the room he'd seen on camera, the one filled with syringeless filters floor-to-ceiling. Thousands of ghosts stared back at him. His face in every vial of the truth drug. Lost in the funhouse. Every shard of the broken mirror.

Was Thinkingcap still here? The Frenchwoman?

Was Marijke?

"Marijke!" he shouted.

No response.

They'd moved her, or she was too drugged to hear him.

"Marijke!" he shouted again, hoarsely.

Nothing.

He felt the cold steel of the blade at the exact same moment as the hot breath in his ear, the whispered Arabic words. The seven-inch combat knife pressed against the soft skin and delicate cartilage of his throat, the high-carbon steel blade sharper than a brand-new razor. It slid slowly, the silky pain at once cold and hot, the sensation delayed for a second; but when it came his entire body screamed in agony.

And the whisper: "The rope of lies is always too short, Mr. Chase."

Thinkingcap.

The terrorist hissed. "Now you will see yourself die a thousand times over."

Chase went rigid, flooded with fear, with adrenaline. "If you'll *listen...*" Chase replied, almost under his breath, the remark intended to distract for a second or two. At the same time he gripped the Beretta at his side, placed his finger on the trigger, and then in one swift arc lifted the weapon and fired backward at his enemy.

There was only a muted click. *The gun was empty.*

Thinkingcap batted the gun away with a flick of his left hand; it went flying off to one side, clattering to the floor, useless.

Chase had lost valuable seconds in reaction time. The blade sliced across the skin of his neck just as Chase hammered the fingers of his right hand upward and under the handle. He grabbed the knife handle, twisting it violently to loosen Thinkingcap's grip; at the same time, he slammed the heel of his left foot into the back of Thinkingcap's right knee to knock him off balance. Thinkingcap grunted, and Chase suddenly sank to the ground, lowering his center of gravity while still twisting the knife blade and Thinkingcap's wrist with it.

The knife clanged against the floor.

Chase reached for it, but Thinkingcap, quicker, scooped it up. Clutching the knife in his fist like a dagger, Thinkingcap plunged it downward, sinking it into the soft meat of Chase's left shoulder.

Chase gasped; the pain was shattering, forcing him to his knees. He swung his right arm toward Thinkingcap's head; Thinkingcap sidestepped the punch easily, moving around him effortlessly, almost dancing. He didn't seem to break a sweat. He shifted his weight from foot to foot, his knees slightly bent, his stance soft and comfortable, the blood-slicked knife blade glittering in his right hand. Chase staggered to his feet, kicked his right foot toward the inside of Thinkingcap's knee. But Thinkingcap sidestepped the kick, backing off just enough to cause Chase to lose his balance, then catching the kicking leg and yanking it hard, forcing Chase down again.

Thinkingcap seemed to know Chase's moves before they happened. Chase shot his arms forward to grab Thinkingcap's legs, but Thinkingcap simply slammed an elbow into Chase's neck, trapping Chase's head between his knees, and slammed him into the ground. Chase's teeth cracked against his lips; he could taste blood, and he thought he might have lost a couple of teeth.

Weakened by the knife wound in his shoulder, Chase's reactions were slowed, delayed. He groaned, thrust out his right arm, and grabbed his enemy's ankle; then locking it in his crooked elbow, he turned it until Thinkingcap bellowed in pain.

Suddenly the Palestinian's arm shot out, the knife aimed directly at Chase's heart. Chase dodged, but not quite in time: the knife plunged into his side, between his ribs; the pain was searing, white-hot.

Chase looked down, saw what had happened, and grabbed the knife handle. He yanked at it and hurled it across the room, smashing a number of vials as he screamed in pain. Now they were both disarmed. But Chase, down on the floor and badly weakened, with broken glass and the solution all around him, was at a disadvantage. Moreover, Thinkingcap was immensely strong, all muscle, a coiled python. His movements were relaxed, fluid. Chase rolled back away from Thinkingcap; Thinkingcap kicked him, hard, in the abdomen. Chase felt the wind come out of him; he almost passed out, but he struggled to his feet, swinging wildly.

Thinkingcap threw his weight on top of Chase, flattening him against the floor; then, jumping into the air, he stomped up and down on Chase's chest, putting all of his weight into it. Chase moaned; he could feel, actually *hear,* several ribs crack.

Thinkingcap went at him again, flipping him over so that his face cracked to the floor again, bringing a number of vials with it. Now Thinkingcap wrapped one arm around his throat, pushing down on the back of his neck with his elbow in a rear choke hold. At the same time the Palestinian went down on his right knee and folded his left leg so that he was in a one-legged kneeling position, extremely stable. He began pulling Chase back toward his left leg. Chase tried to rise, but each time he did, Thinkingcap pushed him back with his elbow. He had no leverage. He was losing consciousness, his strength was fading. The airflow to his brain was cut off; he began to see black-and-purple spots.

Part of Chase wanted to succumb to unconsciousness, a comfortable defeat, but he knew that any defeat would mean death. He screamed, summoned his last reserves of strength, flung his hands into Thinkingcap's face, and jabbed his fingers into his enemy's eye sockets.

Thinkingcap involuntarily released some of the pressure on Chase's throat—not much, but just enough to allow Chase to swing his fists around in an arc, one of them connecting hard with the brachial plexus nerve bundle in Thinkingcap's right underarm area. Chase felt Thinkingcap's right arm go slack, momentarily paralyzed. He took advantage of the brief pause to grab a vial of the solution and smash it in Thinkingcap's face. The choke hold was broken.

Chase wiped his bloody hands on his shirt. He knew the drug was inside him now as it was inside his opponent. The floor was wet with it and they had open wounds. The stuff was flowing in their blood now, creeping toward their brains.

The heart he heard beating was his own, accelerated by the drug. It pounded in his ears and temples. A thrill of pure energy coursed through his whole body. The light was diamond bright and the sound of his blood pulsing had the clarity of a bell. The strength flowed through his limbs and he wanted to shout with it, with the ecstasy of it, of being so strong.

Chase tilted his right shoulder down and body-slammed Thinkingcap up against a wall of the serum. Shattered glass and wetness everywhere. Chase was now moving almost by instinct; his oxygen-starved brain felt distant from his hands, which seemed to move of their own volition. But fueled by rage, Chase managed to force Thinkingcap's head onto the ledge where the vials had been. The two men were entwined, pushing and pulling at each other against the wall, their muscles trembling. Thinkingcap's right arm was dead, the paralysis lasting longer even than Chase had hoped. Chase pushed, shoved as hard as he could, forcing Thinkingcap further into the wall of broken glass, while Thinkingcap scissored both legs around Chase's, locking the two men together.

Keep control. Not easy. Shivering all over.

Slanting light like arrows at the eyes.

Chase was feeble but determined; Thinkingcap had lost the use of one arm. They seemed evenly matched. Chase straight-armed Thinkingcap's neck downward, but Thinkingcap came back up; Chase straight-armed him again, this time keeping him down with all his strength, the muscles in his right arm straining, trembling. The Palestinian's eyes were fierce. He began hammering his good fist into Chase's abdomen. For a few seconds Chase held him down, clutching Thinkingcap's throat and squeezing with all his strength, trying to cut off the air, trying to compress the nerves and induce paralysis, but he was fading; he could no longer summon the strength; the drug was in his bloodstream, radiating, depleting his power further. His hands trembled. Chase summoned one last, superhuman surge of energy, his entire body an instrument of anger, but it was not enough; he didn't have the strength.

Thinkingcap roared, his crimson face contorted in pain and rage, spittle flying from his purpled lips, and he began to rise—

The explosion seemed to come out of nowhere, the bullet lodging itself in his enemy's right upper arm. Thinkingcap's legs loosened their viselike grip on Chase's as he lost his balance and fell to the floor.

Two more shots lodged themselves into the Arab's thorax. The soft copper bullets opened within him, then stopped before they reached Chase.

Thinkingcap grunted loudly and did what the drug wanted him to: he told the truth. "The Russian...Majorca... Skypilot..." The voice was shrill, inhuman, and then it came to an abrupt, gurgling stop.

Chase fell to the ground and crawled away from the body. He fought to get to his feet, but the pain in his head and chest prevented him from doing so. He reached up and felt the sticky, wet blood in his hair.

Dazed, sickened, Chase turned and saw the source of the gunshot. Verena was holding the pistol he'd seen on the inside of her thigh. She lowered it slowly. Her eyes were wide.

"Congratulations, Mr. Chase," she sneered, "your plan was a smashing success."

He felt as if the air had gone out of the room.

He staggered to his feet, made it a few steps, and collapsed.

"No. Not you. When did they—"

Verena ran to Chase and dragged him across the floor. Chase was unable to fight back, powerless to move. He felt his shirt-sleeve being unbuttoned and rolled over. There was the prick of a needle, and in a moment he felt nothing.

THREE

–1–

As he receded into his own past on the wings of the drug, Chase grew younger and younger and smaller and smaller. He felt that this rewinding of his life must end at the moment of conception, when sperm penetrated egg and created the microscopic Jonathan Chase. This event and its meaning were blindingly clear to him. He had been untouched, untrained, untainted then, perfect, the receptacle of all information about himself, an infinitesimal being that was all mind.

This marvelous speck of pure intelligence, traveling down the Fallopian tube, possessed the secret of its own unique genetic nature and fate. Because it was already Chase and could not be anything but what it was designed to be, it immediately set about transforming itself into his body. Chase's rudimentary heart appeared on the fourteenth day, his spine, brain, eyes, ears, alimentary canal, and the buds of his limbs by the twenty-first, and then, day by day and organ by organ, all the rest of his parts sprang into being. Floating in the fragrant amniotic fluid, Chase heard voices from outside, saw light filtered through membranes, heard the beating of an enormous heart above his head, felt his mother's emotions coursing through his own body and so learned that there were others like himself.

Was it possible to go farther back than this, beyond the muted rosy light inside the womb, was it possible to break into two again and rise up through the blood vessels and cells of his parents' bodies, to swim into their very brains and find the storage places of their own original memories of themselves, in which, surely, he himself was already present along with all his ancestors and all his descendants that he would never have? Was it possible to go farther back, even, than that, possible to know everything by crossing the brilliant constellation of these innumerable generations of tiny minds like stepping-stones to their source, the Original Mind? Was knowing what Chase had known in the first microsecond of physical being, before he set about manufacturing himself and forgot the secret of life in the travail of breaking its code, the same as knowing everything? Was this knowledge the bliss of Samadhi, satori, salvation, Inward Light? Was he on the threshold of understanding the infinite?

Even under the influence of the gas that had been released into his bloodstream, Chase could not bring himself to think so. If he was traveling through the infinite, how was it that he remembered things about the nature of the infinite that the speck-mind of the fertilized egg could not possibly have known and had no need to know? He fought to bring his brain back to equilibrium. His conscious mind began to function again. A brilliant light shone above his eyes. He saw strange figures around him and knew they were his captors. Where had he been? Had he gone further back than he knew? Was he not where he thought he was now, but somewhere else? Where was his childhood dog Bucky? Where were the Marines of his patrol, Corporal Erskine and all the others? Where was Frankie? Where was the red-haired girl? Where was Brewster? Where?

"Wake up, Jonathan."

His right eye focused, briefly, and he glimpsed Verena's face.

"That's right. Wake up." She aimed the beam of a flashlight into his other eye.

A second later he was back.

Evidently it was midday, because the light was almost unbearably bright.

The room was white and splendidly decorated, with glass tables, white soft armchairs, and what appeared to be excellent original paintings on its walls, a deep pile of white carpet covering the floor. The place reminded Chase of the palace of an emir where he had once stayed in the Sudan. It had the same stillness, the same sense that the house and everyone in it were suspended out of ordinary time and place. Each was ruled by a man whose absolute authority was never exerted because it was never questioned. But the central feature here was a large, comfortable, customized armchair with controls on a panel at the right armrest and buttons that could, obviously, do all sorts of sinister things.

It was evident that the Mirza loved Verena Rautavaara. His face, tanned like a fine hide by decades of exposure to the weathers of the Mediterranean, glowed with joy when his agent, code-named Snow Queen, entered the room from a side door. Her hair was once again its usual platinum blond and she wore a low-cut straight white cotton dress with long sleeves and gold embroidery. She carried an Uzi on a strap over her back. He gathered her into his arms and kissed her on the forehead and both cheeks, then stood back from her, with his hands on her elbows, and examined her musing face.

Chase felt the gut twist of impotent horror as he watched. And then the lead of despair deep inside. He had sent himself into a compromising situation, and there was no one else to blame. Like Chase, Brewster had almost certainly been duped by what had transpired. Verena Rautavaara: the Mirza's little helper.

The despair came from the knowledge that he had let his country down, and failed I-Division. In Chase's book these were the cardinal sins.

"Perfect." The Mirza turned to Chase, who was slumped to his knees on the floor, hands cuffed to his ankles. "My dear Mr. Chase, you have had the chance to love the only perfect woman who has lived on this earth since ancient times."

He spoke English like an Englishman, with a public school accent. Champagne was brought to them and they drank, standing, looking down at Chase. He could see now the paintings were by the Spanish masters; most of the men, conquerors, were painted full-length. They all looked like the Mirza—thin figures in close-fitting black, like columns of smoke against the landscapes behind them, with cruelty sleeping in their immobile faces.

"Well, Chase, surprise. I'm sorry it had to be like this. You have lived up to your reputation. Every girl should have one." Verena's eyes were as cold as the North Sea in December, and the words meant nothing.

"Not as sorry as I am." Chase allowed himself a smile that neither the muzzle of the Uzi nor Verena deserved.

"Not really a surprise, either." Chase managed to smile again. Bluff seemed the only way now. "My people know. They even have the location of this place." His eyes switched to the Mirza. "Should've been more careful. You're all blown."

For a split second he thought the Mirza's face showed concern.

"Bluff, Jon, will get you nowhere," said Verena.

Leaving the Mirza at his throne, Verena approached Chase. "Black doesn't suit you, Jon. You're covered in blood. I'm going to take off those cuffs, and—very slowly—I want you to take off your clothes so we can bandage you up."

Chase shrugged. "If you say so."

"I do, and please don't be fooled. The tiniest move and I'll have no compunction about taking your legs off with this." The muzzle of the Uzi twitched. "Don't worry if you're naked underneath. Remember I've seen it all before."

The Mirza cackled.

There were no options. Slowly, Chase began to divest himself of his torn and bloodied clothing. As he did so, he tried to talk, picking questions with care.

"You really did have me fooled, Verena. After all you saved me several times."

"More than you know." Her voice was level and without emotion. "That was my job—or, at least, the job I said that I'd try to do."

"My God," Chase laughed. "Have they really got you at it, Verena? Come to that, why didn't you let the goons finish me off at your apartment in Zurich?"

"Those were Thinkingcap's men. You were too good for them. Anyway, the deal was to bring you alive, not dead. I was simply your guardian angel. Guiding you here, to the Mirza. That was the job."

Chase sighed. "What a pity. What a waste of such a pleasant girl."

"Chauvinist."

He finally pulled off his clothes, standing there in his black undershorts.

"So why kill Thinkingcap, one of your own men?"

"Quite simply, we needed him in his capacity as a pharmacist. That part of the operation is now over. And you—conveniently for us—have eliminated him."

"You're welcome."

"My father, too, was a beginning to be a hindrance. Once we'd made use of his contacts, we were quite happy for you to put an end to him."

"So you couldn't betray them until your purpose was achieved."

"Thanks to you, we never had to."

Chase, hands splayed against the white wall, leaning forward, heard Verena move, but he knew there was no chance of his taking any precipitate action. She was fast and good with weapons at the best of times. Now, with her boss here in the room, she would be very itchy with her trigger finger.

For one of the few times in his life, Chase felt out of control. Mostly it had to do with recognizing the beginning of emotional feelings toward Verena. He hated himself for that. But he was already too much in love with the hate to squander it.

"Turn around—slowly—with your arms stretched out and feet apart, then lean back against the wall."

Chase did as he was told, regaining a complete view of the room just as the door to his right opened.

The hoods who entered carried medical supplies and some sort of outfit for him to wear. They cleaned and bandaged his shoulder and ribs as he dressed—in a sort of safari-style khaki shirt, twill khaki trousers, and white slip-on tennis shoes. All the while Verena covered him with the Uzi.

The Mirza studied Chase. Verena studied the Mirza. She appeared tense, as if something about Chase's presence seemed to threaten the strange dynamic between the two of them.

"I understand if it is difficult for you to be around the naive and headstrong American. We're only keeping him alive for his conditioning. I can remove him from your sight at any time."

The Mirza smiled and relaxed in his chair, steepled his fingers, tapped their ends together. "No, no. Chase and I are going to have a quiet conversation. It's a rare opportunity for me to view the proverbial bug under the microscope."

The Mirza signaled to the goons to leave. "Give us an hour."

Snowqueen kept the Uzi trained on Chase.

An intangible aspect of the exchange between Verena and the Mirza told Chase everything he needed to know about his predicament. Women involved with men like the one holding him captive did not offer themselves to others without good reason. The Mirza was like some Victorian millionaire martinet. And whatever he said about using Chase as a case study, it was clear he was jealous as well.

"I am a believer, Mr. Chase, in B. F. Skinner's theory of operant conditioning, which holds that any organism will naturally repeat behavior when it is reinforced by properly designed rewards. By 'organism,' Skinner meant any sentient being, from pigeons to the members of the IQ Elite.

"Men and women, though capable of far more complex behavior than pigeons in response to much more subtle stimuli, will nevertheless behave in the same predictable fashion in response to a well-designed program of stimulus and reward. I, myself, am interested in reinforcing a certain kind of liberal political behavior, based on a system of beliefs that have already been instilled in my subjects by earlier teachers. My predecessors have created a tribe of young believers by bestowing such irresistible rewards as personal encouragement and praise, higher grades than were strictly deserved, honors, prizes, and so on. For example, in America, you have the Students for a Democratic Society, the Weather Underground Organization, and the Youth International Party, or the 'Yippies.' In Europe, we have the Prague Spring, The Situationist International, and the Provos. I have built my organization on groups such as these by offering a higher order of rewards. These include knowledge of secrets and the trust this implies, praise, power, the psychic support of a like-minded tribe—and, of course, sex and money. Through my organization I give my pupils a purpose in life: the reinvention of society, and, by exercising my influence to get them jobs in the right places, I've made it possible for them to fulfill that life purpose."

Chase interrupted, "Tell me about this 'reinvention of society.'"

"From an early age I wanted to change the world, but I always realized that it could only be changed piecemeal, according to a systematic plan. A frontal assault on the establishment could never succeed. It must be conquered camp by camp—first academia, where minds are formed; then the news media and the arts, which transmit the orthodoxy to lesser minds; then a whole apparatus of special interest groups to bring irresistible pressure on the government in concert with all of the above; then, at the Omega Point, the whole world."

"So killing all the spies was..."

"Do not interrupt me again, Mr. Chase. We will get to that. So, above all, it required endurance. You see, Mr. Chase, my family were Bukhari: a tribe of Jews from Afghanistan who emigrated to Spain and pretended to be Muslim for more than a thousand years, ever since the Arab conquest of the western Sahara."

"A thousand years?" Chase said.

"There's nothing so unbelievable about that," interjected the Mirza. "At least a hundred thousand Spanish Jews were baptized as Christians in the 1390s. Over the next three centuries the Holy Inquisition burned more than thirty thousand of these converts at the stake on suspicion of insincerity, and tortured another thirty or forty thousand. Nevertheless, secret prayer houses that had been in constant use by Jews since the days of the Inquisition were discovered in Spain as recently as the nineteenth century, and groups of secret Jews, the descendants of these false converts, or 'Marranos,' were found even later in Portugal and as far away as Mexico.

"So you see, Mr. Chase, from my family—especially my grandfather—I learned to think like a man surrounded by enemies and to believe in the treachery of all who ruled over others with money and laws. My grandfather told me how Romans, Franks, Venetians, Turks, and their slaves the Albanians had all tried to subdue our tribe in our mountain fastness and all had failed in their turn.

"They tried for two thousand years to starve us out, so we learned to live without eating; they tried to turn families into spies and traitors, so we learned to live without trust. My grandfather said to me one day, 'When I die, you will be alone. Trust no one. Make the world safe for yourself, just one Bukhari among all the thousands who have been oppressed. Rise above our enemies, who are everyone and everywhere, and I will be with you at the head of an army of ghosts.'

"Later on, at Oxford, I came into contact with the driving political idea of the twentieth century, that everything is personal and that nothing in the visible world is what it seems to be. I understood that the world's greatest minds—Pasteur in medicine, Einstein in physics, Freud in psychology, Marx in economics—had validated my grandfather's teachings.

"To achieve this forbidden personhood, to pay back my family's oppressors, became my purpose in life, though I concealed it from the world for many years. You see, I was born in 1910—of a good family—who soon left me an orphan. I was sent to England in 1919. My uncle, the diplomatist, had a Spaniard's abiding suspicion of the British espionage service; it seemed inevitable to him that the English would, sooner or later, attempt to make use of a wealthy Spaniard—obviously not knowing he was a Jew—who had been wholly educated in their country and who might, the force of nature being what it is in young men, even marry an Englishwoman. Therefore I was registered at my schools not under the name my family used—but under the name that belonged to one of the minor titles that my family had acquired in antiquity through marriage.

"The result was that, although I knew a lot of people in England, none of them knew me by my real name; and though everyone in Spain knew my more famous name, almost no one in that country knew me by sight.

"Between school and Oxford, I performed my military service. Spain was in political uproar. I took no particular interest in the rise and fall of dictators, the rebellion of garrisons on the peninsula. This had always gone on. The Bourbon king abdicated. It had nothing to do with his family, or with the other ancient families connected to his family. His uncles believed that the real threat to Spain—and to Catholicism, which was the same thing in the mind of the archbishop—came from outside Spain. They were greatly afraid of communism. Of anarchism, too, and socialism. All were the same thing in their eyes. My uncle the archbishop, then only monsignor, had seen forty-eight churches burned in 1909 in Barcelona, and drunken workers dancing in the streets with the corpses of nuns they had taken from the catacombs.

"They were nobles and prelates. They decided they needed an agent in the enemy camp. I was engaged by arrangement to the daughter of a duke who was a party to the conspiracy, and sent to Oxford. I studied Arabic for my own pleasure, and Russian in preparation for my mission. I was instructed to ingratiate myself with the English Communist movement that was flourishing at Oxford in the 1930s. It was an easy job; many of the people the Communists were recruiting at the university were from the aristocracy or its fringes, class renegades. Outwardly, I became like them. In 1934 I was introduced by one of my dons to a Russian, who recruited me as an agent of the Comintern. The resources of the NKVD were not sufficient to discover my real identity, much less my real purposes. The Russians knew that nations had intelligence services; they never suspected that a class, even the class they were hoping to destroy in Spain, should send secret agents against them.

"I went down from Oxford in that year. I spent the next months in Barcelona being trained as a terrorist; there I met many other Spaniards, all of them of a different class and all of them going under false names. I memorized all their faces. In 1935 I was sent away from Barcelona with a false English passport supplied by the Russians, with instructions to go to Madrid and wait. I did so. When war broke out, in the summer of 1936, I was in place.

"During the siege of Madrid, I was an agent of the Comintern and the leader of the fascist fifth column. Because I had so many languages—Spanish, English, Russian, German, French, Arabic—and had them so well, I was assigned in Madrid to the foreign community. Foreigners were pouring into the capital—journalists, spies, soldiers. Moscow wanted them watched; sometimes it wanted one of them killed. The Soviet controllers especially wanted a watch kept on Russians. It was better for a Spaniard to do it than a Russian, because Russians generally believed that Spaniards were children.

"I was arrested by the victors at the end of the war. I was sent to prison for an interval. There I learned a number of things, a prisoner's skills and tricks. After a time I was condemned to death. I was taken out of my cell by the guards. The other prisoners saw a man killed by a firing squad in the prison yard. It was not me.

"Elsewhere in the prison, I was being fitted secretly into the uniform of a major in the Nationalist army, and in those clothes I walked out of the prison and back into my true identity. In 1941 I volunteered for the Division Azul, the Spanish force that fought in Russia with the German army, and was wounded again.

"While recovering in a French hospital, I got the news my grandfather had died. Never a day had gone by that I hadn't remembered his lessons. I had studied with some of the finest minds in England, but the wisest man I had ever known was my grand-father.

"The first prophetic proof of the soundness of my plan to rein-vent society was my own recruitment by a Frenchman into an organization that was then merely called 'The Directorate.'

"This man knew my true name and my true heritage. In Herat after the war he had encountered local people who believed that they were descendants of an Israelite tribe that had been captured and marched to Babylon by Nebuchadnezzar after the destruc-tion of Jerusalem in 586 BC. Eventually these people made their way into western Afghanistan, founded Herat, became the tribe called Pathan, and started conquering their neighbors. Like their purported ancestors under Joshua, they were merciless warri-ors and conquerors. They called themselves the sons of Israel. Their legendary history and law were recorded in sacred books. The Frenchman had met the hereditary keeper of these texts in Habibullah and seen them. Our original family name was there.

"This Frenchman made it plain that I had been chosen for the Directorate for what I was, because the Directorate thought it was essential to have people like me inside the perimeter of the privi-leged classes. 'You must be our conscience,' he told me. 'Never be tempted to be like us; we're the ones who should try to be like you.'

"Listening to this unmanly speech from a rich man's spoiled son who wanted to play at being spies, I thought to myself, Grandfather, they are so weak! But I knew that Grandfather, killer of Turks, would have replied, 'No, they are just washing your feet for the sake of their own souls. Beware the enemy who pretends to be humble.'"

The man was unhinged. Chase knew that, but possibly so did many others. Listen, he thought. Listen to all the Mirza has to say. Listen to the music, and the words, then, perhaps, you will find the real answer, and the way out.

He let out a loud sigh. "Look, I've seen a lot of men die for politics, and politics was usually the excuse their murderers used. Men kill not for an idea but because they can't live with a personal injury. I can tell you've had your feelings hurt a lot over the years and because you've been a spy your whole life, you naturally assume you know more than anyone else, but..."

The Mirza cackled, "So, the American is a psychologist now?"

"Well, I'm curious about this mystical idea of a secret, ancient nationhood you have. It seems like something only a privileged man could invent."

"How would you know?"

"It's just the tendency to dramatize the hidden side of your nature. You clearly take pleasure in tantalizing outsiders with your national mystery. As if it were something hidden, but in plain sight."

"And what, in your opinion, is that mystery, Mr. Psychologist?"

"You're a murderer. Don't worry, I'm one too. I'm paid to be. But you take pride in your murders. It's not a quality that's confined to you."

"You think my motivations are as simple as that?"

"I think the human question is simple as that, Mr. Mirza. Intellectual systems are developed to justify the exchange of death. In Germany, two thousand years of Christian teaching produced the SS. In Vietnam right now, two thousand years of colonialism produced this slaughter of peasants Ho Chi Minh calls a revolution. It required only a hundred years of technology to produce the Hiroshima bomb. All achieved the same results—murder without guilt."

"You believe in nothing, then?"

"I believe in the truth."

"You must be crazy, Mr. Chase, to speak to me like this."

"In some respects, maybe. But I've got to say this 'reinvention

195

of society' of yours sounds as full of holes as a Swiss cheese—you know that, don't you?"

A smile bent the Mirza's lips.

"You want me to believe in these higher motivations for killing off spies all over the globe. But there's no motivation. It's all been one big decoy, hasn't it? Misdirection on a global scale. You're trying to bring off an operation, a major operation I'll hand it to you, and you need prying eyes out of the way."

"Well, Mr. Chase, your theory, as a theory with no hard facts to support it, is sound enough."

"You want hard facts? Here's some: Majorca. The Russian. Skypilot."

The Mirza's eyes widened at the words, and then he laughed. "You're a fool, Mr. Chase. What do you think this is—a film? We tell you everything, you escape with the truth, the world is saved? I believe you are insane."

"Then you should be frightened," Chase said. "You are old. Even if I have no weapon, I could kill you with my bare hands before anyone stopped me. You don't seem to be afraid of that."

"Nothing is gained by this. Why exchange these threats?"

"You said it yourself. The truth."

The Mirza moved his face into the light and with a wheezing cackle, slammed a button down on his armrest.

It was then that the floor opened up underneath Jonathan Chase.

✦

The dark, windowless room where Chase was held had walls of unplastered rock and a concrete floor. He knew this much from having explored the space around him with bare feet. He was handcuffed to the head of the iron cot on which he was lying. The cell was so cold and damp, and such a good place for the rats he thought he heard scampering in the darkness, that he supposed he was in a cellar.

A very thin man in a tweed jacket and black balaclava covering his face opened the door and turned on the feeble lightbulb that dangled from the ceiling. He checked Chase's handcuffs to make sure they were still locked, then leaned against the rough wall and looked him up and down.

"Are you all right?" He asked in brisk Oxbridge English.

"I have to use the toilet."

"Of course you do, you poor thing. It's been hours."

The man's tone was filled with solidarity, as if he himself had often been handcuffed to a bed in a dungeon while longing to urinate, and only the two of them could understand the feeling. He freed Chase's left wrist, snapping the empty cuff back on to the frame of the bed, and set a galvanized bucket closer.

"Don't be embarrassed. I am beyond disgust."

"Lucky you."

The man behind the mask laughed, very brightly. "You sound like your chief."

"You know my chief?"

"We used to work together."

"Where was that?"

"This is a very strange conversation, Jonathan. Do you always try to catch people you've just met in lies?"

"It depends on the circumstances."

Chase pushed the bucket away and sat down on the bare straw mattress. The effects of the drug had worn off.

"You resemble Brewster. He'd do anything for old men when he was young."

"You don't really sound like a friend of his, you know."

The man in the black mask laughed again, evidently delighted by Chase's spunk. "Oh, but I'm not; I never was more than a useful acquaintance."

"Anyway, I'm glad to meet you," he said. "You may think, considering the circumstances, that it would have been better if we never met." He waited for Chase to say something, but he did not. He shrugged and continued. "All I can tell you is, I did my best to prevent it when you were recruited. But Brewster wouldn't listen. At the time he was a member of the all-time CIA backfield, the best ever at what he did. The question is, are you really Brewster's favorite son?"

"It's cold in here."

"Were you harmed in any way?"

"It's hard to remember. My head was swimming."

"Allah is merciful."

"Does Allah have something to do with this situation?"

The thin man laughed at this new defiance. "No. All appearances to the contrary notwithstanding, nothing. Much older gods than him are at the bottom of this. Now turn your back, please, while I unlock the handcuffs."

Chase felt the muzzle of a pistol pressed against the base of his skull. He expected to feel the sting of another injection at any moment, but this did not happen. The man in the mask grasped Chase's jaw and gently turned his face this way and that.

"Do you know what I think, Jonathan?" he said. "I think we're going to be great friends. We have a lot more in common than you may realize."

Chase did not speak or make a gesture. His hands were free now; he knew that he could overpower this frail man, kneel on his back, break his neck, take his weapon. It was the wrong time.

"Do you?" Chase said. "Do we?"

"Oh, yes. You're going to be astonished at what a long way we go back, you and I."

2

The room into which Chase was shown was used for dining. Handsome carpets, heavy and thick, covered the floor. There were big Bedouin pillows and a long, low dining table. Tapestries embroidered in gold thread hung from the eaves. Hidden musicians tuned their instruments. Servants scurried about. One of them brought Chase a gin and tonic in a tea glass. Another offered him figs. Behind the table, all in a row, a half dozen hooded peregrine falcons perched motionless on shoulder-high T-shaped perches inlaid with what looked like ivory and lapis lazuli.

"How nice of you to join me for dinner, Mr. Chase." Even the Mirza's voice seemed to take on sinister undertones—a voice of honey and milk, mixed with strychnine. He had changed into camel's hair robes. A servant followed, carrying a large, hooded falcon on his arm. Other servants marched in with more falcons and placed them gently on the perches.

"Did I have any alternative but to dine with you?" As he looked him in the eye, Chase consciously summoned a vivid picture into his head—this time the Mirza was at his mercy, strapped to a table. Chase held a huge branding iron just above the flesh on his chest. If he brought images such as this to file in and out of his mind, he had little to fear from the man. It was when you allowed your eyes to meet his that you became vulnerable.

He sensed the Mirza wince inwardly. "You are a very clever man, Mr. Chase." It was as near as he would allow himself to reveal weakness. "I was warned of that by Verena, but I imagined you were merely a strong physical man, used to violence, an able fighting opponent. I had no idea you had willpower as well."

When the thin man in the ski mask had arrived at his cell, Chase was taken along the corridors of the strange compound, through to the Mirza's bare, austere study where the masked man went straight to the fitted bookcase nearest the window and pulled out a book on the third shelf. There was a click, and that part of the bookcase swung open to reveal a door. Chase was quick to notice that the spine of the false book showed it to be a fat imitation copy of E. M. Forster's *Two Cheers for Democracy*. Somewhere within the Mirza there was a spark of humor.

"I've planned a simple meal for us." The Mirza smiled now, and Chase thought he could detect the leer of one of the Borgias. "Very simple. Especially for you, Mr. Chase."

Chase held up a hand. "Just one thing..."

"Yes?"

"Who was he? That man in the ski mask?"

"That, Mr. Chase, is a question with a very long answer. And an answer best suited for another time."

"He said he knew me."

"He knows a great many people. Was there anything else?"

Chase looked up, into the full power of the man's eyes. From a long way off he heard the Mirza repeat, "Anything else?" Then he tore his eyes away, concentrating on a Mirza whose body was being riddled with bullets.

"When you sup with the devil, they say you should use a long spoon. I'm sorry if I seem to abuse what you call your hospitality, but I shall require you to taste every course set in front of me."

The Mirza laughed. "I can do better than that. A servant will taste it for you. I shall see to it. You have no need to fear me, Mr. Chase."

"I don't fear you."

"Funny, I had the impression you did. Why else would you have need of a food taster at my table?"

"Because you are an expert in the use of a certain kind of drug that makes people happy to confess things; an expert in manipulating people, so that they believe the 'radical' hodgepodge you throw at them. You are—let's cut the formalities—you are expert in sending impressionable people to their deaths, along with innocent victims; and you do it for money and political influence, right?"

There was silence for a second, no more. "Do you know about falcons, Mr. Chase?"

"They are used for hunting."

"For training purposes, only a wild falcon will do. It must be a female because in all species of hawk the female is larger, stronger, and fiercer but easier to dominate."

Chase nodded.

"She falls in love with her master," the Mirza said. "That is the object of the training. You keep her in a dark room, always hooded, with a bell tied to her leg by a leather thong. The thong is tied to the perch. Of course the bird falls asleep. You go in and speak to her in the dark. She wakes up. She must hear no other voice than yours."

"And this, metaphorically speaking, is how you built your army?"

"I'm glad you bring it up, Mr. Chase. Our last conversation left me thinking about the similarities between this American hippie counterculture of yours and the Hitler Youth of the thirties and forties."

"What similarities?"

"This counterculture is clearly totalitarian in its impulses and methods."

"Fascinating. I was under the impression it was about peace and love."

The main dish arrived, succulent and lean lamb chops, cooked with rosemary and other herbs, served on a huge salver, surrounded with small roast potatoes and beans. The server tasted everything before Chase took his first bite.

"Shocking thought, isn't it? These past few years have puzzled me, this army of foulmouthed runaways, all dressed up like the proletariat, squirting urine on the police and waving marijuana lollipops at television cameras. Why do these bourgeois children who have everything decide to hate everything they might ordinarily be expected to love—freedom, country, family? It can't just be puerile self-hatred; that's far too simple an explanation for a movement of this magnitude. I keep wondering where this mass temper tantrum is coming from. And then, recently, I stumbled onto the most amazing book about the Wandervogel, the pre-Nazi German youth movement. This was the precursor to the Hitler Youth, of course, but it began before the First World War as a reaction to post-Bismarckian industrialization. A schoolteacher named Karl Fischer got it started as a sort of back-to-nature thing in 1896. Wandervogel means 'birds of passage.' Very apt."

"I should just warn you, that if you're trying to goad me in some way, it's not working. As you can see for yourself, I myself am not a hippie or a student radical."

"Let me finish. It's all very interesting. How the German youth movement became the Hitler Youth. The Nazi Party, portraying the movement as one of youth and for youth, sensed the tensions between the generations in German society, played the young and new against the old and decayed with consummate skill, and denigrated 'the system' as the vile creation of a declining, older generation. The alternative was the destruction of the republic by the dynamism of National Socialism and its replacement by the Third Reich. The goal of the Hitler Youth was to rouse youth and direct their resentments against the state."

"So change a couple of proper names and you're the Jewish Hitler. Except you still have to rely on insane Arabs to do your heavy lifting. Is that what I'm meant to infer?"

The Mirza laughed, a low, deep chuckle. "Yes, Mr. Chase, the question is always 'who benefits?' Is it not? But have you ever thought that maybe being covert action assets is the fate of all idealistic, romantic folks? Not just Arabs. You yourself seem to have been weaned on it."

"You're right. I was. And most of its nonsense we inherited from the Brits, who adore it. When I was new they told me to be careful what I said and who I said it to on this subject. Nobody laughs at the rigmarole; it's very bad form. Everyone expects it; it's part of the forbidden atmosphere, like fake beards and cyanide pills. Mumbo jumbo that makes the whole process seem more serious. More connected to some invisible power.

"Like you, no doubt, Mr. Mirza, I quickly perceived that the world of espionage was a mirror image of the ordinary world, that tradecraft closely resembled the everyday behavior of people who live in small towns like the one I grew up in and must hide their real selves from prying neighbors. That little town in New Hampshire's adulterers, embezzlers, and drunken wifebeaters employed lies and deceptions, clandestine relationships, code words, false identities, and other tricks of the world of espionage as a matter of course.

"Had my mother really met and married an American named Chase who was killed in a car accident after a star-crossed honeymoon, or had she simply succumbed to the advances of some traveling salesman who gave her his Croix de Guerre in return for her favors? Was everything she told me about my father a cover story? Many in Keene suspected she'd never been married, that I was a bastard, that she'd made up the whole romantic story of her brief marriage in order to claim the Chase family seat on Silver Lake. But no one dared say so to her face because no one in town knew the truth or possessed the resources to discover it."

"I'm sure they told you, as they told me," the Mirza interjected, "that suspicion is not proof. It doesn't matter what the opposition thinks as long as it doesn't find out the real truth."

"Are there truths that aren't real, Mr. Mirza?"

"They're the whole basis of a good cover. Every truth about you, for instance, Mr. Chase, is out in the open and therefore beautifully misleading because, taken as a whole, they seem to explain everything about you. You come from an all-American village in the Northeast, from a good family, you're an Ivy League boy who joined the Marines, got captured in Korea and won the Silver Star, and then went back to Yale on the GI Bill of Rights. It's a story that presses all the right buttons, which is one reason—your brain being the other—why your man Brewster took such an interest in you. Who would ever think to ask if there's anything funny about you? How could there be, behind the smoke screen of all those credentials and honorable wounds?"

"Is there something funny about me?" Chase asked.

"Of course there is. You're a spy. What's more, you're a graduate of the so-called Assassin Factories of An-Tung—don't look so surprised, Mr. Chase, I've been in this business many years—Assassin Factories where young toughs are captured, brainwashed, and trained by renegade masters to be empty-handed killers, sparring and exercising for eighteen hours a day, living on iron bowls full of vegetables and cold rice and sleeping each night in a shallow pool of iced water. Those whom the regimen doesn't kill are very difficult to kill indeed. But espionage and assassination are criminal activities, my young American. Therefore, you've agreed to live the life of a criminal, at least during business hours."

"I have? Wish someone had told me all those years ago."

"I'm not suggesting that you really are a criminal, only that what you have agreed to do for your country will be regarded by its enemies as criminal. When a case officer recruits an agent, he suborns him to treason. That's a capital crime in every country in the world. Never forget that. Once you set foot on the territory of any country but your own, you're under sentence of death the minute suspicion of your true purposes turns into proof."

"I suppose your point is that we're not so different, you and I?"

"Let's see. If I were you and on your case, I would have started by sorting out the evidence I needed to illustrate the truth I already knew in my bones. I wouldn't yet have discovered the details—how money was handled or whether it was even necessary, how the Directorate found its assassins and perfected their will to kill. So I would follow leads, I would go to Europe, I would find bit players like Lazarus and Thinkingcap. How am I doing so far, Mr. Chase?"

"Please, go on."

"Now, these assassins, these small fry, could not have told me their reasons, or who the large fry were. But they would try to convince me that nothing was left to luck, that they had the power to rescue me, if I ceased my inquiries. I myself would by then understand something much larger was at work. That diversions had been planted everywhere. I would be able to see why this was the case and why it had been inevitable. The next step, putting faces to my theory, would be a matter of professional routine. I would know where to go and whom to contact."

"And here I am."

"And here you are. You have your faces."

"One thing you missed—I mean would have missed, if you were me—is a Plan B."

"Plan B? How mysterious you are, Mr. Chase."

"We've already achieved what we wanted. As we speak, the White House is announcing that American Intelligence Services have been irreparably compromised by the capture of a high-ranking asset, and that they must be replaced by a new intelligence service that can operate in a world in which there can be no deadly enemies."

"You already mentioned this in your interrogation. Quite simply, I don't believe it."

"Then you can continue to interrogate me all you like. My memories are no longer an asset to you. It's already too late."

"It's absurd."

"This new agency will be involved in the search for pure knowledge, as opposed to the pathological appetite for secrets that has driven all spies throughout their short, antidemocratic, maddeningly obscure histories. There will be no more room for old bores like you."

"I am now seeing the humor in this situation. You find me a bore. You are bored. Victims bore you as they bore all Americans. But you don't have the faintest notion what Skypilot really is, do you?"

"Villains bore me. I've always thought they smell like corpses. It's a particularly Central European malady."

"Verena!"

"Oh, not her again."

"Don't be frivolous, Mr. Chase. She can make it very unpleasant for you."

Verena appeared immediately. "Let's go." She came quite near to prodding Chase with the Uzi. "Hands above the head, fingers linked, arms straight. Go for the door. Move."

Chase walked forward, passing through the door to find himself in a curving passage, deep pile carpet under his feet, the decor changing to sky blue. The passage, he reckoned, ran around the entire story, and was probably identical to others on the floors above. The compound, whatever it looked like on the outside, appeared to have a circular core.

They came to a set of elevator doors—brushed steel, curved like the wall itself. Verena commanded him to take up the hands-on-the-wall position again while she summoned the elevator, which arrived as soundlessly as the doors slid open. Everything appeared to have been constructed in a manner that made silence obligatory.

She ushered him into the circular cage of the elevator. The doors closed and he could hardly tell if they were moving up or down—deciding that up was the only possible way they could go. Seconds later the doors opened again, this time onto a very different kind of passage—bare, with walls that looked like plain brick and a floor that gave the impression of being made of flagstones, although no noise came from treading on them.

"I'll take you to your final resting place, then, Jon."

They entered a large, bare room with tiled walls. One wall was taken up by a row of deep comfortable chairs, like exclusive theater seats. There was a medical table and a hospital gurney trolley, but the centerpiece, lit from above by large spots, was a throne. Not just any throne would do for Mr. Chase, though; this one was tricked out with rows of shiny hypodermic needles at the head and armrests.

Chase's first reaction was to remember something Brewster had said about the other ZD victims: "Afterward, they can't remember anything, except that it was the most pleasant experience of their lives. Apparently you could have your leg sawed off under the influence of this drug and not remember a thing."

How far things had come from Manchuria. No hard-nosed moral suasion here. No violence, no threats, no sleep deprivation or strange hours, no insistence on confession for your own good, just drugs and needles.

There was no doubt that it would do the job, though. The whole thing was macabre and unnerving.

One of the Mirza's hoods, the one with an eyepatch, stood by the chair in full evening dress and white gloves. Behind, and to his right, another hood, balding and also in tails, held a white blindfold on a heavy silver dish.

They were going to do this in style, Chase thought.

Verena took her place behind the balding hood, and for the first time Chase saw her, under the glare of the lights, as she probably was in reality. Her hair was loose and face overpainted with makeup so that it looked more like a tartish mask than the face of the charming girl he thought he had known.

Her smile was a reflection of horrible perversity. "The Chair awaits you, Jonathan Chase," she said. He squared his shoulders and stepped into the chamber. Two more big men had joined the party, each with a familiar stone face, one carrying a handgun, the other an Uzi.

"She awaits you," Verena prompted, and Chase was forced into the chair and strapped down. "Blindfold him," Verena commanded.

Chase's eye flickered around the group once more as the white cloth came down, just in time to see Verena reach for the chair's control box. He saw, as if in close-up, her fingers press down on the button.

✦

For a few seconds, Chase thought he was blind, deaf, and possibly dead. He was aware of a burning eruption of flame into his bloodstream as the needles pierced the skin. Then his vision went white, and it was as though someone had clapped cupped hands, hard, over his ears.

Time stood terrifyingly still, so that—once he remembered he'd been blindfolded—everything took on a dreamlike quality, the sounds around him and the actions of all concerned appeared to be telescoped into slow motion.

"Thiopropofal, in case you were wondering. It's a benzodiazepine from the same family of tranquilizers as Valium, but much more powerful."

"I've noticed." Chase could feel the intravenous fluids drip into his arms. It felt as if they'd shaved all the hair there. Perhaps all his body hair.

The chair had been adjusted so that his head and shoulders were propped upward, and he and the woman who called herself Snow Queen could commune face-to-face. Blindly, in his case.

"It depresses the central nervous system. When administered in sufficiently large doses it induces euphoria, suggestibility, and a tremendous sense of cooperativeness. The subject will do anything. Anything. It's hangover free. The subject doesn't remember a thing that he did or said afterward or have the slightest feelings of guilt or remorse. The beautiful part is that once a subject has been dosed, the Thiopropofal is in them for life. Most usually, it lies dormant. But it can also quite often bide its time, waiting to take effect due to the trigger of certain stimuli."

"Is there an antidote?"

"Oh, Jonathan, if there was, would we tell you?"

"Humor me. I'm not going anywhere."

"In an unscientific manner of speaking there is. Thiopropofal in big doses *is* an antidote to the natural responses of the brain. It turns off the conscience."

"Can it be overcome with another drug?"

"In theory, yes. Amphetamines might work. But no sane person would administer them for that purpose."

"Why?"

"You could stop the heart or damage the brain and turn the patient into a vegetable."

A wall of agony—almost a keening—interrupted Verena's disquisition, but she was undeterred. "Now that's the Naltrexone drip. It can be very useful with men like you. It allows you to experience a level of pain that the human body was never meant to know."

Chase felt like he was being raped by pain, felt that the very fiber of his existence had been violated.

"Now, now, Jonathan. Pace yourself. We're just prepping you here. This will be nothing compared to your final ordeal. You know what Emerson says of the great man, Jonathan? 'When he is pushed, tormented, defeated, he has a chance to learn something; he has been put on his wits, on his manhood, he has gained facts; learns his ignorance; is cured of the insanity of conceit.' Would you concur?"

The muscular convulsions that rippled his spine only magnified the already unendurable pain.

"Now, my lovely Jonathan, we must prepare you for your introduction to high society!"

◆

Part of his brain, somehow, took in the fact that, in reality, events were moving at high speed; also, in the foremost of his mind he realized he was moving.

The chair was moving.

After the silence of the execution chamber, it was startling suddenly to hear noise. Men's and women's voices echoed from above and to the side. The voices were very loud and seemed close at hand and reminded him of something, and it took a moment to sort out the various combinations in his head—the lively chatter, the clink of china. Some sort of party going on?

Sound helped thought.

The voices receded, the clarity blurring, then vanishing altogether. Chase heard boots clicking on the floor. He was still moving. The chair like a seat in a roaring roller coaster swinging around the sky.

Shaking all over. Stinking of sweat.

Lying silent in the whiteness of his roaring torture-chair, Chase tried to think: they had to open him up soon or it would be too late and the Mirza knew that.

Guess again. Guess again.

Think. *Think anything:* the Mirza had planned, using his great knowledge and privileged information. He had mustered his forces through the most elusive international terrorist organization in the world and set up a complicated and admirable tactical operation.

There was little to stop him at this stage.

Think. Why were they keeping him alive?

For his own safety, the Mirza would have to get rid of Chase. Why the Mirza had not already killed him was almost beyond Chase's comprehension. Chase could only presume he was still alive because the Mirza's vanity needed to feed on the applause of a doomed witness.

Was that it?

3

He woke with a start. Noise around him—the babble of conversation. Wherever he was, there was a large audience—male and female voices—already gathered.

A minute or so later, the murmur of the audience subsided. Applause took its place, rising to a thunder as Chase heard feet, heavy, on wood planks—a stage?—to his immediate right.

Slowly the applause diminished. There were some coughs, a clearing of throats, and then a voice—not the Mirza's, but Verena's.

"Ladies and gentlemen. Fellow members of the executive council of Zero Directorate. World section heads of our organization. Welcome." Verena paused. "As you see, our Leader is among us, but has asked me to speak to you. It is I—along with former agent Neville Scott—who have been at the center of planning for the operation which, until now, we have spoken of simply as Skypilot. Also, please help me welcome our guest of honor: this trussed-up specimen here is the American spy Jonathan Chase."

Laughter erupted all around him.

"Mr. Chase has committed himself, through tenacity and can-do spirit, to being our very first volunteer for Skypilot. But more about our sacrificial lamb later."

More laughter and an outbreak of applause, which then died as quickly as it began. Verena seemed to be shuffling and rearranging her papers. Chase heard her clear her throat and begin again. "The world, as we all know, appears to be on a permanent brink of chaos. There are the usual wars, skirmishes, rumors of war. The people are afraid. It should be quite plain to us all that many of their fears are fomented and manipulated by the military men and politicians of the so-called superpowers.

"We see marches, demonstrations, and pressure groups building, particularly within the Western powers. These action groups are motivated by fear: fear of a nuclear holocaust. So, as we hear and see, people take to the streets in an attempt to halt what they see as a nuclear arms race.

"We, of course—like the great military strategists—know that the whole business of a conventional nuclear arms race is a piece of neat misdirection. The so-called arms race is purposely being allowed to dominate the public mind, while the superpowers pursue the real arms race: the race to provide the true weapons of attack and defense—most of which will not be used here on this planet, Earth, at all."

She gave a tiny dismissive cackle of laughter. "What they do not see is that the bogeymen—the neutron bombs, cruise missiles, and so on—are merely makeshift weapons, temporary means of attack and defense. The same applies to the coast-to-coast tracking systems and the idiocies that are proclaimed about the airborne early-warning systems. All these things are like slingshots, to be used as stopgaps until the real armament is unleashed.

"The problem at the heart of this is fear—fear that homes, countries, lives are at stake. Those who take to the streets and demonstrate can think only in terms of war here on this planet. They do not see that in a matter of a very few years now, nuclear warfare will be negated, outdated, useless."

There was a confused shuffling among the audience before Verena Rautavaara continued.

"What I am about to tell you is already common knowledge among the world's leading scientists and military experts. The arms race is now not directed toward the stockpiling and tactical deployment of nuclear or neutron weapons, though that is exactly what both Soviet and American propaganda would like people to believe.

"No." Verena thumped her lectern, sending vibrations though the joists and boards near Chase's head. "No. The arms race is really concerned with one thing—the perfection of an ultimate weapon which will render all existing nuclear weapons utterly impotent." Verena gave her wicked laugh again. "Yes, ladies and gentlemen, this is the mad scientist's dream, the plots of science fiction for years past. But now the fiction has become fact."

Chase held his breath, already knowing what was to come. Disoriented as he was, Verena would, he was certain, talk about the ultrasecret Particle Beam Weapon.

"Until recently," Verena went on, "the United States was undoubtedly ahead in its program for the development of what is known as a Particle Beam Weapon, a charged-particle device, very similar to a laser, combined with microwave propagators. Such a weapon is indeed well on the way to finalization, and this weapon can, and will, act as a shield—an invisible barrier—to ward off any possibility of nuclear attack.

"As I have said, the Particle Beam Weapon, or PBW, was thought to be more advanced in the States than in the Soviet Union. We now know that both superpowers have reached roughly the same point in development. Within a few years—a very few years—the balance of power could either swing dramatically in one direction or become absolute on both sides. For the Particle Beam is designed effectively to neutralize any of the existing nuclear delivery systems.

"The superpowers can escalate with millions of cruise missiles or rocket-delivered neutron bombs. Much good will it do them. Therefore they are not stockpiling these arms. The PBW—once operational—will prevent any country from launching a conventional nuclear attack. PBW means absolute neutralization. Stalemate. Billions of dollars' worth of scrap metal sitting in silos all over the globe. If one superpower wins the Particle Beam race, then that power holds the entire world in thrall."

Chase shifted uneasily, as the facts began to come back to him. He knew that all Verena was saying made complete sense, even though, for a nonscientist, it did sound like high-flown fiction. Chase had the advantage of having already been briefed, along with Brewster and Number One. He had spent hours poring over pages of technical data, and reading long, if simplified, reports on the Particle Beam Weapon. As Verena said, it was a fact, and both the United States and the Soviet Union were now neck and neck in this, the most important arms race in history.

Verena now started to talk about the current satellites actually in space, some since 1957, orbiting or stationary, operational and fully active: the whole series of hardware which made an immediate nuclear confrontation possible.

"It is really a question of old military strategy," she continued. "History can always teach mankind. The problem is that to learn from history—particularly in military matters—mankind must adapt. For instance, World War Two began as a failure for the greater part of Europe because the military thinking of the so-called Allies was based on the strategy of former wars.

"Now, at this crucial point in history, we have to think, strategically, in a very different environment. An American senator once said, 'He who controls space controls the world.' There is also an old military maxim which says you must always control the higher ground. Both these statements are true. Now, the high ground is space, and space controls the nuclear potential of nations until the PBW race is won or lost.

"So, members of Zero Directorate, it is our task to provide our present clients with the means to control space until the race is won."

Verena continued, giving a great deal of information about the present satellites in use—the reconnaissance satellites: Reconsats and electronic ferrets, Big Bird and Key Hole; the radar satellites, such as the White Cloud system; the Block 5D-2 military weather satellites which carry banks of solar cells, giving each a greater longevity, plus a broad and very accurate coverage of world weather conditions.

Chase's anxiety increased. Acute awareness of danger. The overwhelming urge to scream. The facts—simple and incomplete—concerning these satellites were easily obtainable. But Verena showed a knowledge far and above any published data. The information she now passed on to the Zero Directorate audience was of the most highly classified variety. The woman, Chase could hear, knew exactly what she was talking about; and the bulk of it was considered highly secret, and sensitive, on both sides of the Atlantic.

He was surfacing, but everything was mixed as if three or four facts at once were being superimposed.

For the past few minutes, he'd been guessing that Zero Directorate's plan centered on the United States' progress with the Particle Beam, but this, he now surmised, was wrong. They were after the satellite systems already in operation. The primary targets in any conventional nuclear war—which would all be changed on the advent of the Particle Beam—had to be the communications and reconnaissance satellites, for they were the heart of military strength in an age of long-range warfare.

The answers were coming to him mixed up because of the drugs, but he was piecing the images together like an expert.

Where would Zero Directorate wish to strike? How, and what, would be their target? Slowly Jonathan Chase realized the full implications of Skypilot. But before Chase could follow through along this line of thought, Verena continued:

"The control of space, ladies and gentlemen, means the ability to neutralize the enemy's eyes and ears. It has been considered, for a long time now, that the United States had a fair, if limited, capability for space control. They were able, in theory, to neutralize Soviet satellites within a twenty-four-hour time scale. It was also thought that the Soviets had no such capability. In the past eighteen months, however, this has proved to be incorrect. The killersats, as they have been called, have now emerged as the current essential weapons. Powerful weapons. That power, my good colleagues, lies totally with the Soviet Union.

"It has, of course, been denied that any such satellites are in orbit. But there is no doubt that the Soviets have at least twenty laser-equipped killersats already in space, disguised as weather satellites. They also have the capability of launching over two hundred of these weapons in a matter of minutes."

Verena paused. Chase felt the anxiety in his throat and a twanging, like a plectrum, at his nerve ends. Although still shaky, he could feel the down-curve coming. Once more: he had seen the documentation and knew the truth.

"Our problem," Verena continued, "or, I should say, our client's problem, is that these satellite craft are hidden under one of the most successful security schemes ever mounted by the Soviets. We know the satellites are laser-armed; that they have a superlative chase capability; and that these facts are held on computer tapes and microfilm—their numbers, place, present orbital patterns, position of silos, order of battle. All this information exists, and is, naturally, required by our clients.

"The full intelligence concerning these killersats is held in Moscow. But the Soviets have been so careful as to isolate each section of information that our two sources inside the Kremlin reported, some months ago, that theft was virtually impossible. In fact, we have lost a great deal of time attempting to procure microfilm and other documentation in this manner. Each attempt has led to failure.

"However, there is another way. By the year 1973, these weapons—known in military jargon as Star Killers—will be controlled and operated through GLONASS, an abbreviation for the lengthy title Global'naya Navigatsionnaya Sputnikovaya Sistema."

There was polite laughter, which seemed to ease the tension in the hall. Verena went on to say that GLONASS was already under construction. Vast modifications were being carried out at the Rogachevo Air Force Base near the arctic circle and not far from the existing GLONASS headquarters, deep within Mount Narodnaya in the Urals.

"And until the program becomes operational, until Rogachevo base is converted, the Star Killers are controlled from GLONASS headquarters in the Ural Mountains. That, fellow members of Zero Directorate, is the weak link.

"Because GLONASS HQ controls the Star Killers, all information must be available to Rogachevo base. And so it is. Where it has been hidden away, in segments, at the Kremlin, it lies open and together, on the computer tapes in Mount Narodnaya."

It was all true enough; Chase could vouch for that. But the really big question had to be answered. How did you walk into the well-screened GLONASS HQ and lift computer tapes giving every detail of the Star Killers? Chase had a feeling that under the Mirza's instructions, Verena was about to answer the question.

"Operation Skypilot," Verena intoned. "Object: to penetrate GLONASS headquarters and bring out all the computer tapes carrying information on the Soviet Star Killers.

"Method? That is where all your hard work of the past few months comes in, my friends. It was a perfect operation and will be impossible for Chase's people, or anyone else for that matter, to string everything together. For what we needed, and what we have now attained, is something like a patchwork of information that could never have been achieved by the kidnapping and debriefing of one opposition agent alone.

"However, your collective efforts, especially those of you in the Eastern bloc, have allowed us to put all of the dark pieces of the jigsaw into place and to give a face to the thing we needed most. Now, my friends, I can safely tell you that the man we want is a certain Russian colonel called Sergei Aleksandrovich Nikitin. Colonel Nikitin has a very discreet taste for haute couture of which his comrades, for obvious reasons, are ignorant. Through the combined picture all of your tireless efforts have given us, we know he will be in Majorca on November 2nd, the Feast of the Devout, for a preview of the Simon Gaudet line of spring fashions. Our interest in Colonel Nikitin lies only in his left hand. His, and only his, left hand can be used for a state-of-the-art biometric scan. This biometric scan is, in turn, the only means of bypassing the passive infrared and hybrid combination security scanners deep inside GLONASS HQ.

"The actual abduction will be handled by a team of Zero Directorate employees, all highly trained commandos including myself and the assassin known as La Flamme. We will seize him by the catwalk, give him an injection, throw him into an unregistered van with a high-speed motor, ferry him to an airplane hangar, and remove his left hand.

"Our only foreseeable problem will be Nikitin's security detail. It is said to be, understandably, massive. Most likely this is due to his somewhat peculiar tastes. In organizations like the KGB, the right hand doesn't always know what the left hand is doing, and it seems our friend Nikitin has acquired a small army for traveling companions. Breaking through to the man himself will doubtless be quite a task for La Flamme and myself.

"This is where we have our leader to thank for a dazzling act of intellectual jujitsu: he has thought up a way to create a diversion, to lead investigators, perhaps some of Nikitin's detail even, away from the true operation, away from the real reason—the colonel's capture—away even from the people truly responsible. We believe that the implementation of this diversion will drive the very fact, the very existence of Nikitin's abduction out of the consciousness of the world.

"And this, friends, is where Mr. Jonathan Chase comes in. Mr. Chase knows everybody in the world, and he's a very senior officer. He requires no support. He's what the Americans call a Singleton—he operates alone, goes where he pleases. He feels about his country and his organization as we ourselves do about the Zero Directorate. He'd do nothing to harm his country. Voluntarily, that is."

Suddenly Chase felt the muzzle of a pistol pressed against the base of his skull.

"However, we have been prepping him, with just the right mixture of Thiopropofal and Naltrexone, for a spectacular confession. A miraculous confession, you might even say. For there is no agent working in the world right now who knows more official secrets than Mr. Chase."

Chase's scream reverberated through the large hall—another scream that ended only because breath itself did.

He could hear the room erupt with laughter.

Then the schism came: Chase felt anger but was powerless to move. He longed to scream, but he couldn't. He felt his tongue aching for the orgasm of speech. *Hold back.* All you've got to do. *Hold back!*

"We will position Chase at a site not far from Nikitin's location tomorrow night. And when he begins his confession, we will broadcast it far and wide. Local authorities and intelligence officers on the ground will be forced to react, once we've tipped them off to the eventuality.

"We have our great leader once again to thank for this stratagem. For it is his theory that broadcasts of any sort, television, film, the news media, have far greater powers of persuasion than any individual government in this day and age. While governments have laws and constitutions, the power of the broadcast is restrained by nothing more than the rules of theater. Because the targets of these broadcasts are usually thought to deserve the punishment they might otherwise have eluded, the broadcaster has no need to worry about the quality of its evidence. And verdicts of 'innocent' based on these rules of evidence are almost unknown. The sentence is shame, degradation, and exile.

"Therefore, while Chase plunges his own country's and perhaps many other countries' intelligence agencies into perfidy and shame, we will scoop up the colonel and be on our way to the Ural Mountains. Now, we must decide on schedules, times, weapons, and escape routes. May I have a map, please?"

Chase tried to guess the time and settled on noon. That gave him one and a half days. One and a half days to get out of this infernal chair, sorting the facts in his mind. And after that? He could either fight his way out, kill himself, or find some way to send a message.

But the doubts were coming. What was real? Was anything?

Ideas floated by: until the real arms race for the Particle Beam Weapon was won or lost, the Star Killers had to remain the province of the superpowers. Letting them fall into rogue hands was tantamount to collective global suicide.

Panic. Then control. Then anger.

So far, he had held out pretty well. He'd displayed the euphoria that was one of the drug's effects, but had fought hard against the urge to confess. When he talked at all he quoted long passages from books, recited lists of wines, and conversed with unseen companions about baseball.

But at the broadcast itself? *Could he hold out?* Now that they'd started using the painful Naltrexone? He wasn't sure...

And in the middle of that thought, the realization of a chilling prospect: the one person in all the civilized world who might yet be able to avert disaster was...Jonathan Chase.

–2–

Chase kept hearing Verena's voice and smelling the smoke from the Mirza's cigarettes, but he knew these sensations were only a dream. In reality he was listening to the Korean girl sing on the sun-drenched Yalu River. With grave Asian courtesy his teacher Jeong said, "She is singing that God is the smallest thing in the universe, so small that he cannot be imagined; he does not wish to be imagined, so he fills the sky with the stars that are his uncountable thoughts and we look not at the place where he is, but at the places where he has never been." Chase nodded sagaciously; this much of the truth he had already perceived. Chase understood it was immensely small, although it contained innumerable collapsed universes with all their indescribable luminosity; inside, as from inside his mother's womb, the light was rosy, but vast.

The Korean girl stood in the bow of the sampan with gossamer sails billowing around her. "Oh, Jonathan, I am so happy for you," she said. Chase opened his lips to thank her for her patience and understanding, and once he began to speak he could not stop. He told her over and over again. He had never been so happy as he was now, even though he heard mortar shells exploding around him in the jungle and he knew that he was dying at last.

"Jesus, doesn't this guy ever shut up?"

"I shoulda finished him off long ago, boss."

"I think not." A familiar voice spoke softly. "When the time comes...after the transmission of his debriefing."

The Mirza cackled.

Chase opened his eyes.

He was on a plane. Sitting toward the rear of the aircraft, it was impossible for him even to attempt to follow a flight path. Most of the time they had been above layers of cloud, though he was fairly certain that he had caught a glimpse of Cairo an hour after takeoff.

From the moment of his drugged departure from the compound, Chase's mind hardly left the subject of a possible breakaway. That, however, hadn't been the time to try anything—locked away in what seemed to be a very solid bunker, in an unknown location, kept close with armed men, one of whom wore an eyepatch. Chase sat looking at this guard, privately dubbing him "The Pirate" and giving him the occasional smile, but receiving no reaction. Sometime around four o'clock there were noises from above—a helicopter very low over the building, chopping down for a landing. Then, a few minutes later, the Pirate entered with the other guards. "You'll be joining the Boss now." He was ordering Chase, not telling him. "It's only a short walk, so you won't need the irons. But I warn you—any funny business and you'll be scattered to the four winds." The Pirate sounded as if he meant every word and would be more than happy to do the scattering personally.

Chase was marched up the passage, between his original guards, and through the door. The security truck had gone, and they were standing on the edge of a small airfield. It was clear now that they had come out of the basement of what must be a control tower.

A couple of Hawker Harriers and a Corsair stood nearby. Away to the left Chase saw the helicopter, which he presumed was from the Zero Directorate compound. In front of them, at the end of a paved runway, a sleek executive jet shivered as if in anticipation of flight, its motors running on idle. It looked like a very expensive toy—a Learjet, Chase thought—in its glossy cream livery, which read "Prince Industries, Inc."

The Pirate nodded him toward the jet and, as they walked the few yards—at a smart pace—Chase turned his head. The neat board on the side of the control tower read "Prince Industries, Inc. Flying Club: Private."

The Mirza and Verena were already seated, as was La Flamme, when he climbed into the roomy little jet. The pair did not even turn to look around at their captive, who was placed with a guard on either side, as before. A young steward passed down the aisle, fussily checking seat belts, and it was at this point that La Flamme turned to lock eyes with Chase. During the flight she repeated the action several times, on two occasions adding a wan smile.

They had hardly settled down when the door was slammed shut and the aircraft moved, pointing its nose up the runway. Seconds later the twin Rolls-Royce Spey jets growled, then opened their throats, and the aircraft began to roll, rocketing off the runway like a single-seat fighter, climbing rapidly into a thin straggle of cloud.

Now, hunched between two of the Mirza's muscular young men, he watched the wing tilt and saw that it seemed to be resting on sea. Craning forward, Chase tried to get a better view from the executive jet's small window—the horizon tipping over, and the sight of a coastline far away. A flat plain, circled by mountains; pleasure beaches, and a string of white holiday buildings; then, inland, knots of houses, threading roads, a sprawl of marshy-looking land, and, for a second only, a larger town. Memories flicked through the card index of his mind, but his eyelids were heavy. He knew that view. He had been here before. Where? They were losing altitude, turning against the mountains inland. The jagged peaks seemed to wobble too close for comfort. Then the note of the engines changed as the pilot increased their rate of descent.

The brunette called La Flamme sat at a window, forward, hemmed in by one of the Mirza's private army. He had brought four of his men on board, plus the Pirate acting as their leader. At this moment the Pirate's bulk seemed to fill the aisle as he bent forward, taking some instructions from the Mirza, who had spent the entire flight in a comfortable office area with Verena, situated just behind the flight deck door. Chase had watched them, and there seemed to have been much poring over of maps and taking of notes. As for La Flamme, he had been allowed no eye contact, though she had looked at him with eyes that seemed to slowly undress him—or devise cunning ways to kill him. Chase could not make up his mind which.

"At last he awakes! Our modern Prometheus!" The Zero Directorate henchmen seemed dazzled by their leader's cleverness, the aperçu received with uproarious merriment. Accepting two flutes of champagne from a waiter and handing one to Verena, the Mirza made his way down the aisle toward Chase.

"Prometheus, you may recall, stole the gift of fire from the gods and gave it to downtrodden mankind." The Mirza's voice was calm, soothing almost.

"Verena tells me you're a formidable linguist, Mr. Chase. You must know, then, the etymological derivation of the name Prometheus. It means foreseeing, or forethinking. It seems as apt a name for you as it does for me. As you told us in your drugged state: you choose to live in the future. You feel it with the back of the neck. Prometheus, according to the classical tradition, gave man civilization and brought us from savagery to civility. This was the meaning of the gift of fire—light, illumination, knowledge. Making visible what had been concealed in the shadows. Prometheus, the Titan, willfully and knowingly committed a crime when he brought fire down from the heavens and taught the mortals how to use it. It was treason! He was threatening to put humans on an equal footing with the gods themselves! But in so doing he created civilization. And it is our task to make its continued existence secure."

Chase eyed the Mirza emotionlessly. "So what do you have in mind?" He said. "*Stasi* on a global scale?"

"*Stasi?*" the Mirza replied scornfully. "Organize half the populace to spy on the other half, no one trusting anyone? I hardly think so. The East Germans' approach has been strictly Iron Age. No, we have at our disposal something much more subtle. It's called a miniaturized broadcasting chip. The latest Russian satellites have all been equipped with these silicon marvels. Once our work is done at the Rogachevo base, we will have the ability not only to put everybody under the microscope, but by activating these chips, to broadcast—using a prototype technology called Video—what we see. There will be no more secrets. What at first we did simply with spies, we will now do with whomever we choose. And you, Mr. Chase, are going to be our guinea pig. Our very first broadcast! What we tape tonight will be the first thing we send out over the satellites. No doubt you were wondering why you were still with us?"

"And you'll be making Big Brother look benign."

"Come now, Mr. Chase. You Americans teach your children about Santa Claus—'He knows when you've been bad or good, so be good for goodness' sake.' Whether you acknowledge it or not, the ethical principle has always been linked to what is known about us. The all-seeing eye. Good conduct tracks with transparency. When everything is visible, the need for spies, for politicians, for lies, disappears. All will be held accountable. We can broadcast their secrets whenever we choose."

"And who will be watching?"

"Everyone and anyone. There's never been anything like it."

"And at the center of it all is despot-voyeur, the Mirza, orchestrating his stolen satellites into thousands of Peeping Toms."

"Perhaps you are not capable of seeing what this will do for humanity. Humanity! First we have to live through millennia of marauding tribalisms, and when the Enlightenment arrives, the Industrial Revolution hunkers down. Industrialization and urbanization bring a whole new wave of social disruptions, unleashing toil and death on a scale never before seen. Two world wars, more atrocities on and off the battlefield. And when there are no more hot wars, there comes the Cold one; espionage breaks out. Is this any way to live? The members of the Zero Directorate come from every rank in every espionage agency in the world, but they all understand the paramount importance of ending the arms race and the Cold War. Of ushering in a new freedom."

"I'm not sure I'd consider the threat of random forced confessions freedom."

"Ah, Mr. Chase, real freedom is freedom from. We seek to create a world in which its citizens are free to be at their best behavior — the way they are when they know somebody is watching."

"And so goes our privacy."

"The real problem with privacy is that we have too much of it, thanks to people like you. It's a luxury we can no longer afford."

The facts fought each other in Chase's brain, as though trying to drag him into despair. He recognized the symptoms: as when, caught in the sea, a man decides he can swim no farther; or feels the onset of fatigue in snow, making him lie down exhausted, to be encompassed by that strange euphoria that comes before death by freezing.

Don't let yourself go, Chase told himself. Keep alert. Do anything; try to combat the inevitable.

Now they were reaching the end of the journey, with the sun below the horizon. The mountains were above them, seeming to lower over the bucking aircraft. Chase still peered out, trying to place their location. Then suddenly, he recognized the long, flat breast of the mountain to their left. The Tramuntuna, near Soller. No wonder he recognized it, knowing the area as well as he did. Majorca—that island plain circled with mountains, hunched against Spain. They were over Majorca—the other Balearic Islands in the distance, and the old town he had spotted was Palma, onetime seat of James II of Aragon. He should have spotted the towers that remain of the old wall and the vast fortress of the Bellver Castle set among the clustered terra-cotta roofs and narrow streets.

Thinkingcap had told the truth! It was down there at the ancient castle, dating from medieval times, when the area had been an independent kingdom, ruled over by the Crown of Aragon, that La Flamme was to administer death and dismemberment—tonight—a day and a half before Operation Skypilot. The target? Colonel Sergei Aleksandrovich Nikitin and his left hand. The situation was altered beyond recognition. Whatever the risk, he must take the first chance, without hesitation. More than at any time during this whole business, Chase had to get free.

Of course. They were on the final approach to Palma airport, near the village of Santa Cruz, and only three or four miles from the town itself. Chase had even been here in the winter, for mountain climbing, as well as spending many happy summer days in the area.

The engines flamed out and the little jet bustled along the main runway, slowing and turning to taxi away from the airport buildings, out toward the perimeter of the airfield.

The aircraft turned on its own axis and finally came to a halt, the guard next to Chase placing a firm restraining hand on his arm. The top brass were obviously going to disembark first.

As the Pirate came level with Chase, he gave a little swooping movement and his bulldog face split into a grin. "I hope you enjoyed the flight, Mr. Chase. We thought it better to have you with us, where we can keep an eye on you during this most important phase. You will be well looked after, and I'll see you get special treatment and more this evening."

Chase did not smile. "A hearty breakfast for the condemned man?" he asked.

"Something like that, Mr. Chase. But what a way to go!" Verena, following hard on the Mirza's heels, gave a twisted little smirk. "Should've let me do you in when the going was good, Jon." She laughed, not unpleasantly.

The Mirza gave a chirpy smile.

"We shall see you tonight then," and he was off.

They were parked alongside a huge hangar, with adjacent office buildings, topped by a neon sign that read "Prince Industries (Spain), Inc." Chase wondered what had prompted the Mirza to choose one of the Balearic Islands as his headquarters for this part of Europe. Simon Gaudet's fashion show, for sure, but was there some other reason? His own potential broadcast confession? Chase wondered how much it concerned Skypilot.

The guards acted like sheepdogs, closing in around Chase, trying to make the walk from the aircraft look as natural as possible. The hangar and offices were no more than a few yards from the perimeter fence of the airport, where a gaggle of ancient Britannias rested, herded together like stuffed geese, each with the legend "European Air Services" running above the long row of oval windows. The fence was low, and broken in a couple of places. Beyond, a railway track with overhead wiring ran straight past; behind that, a major road—the Paseo Maritimo—slashed with cars, moving fast. Going to, or coming from Palma, Chase thought; for in this area all roads led to that town.

At full stretch he could be away and through that fence in a matter of twenty seconds. But he knew he was still far too shaky from the drugs to reach anything like a full sprint. Twenty seconds: he actually considered it as they neared the offices. The muscular North Africans around him would be prompt in their reaction. Yet Chase was almost hypnotized by the idea of escaping this way through the fence, should opportunity present itself. Was he lucid enough?

It was to happen sooner than he expected. They were within a few paces of the office doors when, from around the corner, in a flurry of rough conversation and laughter, there appeared a large group of men—in the green and red uniforms of the French Foreign Legion. They were close enough for Chase to make out the letters LP entwined in gold on their caps. That would make them, he realized, the 10th Colonial Paratroops, the dreaded red berets commanded by General Massu and known simply as *les paras*. A fragment of Spanish floated from the conversation, then a quick response in French, for the soldiers were accompanied by two young Catalan customs officers—the whole group strolling hastily toward the Brittanias.

Verena and the Mirza were almost at the office door, accompanied by one of their guards; behind them, La Flamme was walking with her guard, and the Pirate walked alone between her and Chase, still flanked by his two men.

It would be one huge gamble. The odds flashed through his mind: putting everything you own on the flip of a coin; on the nose of a horse. Chase wasn't a gambling man. To gamble now would be to gamble everything he owned: life itself on the drugged-up apparatus that was his body. The Foreign Legion were mostly hardened criminals, career mercenaries, veterans of the worst prisons in the world, Chase knew. Eight years in Indochina, Dien Bien Phu, and Hanoi had not helped to make them any more cheerful. If the Mirza's men could be so shocked into holding fire or chase, even for a few seconds, because of these grim *parachutistes,* he might just make it. In this fraction of time, Chase weighed the chances. Would the Mirza wish to call attention to himself and his party? Would they risk a confrontation with this grizzled military force? It was a matter of audacity and nerve.

Later, Chase thought the appearance of the train probably made up his mind; the sound of a horn in the distance, and the sight of the long railway train snaking its way along the tracks, about a mile off.

He slowed, dropping back a couple of paces, causing one of the guards to nudge him on. Angrily, Chase shoved the man. *"Ar-rête,"* he said very loudly. *"Je sais que tu détestes General de Gaulle!"* Then, looking toward the group of Foreign Legion and customs men, he raised his voice and shouted *"De Gaulle!"* already taking one step away from the nearest guard, who moved a hand to grab him. Chase was quick. The bet was laid. *Le maximum: faites vos jeux.*

Chase had stepped away and was moving in great long strides, his hand up, toward the group of soldiers. "Get back here." The Pirate tried to keep his voice low as he stared forward; and Chase heard him hiss, "Get him. For God's sake. Take care." But by this time Chase had reached the group, and when the hood on his trail came straight at him, sidestepped, attempting a trip with his ankle as he did so. The hood collided with the legionnaires.

Chase weaved through the group of stunned Frenchmen as the

Mirza's hood was lifted into the air and unceremoniously thrown back in the direction of his confederates. Although slightly off balance, he managed to pass through the phalanx just as he heard the first blows begin to rain down on the Mirza's people. Like wounded animals, the Frenchmen were enraged enough now to maim and mutilate for the sport of it.

Using the group of legionnaires for cover, he was off, going flat-out in a low crouch, weaving toward one of the jagged gaps in the fence. There were shouts from behind him, but no shots. Only the sound of pounding fists and snarled curses. Chase dived through the gap, sliding down the small embankment onto the railway track—the train now bearing down on him, its roar shaking the gravel, the sound covering everything else. If there was going to be shooting, it would happen in the next few seconds, before the train reached them.

The big engine was coming from his right—from the direction of Palma, he thought. There was no time for further reflection. It was now or never, in front of the train looming above him. Chase chanced it, leaping in two long strides across the track and doubling his body into a ball, rolling as he reached the far side, the engine almost brushing his back as it passed with a great toot of its horn.

In an instant Chase was on his feet running down the far bank toward the Paseo Maritimo, his thumb already up in the hitchhiker's position. But luck was still with him. As he reached the edge of the road he saw a small battered pickup truck pulled to the side. Two men were being dropped off, and there were four others in the back, shouting farewells to their comrades. They looked like farmworkers going home after a long backbreaking day in the vineyards.

"Going to Palma?" Chase shouted in Spanish.

The driver, a cigarette stuck unlit in the corner of his mouth, nodded from the window.

"A lift?" Chase asked.

The driver shrugged, and one of the men in the back called for him to jump up. Within seconds they were edging into the traffic, Chase crouched down with the other men—thanking providence for his own facility with the Spanish language. He sneaked a peep toward the airport side of the train tracks. There was no sign of the Pirate or the others.

No, Chase thought, they would be running for cars—the Mirza would be well organized here. His men would already be taking short cuts into Palma to head Chase off.

Cars already had their headlights on, as the dusk gathered quickly around them. Chase asked the time, and one of the workmen told him it was after nine, holding out his wristwatch with pride, explaining it was a gift from his son. "On my saint's day," he said. The hands showed four minutes past nine. "We'll have to move if we're going to see the fun," the man said.

Fun? Chase shrugged, explaining he had just come in on a flight, "with freight." He was very late and had to meet a man in Palma.

"All men are in Palma tonight. If you can find them," laughed one of the workers.

Chase scowled, asking why. "Something special?"

"Special?" the man laughed. It was Palma's night of nights.

"Fiesta," one explained.

"Feast of the Devout," said another.

A third gave a bellow, lifting his arms histrionically: *"La Llama ha llegado a Palma!"* They all laughed. The Flame has arrived in Palma. They didn't know how right they were.

Chase suddenly remembered that he had been here before for the fiesta. Every town in the Mediterranean had its own rituals, its battle of flowers, processions, carnivals—usually religious. In Palma it was the great Feast of the Devout, when the whole town was crammed to the gills, and there was dancing in the streets, singing, fireworks, spectacle. The festivities started when bonfires were lit by a flame brought, with Olympian ceremony, by runners from a high point in the Tramuntuna Mountain itself. He could not have arrived in this ancient place at a better time. There would be crowd cover until the early hours—with luck, enough breathing space to find a way of making contact with Washington and Brewster.

2

Jonathan Chase was alone now, and that was to his advantage. He controlled the rhythm of the operation. It is almost impossible for a national police force to keep track of a single agent who continues to move, if the agent takes elementary precautions. For Chase's opposition, who dared not go outside their own circle for help, it was hopeless. They could not know where he was going or what he was doing. Their only chance was to catch Chase in the open and kill him. He didn't think they would be able to do that.

They dropped him off on the corner of the Plaça d'Espanya, which was already full of people standing shoulder to shoulder, pushing along the pavements. There were plenty of police in evidence, directing traffic, closing off streets, and—presumably—keeping an eye open for troublemakers.

Chase stepped back into the crowd. It was some years since he had been here, and first he had to get his bearings. In the middle of the crush of people, Chase realized, with a sudden stab of fear, that his legs were shaking. Directly in front of him there were three great bonfires ready to be lit. To the left he saw a bridge spanning the well-kept canal, banked here by green lawns and flowers, which ran, above and below ground, through the town—a tributary to the harbor.

A platform had been built over the bridge and was even now crowded with musicians. A master of ceremonies spoke into an uncertain microphone, telling the crowds about the next sardana they would be playing, keeping things going until the flame arrived to ignite both bonfires and excitement. The groups of dancers, some in traditional costume, others in business suits or jeans, formed their circles, clasping hands held high, and launched into the light, intricate foot movements: a dance of peace and joy, a symbol of Catalonia.

Chase thought that if there were to be any future for any of them—or at least a chance of one—he had better move fast. Telephone Washington. Which was the best way? Call from a telephone box on the direct dialing international system? For that he would need money. It would have to be quick, for telephone booths— particularly on the Continent—were highly unsafe and Chase had no desire to be trapped in a glass coffin, or one of those smaller, triangular affairs which would preclude keeping an eye on his rear.

The first move was to lose himself in the swelling throng, which rose and fell like a sea. Above all else, he had to be watchful, for the Mirza's men could be already among the crowds, their eyes peeled for him. And if they saw him Chase knew what he could expect. Most likely they would use dirks, sliding instruments of death through his ribs, covered by the crowd, in the middle of the celebrations. There was no point in going to the police—not on a night like this, without identification. They would simply lock him up and perhaps tomorrow, when it was too late, telephone the American Embassy.

Chase took a deep breath and began to move through the crowd. It would be best to keep to the fringes, then disappear into a side street.

He had just started to move when a large black Mercedes swept into the Plaça, only to be halted by a policia, who signaled that it should turn back. The road was about to be closed. The driver spoke to the policeman in Spanish, then turned to the occupants of the car. Chase's heart missed a beat. Next to the driver sat the Pirate, while three other big henchmen were crammed into the rear.

The Pirate got out, two of the men joining him, while the policia made noises suggesting they get the car out of the way as soon as possible.

Chase tried to shrink back into the crowd as he watched the Pirate giving orders. The men dispersed—diving into the crowd a little to Chase's right. The hounds were there, trying to spot him or sniff him into the open. Chase watched the big man shouldering himself away. Then he moved, taking his time, along the fringe of the crowd, going slowly out of necessity, and because of the density of the shouting, laughing, chattering people.

Chase kept looking back and then scanning the way ahead and across the road. The band had stopped and the master of ceremonies was saying that the Flame, carried from near the summit of the Tramuntuna by teams of young people, was now only a few minutes from its destination. A few minutes, Chase knew, could mean anything up to a half an hour.

The band started up again and the dancers responded. Chase kept to the edge of the crowds, slowly making his way across the now sealed-off road, toward the towering cathedral. He was looking for a street he recalled from previous visits: an ancient square almost entirely covered by tables from the cafés. They should be doing a roaring trade tonight.

He reached the cathedral and saw another bonfire ready and waiting to be lit. A great circle of dancers around it was going through the intricate patterns, slightly out of time to the music, which was distorted on the night air. On the far side of the circle he spotted one of the Mirza's men turning constantly and searching faces in the throng.

Chase held back, waiting until he was certain the man was looking away from him; then he dodged nimbly through the crowd, sidestepping and pushing, until he found a clear path through the archway of La Seu itself. He had just passed the café on the far side and was about to cross the road when he had to leap into a shop doorway. There, walking slowly, scanning both sides of the street, head tilted as though trying to catch his quarry's scent, was the Pirate. Chase shrank back into the doorway, holding his breath, willing the goon not to see him.

After what seemed an age, the eyepatched one walked on, still constantly scanning faces with his eyes. Chase edged out of the doorway and continued up the street. He could already see the intersection for which he was searching, marked by the bronze statue of a nude woman who looked unseeing down the wide road to his right. Crossing over through the thinning crowds, Chase arrived at his goal—Palma's Old City, once the great financial center of the town: its Rialto.

Chase walked straight into the corner *establecimiento* and asked for the toilette. The bartender, busy filling orders and being harassed by waiters, nodded to the back of the bar where Chase found the door marked with the small male symbol. It was empty, and he went into the first cabinet, locking the door behind him and starting work almost before the bolt slid home.

Another piece of luck was that the Mirza's men had returned him his clothes—the black slacks and black bespoke shirt he'd worn for his break-in at the clinic—laundered and pressed without noticing anything funny about his belt. Quickly his hands moved to his belt clasp—a solid wide U-shaped buckle with a single thick brass spike, normal enough until you twisted hard.

The spike moved on a metal screw thread. Six turns released it, revealing a small steel knife blade, razor sharp, within the sheath of the spike. Chase removed the blade, handling it with care, and inserted the cutting edge into an almost invisible hairline crack in the wide U-buckle. With hard downward pressure the buckle came apart, opening on a pair of tiny hinges set at the points where it joined the leather. This was also a casing—for a tiny handle, complete with a thread into which the blade could be screwed. Equipped with this small but finely honed weapon, Chase pulled the belt from his waistband and began to measure the length. Each section of the double-stitched leather contained a small amount of emergency foreign currency in notes. German in the first two stitches, Italian in the next, Dutch in the third...the whole belt containing most currencies he might need in Europe. The fourth section was what Chase *sought.* Spanish pesetas. The fifth section was what Chase *needed.* Dexedrine.

The small, toughened blade went through the stitching like a hot knife laid against butter, opening up the two-inch section to reveal a couple of thousand pesetas in various denominations. Not a fortune—but ample for his needs.

He dismantled the knife, fitted it away again, and reassembled the buckle, thrusting the money into his pocket. In the bar he bought a Coca-Cola for change and downed two capsules of the amphetamine. He remembered, for a moment, what Verena had said: *In theory, yes. Amphetamines might work. But no sane person would administer them for that purpose. Why? You could stop the heart or damage the brain and turn the patient into a vegetable.*

Chase sauntered out into the Plaça, back along the way he had already come. His target was the post office, where he knew there would be telephone booths. A fast alert to Brewster, then on with the other business as quickly as possible.

Music still thumped out from the other side of the cathedral.

He continued to mingle with the crowds, keeping to the right of the circling dancers. He crouched slightly, for the Mirza's man was still in place, his head and eyes roving, pausing from time to time to take in every face in the ever-changing pattern. Chase prepared to push himself into the middle of a group heading in his direction. Then, suddenly, the music stopped. The crowd stilled in anticipation, and the amplifier system crackled into life, the voice of the announcer coming clear and loud from the hornlike speakers, bunched in little trios on the sides of buildings and trees.

"My friends"—the announcer could not disguise the great emotion which already cut in waves through the gathered crowd—"the Flame, carried by the brave young people of Palma, has arrived. *La Llama ha llegado a Palma!*"

A great cheer rose from the crowds. Chase looked in the direction of the watcher by La Seu, who was now searching wildly for signs, not of Chase, but of this great *Llama*. The fever pitch of excitement had got to everyone.

The loudspeakers rumbled again, and with that off mixture of farce and sense of occasion which besets local feasts—from the Mediterranean to little American towns—the opening bars of Richard Strauss's *Also Sprach Zarathustra* climbed into the air, shattering and brilliant.

As the opening bars died away, so another cheer went up. A group of young girls in short white skirts came running, the crowd parting at their approach. About eight of them, each with an unlit brand held aloft, flanked the girl who carried a great blazing torch. Taking up their positions, the girls waited until the torch was set to a spot in the middle of the bonfire. The tinder took hold and flames began to shoot from the fire, rising on the mild breeze. The girls lowered their own torches, to take flame from the fire before jogging away in the direction of the cathedral entrance.

The crowd started to move, backing off to get a better view. Chase moved with them. It was only a matter of turning to his left and he would be at the post office within minutes.

The bonfires in the Plaça went up, other groups of girls having jogged down the far side of the canal to do their work. Another roar from the crowd, and the band started up again. Before he knew what was happening, Chase was seized by both hands, a girl clinging to each, giggling and laughing at him. In a second, Chase was locked into part of the large circle of sardana dancers which was forming spontaneously. Desperately, and with much help from the girls, he tried to follow the steps so as not to draw attention to himself, now an easy target for the Pirate and the other goons.

Chase at last freed himself from the two girls, looked around carefully, and set off again, pushing and shoving through the wall of people whose eyes could not leave the dazzling spectacle of star shells, rockets, and Roman candles.

He saw none of the enemy faces and finally pushed through the crowd, walking fast toward the less-populated streets and in the direction he remembered the post office to be. The street was narrow—buildings to his left and trees bordering the canal to the right. At last Chase saw the line of open telephone booths, each dimly lit and empty—a row of gray electronic sentries beside the post office steps. He drove his hand into his pocket, counting out the one peseta pieces from his change. Six in all. Just enough to make the call, if the duty officer allowed him to speak without interruption.

Swiftly he dialed the number. He had already inserted one of the peseta pieces into the slot from which it would be swallowed when contact was made. In the far distance he was aware of the whoosh and crackle of fireworks, while the music was still audible through the noise. His left ear was filled with clicks and whirrs from the automatic dialing system. Almost holding his breath, Chase heard the sequence complete itself, then the ringing tone and the receiver being lifted.

"Duty watchman. International Capital Group," came the voice, very clear, on the line.

"Number Two for Brewster..." Chase began, then stopped as he felt the hard steel against his ribs, and a voice said quietly, "Out fast, or I'll put a bullet in you."

It was the watcher who had been standing near La Seu. Chase sighed.

"Fast," the voice repeated. "Put down the telephone." The man was standing very close, pushed up behind Chase.

Primary rule: never approach a man too close with a pistol. Always keep at least the length of his leg away. Chase felt a twinge of regret for the man as he first turned slowly, his right hand lowering the telephone receiver, then fast, swinging around to the left, away from the pistol barrel, as he brought the receiver of the telephone smashing into the goon's face. The Mirza's man actually had time to get one shot away before he went down. The bullet ricocheted its way through the telephone booths.

Chase's right foot connected hard with his attacker's face as the man fell. There was a groan, then silence from the figure spread-eagled on the pavement outside the open booth. The blood was quite visible on his face. He'd broken the man's nose.

The receiver was wrecked. Chase swore as he rammed it back onto the cradle. In the distance, among the noises of the feast, there came the sound of a horn. It could well be a fire engine, but someone might have heard the shot or seen the scuffle. There had to be another place from which to get a message to Brewster. The last people Chase wished to argue with tonight were the policia.

At the Ayuntamiento he stopped for traffic, looking across the road at an elegant poster prominently displayed on the wall of the large café. It took several seconds for the poster to register: SIMON GAUDET HAUTE COUTURE. GRAND SHOW OF THE NEW GAUDET COLLECTION ON THE NIGHT OF THE FEAST OF THE DEVOUT BELLVER CASTLE. ELEVEN P.M. There followed a list of impressive prices of admission, which made Chase wince. Eleven—eleven o'clock tonight. He gazed wildly around him. A clock over a jeweler's shop showed it was five minutes past eleven already.

The Russian... the catwalk... Skypilot... Now. Brewster would have to wait. Chase took a deep breath and started to run, feeling the Dexedrine coursing through his bloodstream, feeling strong enough to fell ten men. Still, the thought wasn't far away that the solution was still in him, ticking away like a time bomb. As Verena had said, at any moment he might become afflicted. In this case that could mean losing his ability to mount any kind of effective offense, turning him into a blathering zombie at any moment.

Pushing these thoughts away, Chase tried to recall from his previous visits the quickest way to the ancient castle and the easiest clandestine way into it. If he was right, the Russian would lose his left hand very soon. If he was right—and if he did not get there in time to prevent it.

3

The Bellver Castle stood on the higher ground at the southern part of Palma, and was approached through narrow sloping streets. Chase had visited the castle several times before, and knew that the approach was made from the Avenida Joan Miró, up flights of zigzagging steps which took the normal sightseer underground, to the main entrance, and then into the large cobbled courtyard. Above the entrance was *la Galería del Rey,* while to the left were apartments closed to the casual visitor. On the right stood the impressive Throne Hall, while opposite the entrance ran a cloister with a gallery above it. Behind the cloister stood the lower *Capilla de la Reina,* and, above that, off the gallery, the magnificent Royal Chapel, with its series of lancet, equilateral, and drop arches.

Above the two chapels the keep climbed upward to a small bell tower. This was the extent of the Castle usually on view to the public. Chase knew, however, that there was a further courtyard behind the cloister. This area was still used: the yard itself as a depot for military vehicles and the surrounding buildings as billets for some of the local garrison, the bulk of whom lived below the citadel, in the Calle Drecera. On his last visit to the area Chase had fallen in with a Catalan army captain from the garrison. One night, after a particularly lively climbing session, the gallant captain had suggested drinks in his quarters, which lay within the second courtyard to the Castle. They had driven to Palma, and the Spaniard had shown Chase how easy it was to penetrate the barracks by entering through a narrow alley off the Avenida Miró, and from there follow the transport road which climbed steeply to the top of the citadel. It was not possible to enter the rear courtyard through the main transport gates, but you could squeeze through a tiny gap in the long terrace of living quarters forming the rear side of the courtyard. It was on that night Chase also learned of the archway through the rear courtyard, which led to the main castle area.

So it was to the barracks, the Calle Drecera, that he was now running as if the plague was at his heels. He knew there was little chance of gaining admittance to the main courtyard by the normal route. Concerts were held there, and he had few doubts that this was where the Simon Gaudet fashion show was being staged, under bright illuminations, and with the audience seated in the cobbled yard or occupying the windows in the old royal apartments.

It took nearly five minutes for Chase to find the alley that led into the barracks, then another three before he could start the grueling climb up the dusty wide transport track. Chase forced himself on—heart pumping, lungs strained, and thigh muscles aching from the effort required to move swiftly up the steep gradient.

Above, he could see the burst of light from the main courtyard, while music and applause floated sporadically down on the still air. The fashion show was in full swing.

At last he reached the rear of the buildings that formed the very far end of the second courtyard. It took a few minutes to find the gap, and, as he searched Chase was conscious of the height at which he now stood above the town. Far away fireworks still lit up the night in great starbursts of color, shooting comets of blue, gold, and red against the clear sky. Squeezing through the gap, he hoped that the bulk of the garrison would be away, down in town celebrating with the locals.

At last Chase stood inside the dimly lit courtyard. Already his eyes were adjusted to the darkness, and he easily took in the simple layout. The large gateway was to his left, with a row of six heavy military trucks standing in line to its right. Facing the gates in single file and close up, front to rear, were four armored Creusot-Loire VAB, *furgoneta militar,* as though in readiness. Few lights came from the barrack blocks which made up three sides of the yard. But Chase had few doubts that the *furgoneta militar* crews would be in duty rooms nearby.

Keeping to the shadow of the walls, he moved quickly around two sides of the square, to bring himself close to the final dividing wall which backed on the main part of the castle. He found the archway, with its passage, and, stepping into it, he was able to see up the wide tunnel, the darkness giving way to a picture of color and activity.

If his memory was correct, a small doorway lay to the right of the tunnel. This would take him up a short flight of steps and out onto the gallery in front of the Royal Chapel. He was amazed at the lack of security so far, and could only suppose that the Mirza had his men posted around the main courtyard or still in the town searching for him. Suddenly from the shadows stepped a policia, holding up a white-gloved hand and murmuring, *"Señor, este es privado. Tiene usted un boleto?"*

"Boleto, si." Chase's hand went to his pocket, then swung upward, catching the policeman neatly on the side of the jaw. The man reeled against the wall, a look of surprise in his already glazing eyes, before collapsing in a small heap.

It took a further minute for Chase to remove the officer's pistol, throwing it into the darkness of the tunnel, then to find, and use, the handcuffs, and, finally, gag the man with his own tie. As he left, Chase patted the officer's head. *"Buenas noches,"* he whispered, *"Sueño bien."*

Within seconds he found the doorway and the short flight of steps leading to the gallery. It was not until he reached the elegantly arched passage that the full realization of his mission's urgency penetrated Chase's consciousness. So far, he had pushed himself on, thinking only of speed and access. Now the lethal nature of matters hit him hard; he was there to save a life and deal with the shadowy La Flamme, Verena, and Mirza—assassins, unscrupulous killers, and terrorist organizers the lot of them.

The gallery was lined with people who had obviously paid well for the privilege of viewing the fashion show from this vantage point—even though it allowed standing room only. People stood at the high arched windows of the Throne Hall to his left and at those of the former royal apartments on the right of the courtyard. Across the yard, the King's Gallery was also crowded, and below, in the great yard itself, the show was in full swing. The main entrance, below the King's Gallery, led to a scaffold of carpeted steps, arranged to accommodate a small orchestra. A similarly carpeted catwalk stretched out from directly below where Chase stood, probably starting at the edge of the cloister in front of the Queen's Chapel. It ran the length of the courtyard, to end only a short distance from the orchestra, and was flanked by tiered scaffolding rising in wide steps on either side, to give the best-paying customers a good close view—each step being arranged with those small gilt chairs so beloved by the organizers of fashion shows the world over.

Simon Gaudet had certainly drawn a full house, all well-heeled and immaculately dressed. Chase caught sight of the Mirza on the first step to the left of the catwalk, sitting, resplendent in a white dinner jacket and maroon bow tie.

There were six models: three gorgeous black girls and a trio of equally delicious white ones, following each other onto and off the catwalk with amazing speed and precision. As he looked down, Chase saw Verena Rautavaara just prancing off as another girl reached the far end of the catwalk, and yet another stepping on, to take Verena's place. The music was provided to match the dress designs. This year's Gaudet collection had undoubtedly been created to reflect medieval costume and patterns.

Verena reappeared, whirling to a slow dance, clad in a loose gold creation of multilayered chiffon, with a short embroidered surcoat dropping ecclesiastically in front and behind. Chase had to use a surge of willpower to drag himself from his reverie. It must be well after eleven-thirty by now. Somewhere, above or below him, La Flamme was waiting with a light bullet, pellet, or tranquilizer dart, which she intended to use before the show ended.

And where in hell was Sergei Nikitin? Chase realized he'd never even seen a picture of the man. Somewhere, the poor fool was milling around with a massive security detail oblivious to the fate awaiting his left hand, and himself. Chase's eyes moved carefully over the crowds, up to the roofs, and any other possible vantage point for a sniper. There seemed to be no place for a markswoman to hide. Unless... the answer came to him, and he glanced upward, toward the gallery ceiling. Directly behind him lay the Royal Chapel. Above that, the keep rose, topped with a small bell tower. Above the keep, he knew, there was a loft that had once served as the ringing chamber and storeroom. The ringing chamber had at least three unglazed windows, or openings. All these looked straight down into the courtyard.

The door to the keep was set into the wall, to the right of the chapel door, not more than a dozen paces from where he stood. Behind that, a tight stone staircase coiled upward to various landings in the keep, and finally to the ringing chamber itself.

Chase whirled around, toward the Norman arched door, with its long iron hinge-plates and great ring latch. He tried the ring and it moved smoothly, soundless and well oiled. Gently he pulled the door open and stepped through. He was aware of a smell in the darkness—not mustiness, but the scent of oil mixed with perfume, possibly Chanel No. 5. The stone spiral of stairs was narrow and slippery from hundreds of years' usage. Chase started to climb as quietly and quickly as he dared in the darkness. His thigh muscles felt weak after the exertion of the last half hour, but he plodded on silently, cheered by occasional shafts of light at the wider turns in the spiral and on the landings.

Three times he stopped to control his breathing. The last thing he could afford was to reveal his presence by any noise. Even through the thick walls, the sounds from the courtyard floated upward. If the ringing chamber were indeed La Flamme's hideout, the killer would have to be invested with an extra sense to detect him, unless Chase made some unnecessary sound.

As he neared the top of the climb, Chase felt the sweat trickling from his hairline and down the insides of his arms. Holding his breath, he reached the topmost steps, his head just below the aged wooden-planked floor of the chamber. There were five more steps to negotiate to bring his feet level with the floor. Putting all his weight on the right foot, Chase slowly lifted his body so that his eyes came just above floor level.

La Flamme was at right angles to him, lying in the classic prone position of a sniper. The killer's concentration seemed to be centered completely on the scene below, her eyes close to a sniperscope fitted on top of an Anschutz .22 air rifle converted for darts. The butt was tucked against her cheek and pressed hard into her shoulder. La Flamme's finger was on the trigger, ready to fire. Chase could not afford to miss if he dived for her. The rifle could still go off on a reflex action. If Chase jumped the woman, he might only precipitate the sniper's deadly shot.

There was no time for further appraisal of the situation. Chase leaped up the remaining steps, calling out softly but sharply, "Flamme! Don't shoot!"

The sniper's head swiveled around as Chase heard the dull plop of the air rifle, a sound inaudible to anyone but La Flamme and Chase, high in the keep. In the same second, on an impulse, Chase flung himself onto the prone figure of the woman, landing with a bone-shattering crash across her shoulders. In a flash, lying spread-eagled across the female terrorist's shoulders, Jonathan Chase took in the scene below, looking from the sniper's viewpoint down through the rough square opening.

Verena Rautavaara was alone in the center of the catwalk, pirouetting in magnificent white which drooped in long folds, like a snowy waterfall, around her body. Her arms were outstretched, her feet moving to a haunting jig played by the consort. Slightly to her left and behind her, a dignified old man with a silver mustache—Nikitin!—sat partly turned in his chair, frozen for a moment, looking toward the Mirza, who had half risen, one hand at his throat, the other like a claw to his chest. Almost exactly in line with the Russian colonel, he was doubling forward, and in what seemed like slow motion, he teetered, hovered, and then pitched headlong among the chairs.

Underneath Chase, La Flamme was cursing and struggling to free herself from his grip on the back of her neck. "*Merde!* I hit the wrong one. You'll..." Her voice evaporated in a hiss of air as she let her muscles relax, then arched her back and jerked her legs to dislodge her assailant. Chase was taken by surprise and thrown off, his shoulder thudding against the wall on the far side of the chamber. La Flamme was on her feet in a second, her hand dropping to her hip and coming away with a small revolver. Chase, winded from the throw, levered himself from the wall and kicked wildly at the woman's hand, loosening her hold on the gun. It was enough to send La Flamme weaving and ducking down the narrow spiral stairs. Meanwhile, Chase grabbed the air rifle and reloaded it with darts.

The staircase would be a death trap for either of them, and no place for a shooting match. Taking air in through his mouth, Chase regained his lost balance and started after the female assassin, glancing quickly down into the courtyard as he went. The music had stopped, and a small huddle of people were gathered around where he had seen the Mirza fall. He could see Verena, who had come off the catwalk, escorting Nikitin away with one of the Mirza's guards, who stood very close to the Russian. The Pirate was also there shouting orders to the rest of the guards. From the main entrance, two white-clad figures came running with a stretcher.

Chase waited at the top of the stairs until he was certain La Flamme had passed the first landing. Then he began the descent, the .22 held in front of him, ready to fire back, even if one of La Flamme's bullets caught him in the confined space.

But La Flamme was being just as careful. She had a head start. Chase could hear her, cautiously going down, pausing at each landing, then quickly negotiating the next spiral.

At last Chase heard the door close below, and took the last section of stairs in a dangerous rush, grabbing at the door, pushing the Anschutz out of sight and stepping out into the gallery, where a great many people were craning over, or leaving to get down into the courtyard. La Flamme was just ahead, making for the small flight of steps that would bring her into the archway through which Chase had made his entrance. Taking little notice of people around him, Chase went after his quarry. By the time he reached the archway, there was no one to be seen, except the huddled figure of the policia still out cold.

At the far side of the archway, the noise came only from behind. Nothing in front. From the rear courtyard just silence and the shapes of heavy trucks lined up along the wall near the gate to his far right.

La Flamme was there, though. Chase could almost smell her, lurking in the shadows or behind the line of transports de troupes, maybe taking aim at this very moment. The thought quickly sent Chase into the shadow of the wall to his right. Now he must outthink her. This woman was clever, a survivor, if he'd ever seen one. Did she know of the narrow gap between the buildings on the far side, through which Chase had come? Or did she have another way? Would she wait among the shadows or by the vehicles sweating it out, knowing that only Zero Directorate and her present assailant were aware of her presence?

Slowly Chase began to crab his way along the wall, edging to the right, deciding that La Flamme would most likely have made for the cover of the vehicles. Eventually the woman would have to run a long way, for her contract had gone awry in the most deadly manner. A poison dart, Chase thought. That had been the missile, which reached a low velocity as it hit, leaving little or no mark but injecting something—probably untraceable—into the victim's bloodstream. It would have to be very fast-acting, for the Mirza had collapsed within seconds. At least it had been him! Now La Flamme would know that the full might of the Mirza's private forces would be out to hunt her down, just as they were already in full cry after Chase.

He was getting close to the first truck. If La Flamme was hidden there she would certainly keep her nerve, holding back a natural desire to be rid of her pursuer by chancing a shot which could only call attention to her position.

But Chase had misread the hunted woman. Maybe La Flamme had been rattled by what had occurred in the ringing chamber. The shot came directly from beside the rearmost *furgoneta militar,* a single round, passing like an angry hornet, almost clipping Chase's ear.

Dropping to the ground, Chase rolled toward the trucks parked against the wall, bunching himself up to present only the smallest target and coming to a stop beside the great, heavy rear right wheel of the first truck. He had the .22 up, held in a two-handed grip, pointing toward the flash from the shot.

Once more Chase set himself the task of outthinking his enemy. La Flamme would have moved after firing, just as Chase rolled toward the truck, which was only a few yards from the rear-armored *furgoneta.*

What would he—Chase—do in that situation? The trucks were at right angles to the little line of armored troop carriers facing the gate. Chase thought he would have moved down to the second truck, protected by its armor, and then skipped across the gap between the line of vans and the truck behind which Chase was sheltering. If he was right La Flamme should at this moment be coming around this very truck and trying to take Chase from the rear.

Moving on tiptoe in his thin-soled tennis shoes, crouched low, Chase silently crossed the few yards' gap between his truck and the rear *furgoneta*. Whirling around, he dropped to one knee and waited for the brunette assassin's figure to emerge from the cover which he had just relinquished.

This time his thinking was right. Chase heard nothing but saw the shape of the hunted woman pressed hard against the hood of the big truck as she carefully felt her way around it, hoping to come up on her opponent from behind.

Chase remained like a statue, the Anschutz an extension of his arms, held in a vise with both hands and pointing directly toward the shadow that was La Flamme.

Still La Flamme's reputation held up. Chase was staking his life on his own stillness, yet the terrorist detected something. With a sudden move, she dived to the ground, firing twice as she did so, the bullets screeching off the armor plating of the *furgoneta*.

Chase held his ground. La Flamme's shots had gone wide, and the target remained in line with the air rifle's barrel. Chase fired with steady care: two pairs of darts in quick succession, a count of three between the pairs.

There was no cry or moan. La Flamme simply reared up like an animal, her head and torso arching into a bow from the ground, then bending right back as the force of all four shots slewed her in a complete circle, then pushed her back along the ground as though wrenched by an invisible wire: arms, legs, and head flailing and flopping as a child's doll will bounce when dragged along the floor. Being a long-range weapon, the Anschutz certainly packed a punch at such close quarters.

Chase could smell death—in his head rather than nostrils. Whatever was in these darts, four was definitely far over the maximum dosage.

A moment of strange stillness.

Then he became aware of lights coming on, running feet, shouts and activity.

The policia closing in, with press and fashion photographers racing in front of them and shooting wild. It felt like a moving surrealist painting with sound effects—the heavy brutish grunt of the Frenchwoman's body meeting the cobblestones and then the sudden blizzard of camera flashes like white flowers filling the night sky.

Slowly the flashes settled and the sky was filled again as hundreds of pigeons flocked from the alleyway in fright and the press photographers began screaming.

"*Deténganlo!*"

"*Párenlo!*"

Chase shielded his face the best he could as the cameras went off.

And then he ran.

As fast and as silently as he could, springing toward the minute gap between the far buildings, and so down the sandy track to the Avenida Miró. When he reached the Calle, Chase slowed down. He was breathing hard.

He cursed under his breath.

He'd avoided the Mirza's satellite broadcast only to get his picture taken by all the paparazzi the Mediterranean had to offer.

Never run away from an incident, they taught you—just as you should never run after lighting an explosive fuse. Always walk with purpose, as though it were your right to be where you were.

He knew his face would appear in at least two of the local evening papers and that by this time tomorrow he'd get world coverage as the man standing next to the dead body in the alley outside where the Russian colonel had been kidnapped. If Brewster couldn't pull strings to quash the story, it could cost him his life. I-Division didn't officially exist and they operated in strict hush, but after a certain number of missions you became known among the opposition networks and intelligence services — known, recognizable, and vulnerable.

Zero Directorate, of course, already knew him through and through; but all anyone else had to do now was pick up a newspaper, and the next time Chase walked into the street he could walk straight into the crosshairs.

He was in the limelight now.

Chase was already thinking of ways to change his appearance — shorter hair, contact lenses — when he stepped with a smile into the Avenida. He was home and dry. The street was empty.

Chase had walked four paces when the piercing whistle came from nearby. For a second he thought it was a police whistle. Then he recognized the human sound — the whistle of a man who has been brought up in the country, the kind of noise one makes to call in dogs, or other beasts. Now it brought in the Daimler DS420 Limo, bearing down on him, lights blazing.

The car came alongside with its back door open and a very familiar red-faced, bearded bastard said, "Get in!"

Brewster, section chief of I-Division, gave a loud bearish laugh and slapped Chase on the back.

"Good to see you, Number One."

—3—

Chase closed his eyes for a long moment. To Brewster, he looked very tired and less boyish. No expression showed on his face. Fully alert again, Chase gazed at his old mentor, who was now stretching his legs, his hands interlaced behind his neck. Brewster looked supremely comfortable.

Chase waited until the Daimler passed under a street light to speak. He wanted to observe Brewster's reaction.

"Next time, sir, I trust you'll give me a full and proper briefing."

Brewster coughed. "If you're talking about Verena, we had our suspicions, but thought it better for you to find out for yourself, Number One. Flush her out. As you recall, the general idea was to put you in the field and draw the fire."

"It appears we were successful."

"There wasn't a hell of a lot I could do once you got yourself kidnapped," Brewster continued. "I couldn't even warn you about Verena, because I wasn't sure myself. And the information I was getting from Company agents on the ground was pretty half-assed to say the least."

Half-assed indeed, Chase thought vaguely.

"Aren't you dodging the great unasked question here, chief?"

"No, Jonathan. The cowboys on your heels were CIA free-lancers who sell out their talent to the highest bidders—and it was the DNI who hired them, not me."

"So you send me out to do the dirty work and don't object when someone else orders me killed."

"Granted. There was nothing I could do. My thinking was: Verena had your back."

"Had I known she was my partner, that might have been help-ful."

"Survival of the fittest, Jon. Have you never entered two com-petitors in the same race? It's backup contingency planning—redundancy assures victory. In this particular instance I knew con-ventional spycraft was doomed. Either we were the way of the future or Zero Directorate was. One horse had to win."

"And so you put Verena in the field, morality be damned. Whichever horse got you there first."

"That woman was one of the most brilliant spies I ever met. It occurred to me she was worth incubating, worth nurturing as a contingency."

"So you hedged your bets."

"Think of it as political arbitrage. It was the only prudent course. I've always told you, Jon, spycraft isn't a team sport. And I know you have the talent ultimately to recognize the good sense in my reasoning. You're the new Number One, after all. Even if I'll have to give my left testicle to the Servicio Central to keep your picture out of the papers."

"Still pretty rough handling, chief."

"You are now my most senior officer. I have never doubted your skill and accuracy. I knew you'd make it."

"I'm also one of your best and oldest friends."

"Irrelevant in the field, I'm afraid."

"Sir, there were people at that cocktail party. People from our side. The members are clearly chosen carefully—drawn from all around the world. People whose backgrounds are especially conducive to that line of work, to maintaining a code of silence. There must be a great deal of compartmentalization. That way no one operative ever gets to know another more than fleetingly..."

"We've got your list of names and we're rounding up the remnants, Number One," Brewster was saying. "We've scuttled them for good, I think." Brewster sounded pleased. "Even tracked down the base you mentioned. The thing was on an island, believe it or not, near Mauritius. 'Claw Island'—if you can believe it: that was the name on the maps. Anyway, I can't see anyone else reactivating what's left of it now—thanks to you, Number One."

"All part of the service," Chase added sarcastically. But the remark ran off Brewster's back like water from the proverbial duck.

"Of course, we're still looking for this Mirza character. And there'll be the men they bring with them on the Rogachevo raid tonight."

"Don't forget the man in the balaclava I told you about. The one who claimed to know you."

"What was he like?"

"Prep school accent. Northeastern. Slim build. Good clothes. Burberry maybe."

"Could've been Prospero."

"Prospero?"

"I'll tell you about him some other time."

"And the microchips, sir. If we don't stop them at the base, they'll have the capacity to broadcast from any of the hundreds of satellites orbiting the globe. Worldwide surveillance and playback using something called *Video*."

"We know about the broadcasting chips, Number One. So long as technology stays out of the terrorists' hands we'll be fine."

"So it's okay as long as we're the ones watching?"

"Do you know about the Igbo people of Nigeria, Chase? They live surrounded by the tumult of that country, but they are free of it. Do you know why? Because their culture prizes what they call the transparent life. They believe that there is nothing about an upright person that his fellow villagers should not be allowed to know. Any sort of exchange is conducted in front of witnesses. They abhor any form of secrecy or concealment, even solitude. The ideal of total transparency is so highly developed that if a scintilla of distrust develops between two people, they may resort to a curious ritual wherein each drinks the blood of the other. This new technology of ours produces the same results with an altogether bloodless technique."

Chase felt as if he had been kicked in the stomach. "I heard a very similar lecture earlier today, sir."

"Secrets are what start wars, Number One. You once told me you wanted to be an enemy of war."

"A secret is a truth withheld. You could have entrusted my identity tonight to those photographers who had no right to know it, but you didn't."

"Do we really have to do this now? Is it that important to you? Or can I go ahead and assume that you're still with us because you're a pragmatist—and can recognize the way of the future?"

"It can keep, sir. But one other thing, sir: the solution. I was injected several times and was also told it can lie dormant for some time before having any noticeable effect. The wild-card factor may just be too great, sir. For this kind of work."

"We'll hold out and see what the tests say, okay, Number One?"

Chase nodded. Brewster looked out the window. In the harbors of the Mediterranean, junks and other unwieldy sailing vessels moved so slowly over the water that they left no wakes.

As they discussed Chase's plan to get over the Ural Mountains and into one of Russia's most secure military facilities, Brewster was reminded of the eighteen-year-old Marine he'd met so many years ago in Korea. The boy who'd been a machine, an automaton, devoted to nothing other than the execution of a mission. The boy who could clear his mind, sweep away all anxieties, and go in by himself.

Now, listening to Chase explain the mission as he saw it, he realized how much like Chase himself it was: intelligent, subtle, logical. Symmetrical. It was a morality tale in which the sin of pride was punished by a terrible act of vengeance. Only a clandestine mind like Chase's, free from values and concerned with nothing but the results of action, could have conceived what Chase had just laid out.

Brewster had the same sort of mind, but so had Colonel Zhao. And sometimes the old spymaster found that he could only guess at the darker benefits of what Chase had learned in those last days of the Korean War.

2

Chase closed his eyes and tried not to hear the whine of the turboprop engines. He did not want to use any of his senses. In his mind, as if it were a clear photograph projected on a screen, he saw Verena's face, framed in russet hair and filled with belief. He had a sexual thought, his first in days: it was a memory of the sun on her skin.

As he was dropped from the plane over the northern border of Kazakhstan, Chase made a small vow. From this day forward, he would only play it alone, to his rules. He would bend his will to nobody.

The darkness seemed to cling to him, occasionally blowing free to give a glimmer of visibility, then descending again as though a blindfold had flown over his face. It took every ounce of concentration to follow his bearings as he went, the big Pelican snow scooter roaring through the night, making enough noise, Chase thought, to draw any patrols within a ten-mile radius. At somewhere between sixty and seventy mph, swerving and bucketing along a rough track between the trees, Chase tried to stay about thirty feet from the Russian border and parallel to it.

There was little protection apart from a short deflector windshield. Chase kept his head down, and was quick with his reactions. A turn meant considerable energy, especially in the deep, hard snow, as you had to pull the skis around with the handlebars, then hold them, juddering, as they tried to resume their normal forward angle. Occasionally he pulled out too far, sending the scooter rearing up like some amusement park ride, producing a roll first to the right, then left, slipping upward almost to the point of losing control, then sliding back again and up the other side until, wrestling with the handlebars, he recovered.

Chase had done everything within his power to come prepared. He had liked the Anschutz .22 so much, he'd asked to be supplied with one for the mission. He wore it on his side, strapped outside a quilted jacket. The compass hung from a lanyard around his neck, the instrument tucked safely inside the jacket where a jerk on the lanyard would free it. On his back, Chase carried a small pack containing other items—a white coverall complete with hood, in case there was need for snow camouflage, three stun grenades, a Browning, and three L2A2 fragmentation bombs. The rest lay with him—professionalism, experience, and the two vital attributes of the trade: intuition, and being able to think quickly on his feet.

Chase believed in the certainties that had led him to make this final, single move, but if some of them were wrong, if only one of them, the smallest, were wrong, his place would be here: not at home nor at the Rogachevo base nor across the face of the earth—but here, now. It was a feeling he sometimes had, when he'd taken a calculated risk. He thought: this move could kill me, so if I assume that it will, if I assume I'm already dead and finished, I won't have to be worried or afraid. Fear of death could increase the risk of meeting with it.

Laughing to himself, Chase wondered what a psychologist would make of these thoughts: the early history of betrayal and brutality that he had suffered. How deep did the trauma go? *Violence is just something you're very, very good at:* was Brewster's arctic assessment. It was what made him invaluable to his employers. So long as he remained like fix-mounted heavy artillery, directed toward the enemy, he was a godsend.

To them: he was the Singleton. *His methods would always be justified by their results.* That was the rule. And he had been given promotions and medals by his government for playing by that rule better than anyone else had ever done.

But they didn't have to live his life. They didn't have to fight, as he did, to outwit the fear of death at every step.

Alone. Always alone.

◆

The trees seemed to be getting thicker, but Chase kept well up, moving through the gaps in them, twisting left and then right. Soon he would have to break cover. Then it would be a kilometer of open country, into the woods again, and the long dip into the valley, where there was a great swath cut through the forests to mark the frontier and deter people from attempting a crossing.

Out of the trees and, even in the darkness, the transition was unnerving. Within the forest there had been a kind of safety.

Now the blackness lifted slightly as the open snow, showing gray around him, took over.

His speed increased—a straight run with no dodging or suddenly swerving in a change of direction. The cold became worse, whether from lack of shelter or the simple fact that he was making more speed across open country. As he descended, so the feeling of vulnerability became more intense. Brewster had told him this route was used constantly by border crossers, for there were no frontier units within ten miles on either side, and they rarely made any night patrols. Chase hoped he was right. Soon he would flatten out, curving into the bottom of the valley—half a mile of straight ice before climbing up the far side of the trees of Mother Russia.

Several minutes later, he parked the scooter, camouflaging it as best he could. Then he put on his white snowsuit and made his way toward the point where the light now seemed to blast straight up between the trees, behind a slope above him. He moved silently—a white ghost passing into dead ground, moving from tree to tree.

He squirmed in among the deep snow which buried the roots and trunk bases of the trees. Chase was amazed at the sight; from his observation post, the view down to the small clearing among the trees and the huge rocky area of the base's roof was unimpeded. It was plain now that the entrance to Rogachevo base itself was built into a rising wall of rock, like a giant stepping-stone forming a rough crescent in the center of the thick, snowy forest. The trees had been expertly cleared to allow only a minimal open space in front of the main entrances, while other paths were cut through trees, rock, and ice to form routes round the building to higher, more open, ground above.

To the south, and above the huge spur of rock, the thick forest was broken by carefully prepared clear tracks, through which a wide runway pointed a long gray-white finger, from the rock to a threshold which appeared to end abruptly in the heart of the surrounding forest.

There was no sign of any aircraft—Zero Directorate or Russian. Chase presumed whatever craft the Russians kept here were tucked away in concrete pens built into the rock which helped form the roof of the base itself.

Chase took out the Nitefinder goggles.

Nothing there yet. No vehicles or aircraft. No troop activity.

And then . . . a consuming, growling roar surrounded Chase.

The first pair of strike aircraft came in level with the trees, crossing to Chase's right, neither firing nor dropping anything. They streaked through the cold air, little eddies of steam surrounding the wings as the subzero temperatures produced contrails even at this low level. They looked like silver darts, precision-built arrows with large boxlike air intakes, high tails, and wings folded back into a delta configuration joining the elevators to make one long, slim lifting surface.

As if controlled by one person, the two aircraft tipped noses toward the sky and screamed upward in a terrifyingly fast climb until they were only tiny silver dots, banking away to the north.

The first approach growl came from their left, followed almost immediately by a second from what seemed to be directly above. The jets came in pairs with noses down in a classic ground-attack dive. Quite clearly Chase could see the first missiles flash away from the wings: long white flames shooting back, then the orange trails as the deadly darts ripped through the air. Two from each plane, all four catching the front of the bunker, boring in and exploding with wide orange blossoms of fire that reached his eyes before the heavy zoom and *whump* hit his ears.

The missiles were digging well into the rock, steel, and concrete before exploding. Below, after just two attacks using eight missiles, the Rogachevo base looked ready to be broken in two. The thunder of the explosions still echoed from below, and through the inevitable pall of smoke, he could see the terrible crimson glow of fire begin to sweep out of the open main doors, up from the arms stores and vehicle parks.

Okay, the front door is open, Chase thought to himself. All his senses were alert now, and the dart gun was heavy in his hand. He ran forward down the slope and through the trees, crouching and ready for anything.

Before the main doors smoke billowed up and then drifted away; there was the occasional spurt of flame. Apart from the odd crackling noise, though, there was no other sound. Chase made out the remains of the main arterial passage and followed it. The ground, with its tracks around the bunker, seemed to have become one giant garbage dump, though part of a metal chain runway still snaked out twisted and lopsided.

And then he realized: the building set against the rock face was purely a defensive camouflage for the real entrance. Solidly built, reinforced with steel, it formed a tunnel which led into the mountain.

Through the steel tunnel, the world changed. The passage narrowed into a short alley, wide enough to accommodate him. This led to a large, abandoned command post, which in turn led to a next entrance of sliding steel panels.

Chase blew the doors with an L2A2 and was through—onto a wide viewing platform. Below him lay a vast and empty amphitheater with a bank of computer and electronic instruments. Above him—on the far, huge, curved wall—were three massive electronic Mercator projections, each mapping the world. The projections were crisscrossed by slow-moving colored lines— blues and greens, brilliant whites, blacks, orange, even lines which broke up into different, segmented hues.

Chase let out a slow whistle.

He knew the three projections showed the exact number of known satellites and other space hardware in orbit—the left-hand projection being all non-Soviet satellites; the one to the far right showing Soviet equipment; while the center projection monitored all new indications.

Chase started to think...

Another *whomp* sent a tremor through the mountain complex.

Then came a noise that seemed to be headed straight for him. A Soviet jeep, painted in snow-colored camouflage. The driver wore goggles and a white surgical mask. So did the man standing upright in the front seat beside him and two or three riflemen deployed in front of the vehicle.

Chase ran a hundred paces to his right and took up position behind a steel terminal. He lay down to make a smaller target of himself. His intention was to keep moving inward until he was past both the Zero Directorate invaders and the Russians themselves and then, if he heard firing, to close in until he could see them and open fire.

Shouting. The whiny sound of vehicles in reverse, advancing in low gear. The crash of metal against the rock wall of the base. To his immediate front, perhaps thirty feet away, Chase glimpsed a second vehicle and more Russian skirmishers. He tried to ascertain where he was in relation to the biometric authenticator.

A grenade exploded on the other side of the steel terminal. It made a terrific flash and bang, shrapnel flying all over the place, and its concussion sucked a hole in the clouds of smoke that had accumulated. For an instant Chase could see again. Three Russians, one of them fitting another rifle grenade to the launcher on his weapon, were spread out before him. All were in the kneeling position, Kalashnikovs pointed straight at him. If he could see them, they could see him.

Chase opened fire with the Browning and saw one of them knocked backward. Many others, seen and unseen, returned fire, sparks flying from the muzzles of automatic weapons and bullets flying every which way. Chase dug a grenade out of his bag, pulled the pin, and threw it in the direction of the gunfire. As soon as the grenade went off he ran back the way he had come.

After a moment, firing from his general direction began in earnest. Zero Directorate shock troops. Had to be. Chase realized he had been presented with the opportunity of a lifetime—the opportunity of a very short lifetime perhaps, but an opportunity nonetheless. He reached for one of his fragmentation bombs and crawled toward the Russians. It was easy enough to avoid the Zero Directorate men because they were shouting to one another through the smoke and one of them was screaming in agony.

Chase crawled until he could hear voices all around him. He was in the middle of the attacking force, or near enough. He found a tall console, placed the fragmentation bomb on it, and switched it on. Then he hit the dirt in retreat. When it started beeping, fire erupted from all points of the compass. Grenades exploded. Cries of pain broke out, a choir of the wounded, as the Zero Directorate, firing blindly into the smoke, shot at the Russians, and the two forces killed and wounded one another.

Moans, curses, the acrid smell of cordite. Chase was surrounded, with enemies between him and every possible exit. It was imperative that he move before anyone recovered their wits and started closing in. He did so, gingerly. The Russians were making a lot of noise—recriminations, no doubt—but all it would take to undo him was one alert soldier keeping his mouth shut.

Chase ran into him in a matter of seconds. He was crouched, rifle at the ready, with his back to Chase. He wore the Soviet insignia of a general. He must have sensed Chase's movement because he sprang to his feet, firing his Kalashnikov wildly as he spun on his heel. Chase launched himself at the general and clipped him at the knees. The general's assault rifle, still firing, flew from his grasp and he collapsed, shrieking in pain. No doubt, he'd torn every tendon in both knees. Chase kneeled back, seized his chin, and jerked his head sharply backward.

Chase heard his neck break, and winced with the irony of it. The best thing this Communist general, no doubt a patriot, could do at this moment for his Mother Russia was to die at Chase's hand. He wouldn't have seen it that way, of course, staring briefly into the burning face of history as Chase had done.

Chase heard footsteps. A Zero Directorate man plunged out of the smoke, then back into it again, missing Chase by inches. Invisible now, he fired his submachine gun. Someone fired back. Others were shooting, too. Muzzle blasts embroidered the air all around him. Feet pounded, gears clashed, ricochets sang, men shouted and grunted and screamed. Grenades exploded.

Time had lost its meaning and Chase had no idea how soon the Zero Directorate would reach him, but it would be soon now.

He ran.

There was a transition period when his body moved for itself, and memory started recording again only when he was flinging himself along the dark passage, deeper into the stone, with the Browning out to take out obstacles of flesh and blood and his feet driving him forward with the sensation that the energy was coming from somewhere else, streaming into him and leaving him galvanized and frantic for life.

The firing seemed to have ceased—at least the automatic gunfire had. Chase still heard single shots, sandwiched between moments of silence. The fight was over and the winners were hunting down and killing the wounded. Both sides were using Russian weapons or Chinese copies thereof, so it was impossible to tell who was doing the shooting.

Footsteps filled the passage, but the walls echoed and reechoed them in the narrow confines and they might only have been his own. The first of them stopped, perhaps, to check the dead general on the ground, giving Chase time to get clear, as if the general had reached out from whatever cosmic field of consciousness sustained him now, and chosen to offer him grace.

When he reached the door that housed the biometric authenticator, Chase took off his pack and got out the last of the L2A2s. Doing this simple thing in absolute silence, doing it so slowly that he could not possibly betray his position by even the flicker of a movement, required the use of every cell in Chase's brain and the control of every nerve in his body.

He wedged the bomb between the rock wall and the steel door and pocketed the detonator. Then, crawling again, he moved away from the door, lost in thought as he went.

This was the place. *Where was the opposition?*

Washington etiquette went that after the decision was made, the time for criticism was past. But in the absence of a cast of thousands, improvisation was the only option.

Chase tried not to think the thought that was uppermost in his mind. They had opened the gates of Troy to a wooden horse. If Verena and the Mirza had been playing a double game with him all along—feeding him the GLONASS data as misdirection—who knew what or who might be inside it?

Then he heard a gasp, not loud, like air being let out of a bicycle tire. Chase froze. Barely perceptible, a spot on the floor appeared to undulate. Then move slightly toward him. Then disappear entirely. Chase deliberately averted his eyes, drew the Anschutz and waited, attuning his senses to the slightest evidence of motion in the room. Seconds later, a shadowy patch of motion a shade darker than the rest of the surrounding tiles appeared six feet in front of him, moving rapidly, as if floating.

Chase realized the kind of opposition he'd been up against all along.

Her hands and face were dark with camouflage cream and the white-blond high chignon of her hair was now a short, loosely bound club hanging at the nape of her neck. She had Chase covered with a .45, a Heckler & Koch compact in her left hand; in her right was Colonel Nikitin's swollen appendage.

"My god. You bitch." For a single beat in time, Chase thought he had not said it aloud. But Verena only smiled, her teeth white in the ink of the dark tunnel, the deadly eye of her handgun steady and pointing directly at Chase's chest.

Her face had changed. Chase could see that she appeared older. The hair was tousled, and the black fire now burned a hatred in her eyes. It was the eyes which brought the whole thing into perspective. No matter how she had tried to cover it before, even with the use of contact lenses, Verena's eyes were dark: like black ice.

Chase actually jumped as he pushed the button on the detonator. He'd concealed it in his pocket the whole time. There was no way to be accurate...he just pushed it.

There was an explosion of astonishing force that threw him backward, trailing a plume of smoke like a hasty scrawl in the air.

The wall behind her exploded into a fireball, a sulfurous cloud of smoke filling the room. Chase could still feel the wave of intense heat on his face.

Heart pounding, holding his breath, he darted toward the debris.

She wasn't there.

Jesus, she's good! Chase mused, as he cautiously made his way through the fresh hole in the wall. Outside, there was more carnage. Medical teams worked on the wounded and carried away the dead. One of the aircraft was still burning, and there were great gaps in the cyclone fencing.

From down the road, out of sight, came occasional bursts of rifle and automatic fire.

Chase noticed a small helicopter that hadn't been there before—a modern twin-seater version of the old Bell 47. There wasn't anyone seated within its Lucite bulb.

With a shrill scream, from behind the Bell, Verena crouched and then sprang forward, her face contorted, her hands extended like claws, like deadly instruments. She slammed into him, knocking him back into the snow just as he was reaching for the concealed dart gun. At close range, he could see her face was bloody and swollen. When she screamed, blood ran out from the wounds inside her mouth. Her hair was stained with blood and it looked like she had vomited on herself. She's just had a goddamn rocket launcher fired at her! Chase thought, then realizing—as she clawed at his eyes—that Verena was far stronger than he'd ever imagined, something more akin to a wild beast than a woman. She jabbed one thumb directly into his eye socket, the pain immense, blinding him, while she slammed her knee into his crotch, connecting at once with his genitals. Chase roared with agony and determination, summoning his considerable strength, and slammed her into the icy ground beneath them. His right eye was bloodied, but he could still see through it, and what he saw made an eel of fear wriggle in his stomach.

She had pulled out a flashing blade, a long, thin stiletto. It gleamed wetly, as if coated with a viscous fluid. He knew at once that the blade must be coated with the alkaloid toxiferine, which made it an extremely dangerous weapon. The slightest nick or scrape would lead to immediate paralysis and suffocating death.

Chase could smell the blade and its acrid poison as it whisked millimeters from his face; he had jerked his head back just in time to save his life. Now the crazed woman reared up and lunged, and again Chase's evasive action was only just sufficient; a button from his quilted parka was sliced off and went flying into the air. He went at her with both hands, with all of his strength, unable to risk reaching for the dart gun. The stiletto flashed in a blur near Chase's face, but now he lashed out with his left arm, like a cobra, directly toward the blade—a counterintuitive move, because it meant rising up and greeting the instrument of death, or the appendage that held it, rather than retreating from it—and as he seized the wrist of the hand holding the stiletto, Verena was clearly taken by surprise.

But only for an instant. Chase's strength would normally be far superior, but he hadn't slept since he'd been in the chair on Claw Island. And Verena had a mastery of moves he had never seen before. As her arm struggled against Chase's grip, the long blade trembling, her left foot, clad in a steel-toed leather boot, swung around, striking him again in the genitals. He groaned as he felt the pain radiating coldly through his testicles; he felt sick to his stomach. He shoved her again, slamming her back to the floor and knocking the blond wig off her head.

They were locked in struggle. She screamed again, her black eyes wild. She was powerful and extraordinarily coordinated, and she lashed back and forth like a rabid beast. She tried to kick at him again, using her other foot, but Chase had anticipated the move and rolled onto her, locking her legs in place, using his greater body mass, still holding her wrist, the stiletto blade still pointed at him. He had to move carefully around it, keeping all skin, all appendages clear of its lethal point. She was bucking violently, but he concentrated his strength, his energy, on angling her wrist back at her, directing the slickly gleaming blade toward her neck. Her arm shook with all the muscular resistance she could summon, but it was not enough: Chase commanded more brute strength. Inch by inch, he pushed the tremulous blade back toward the soft exposed skin of her neck. Her eyes widened in terror as the blade gently creased her skin.

The effect was immediate. She suddenly went limp against the snow and began to thrash wildly, her mouth opening again and again like a fish out of water, in soundless gasps.

She put a stained finger on his lips. He leaned down to kiss her, longing for her; as the deadening paralysis spread through her body like a white shadow and all respiration ceased.

Near her body, on the snow, was Colonel Nikitin's hand.

Flesh and *Blood,* was all Chase could think, feeling a gorge of anger.

That's what it was down to.

All of them—himself included—had seen the world as a chessboard. And with the blithe certainty that what worked on the page would work in the real world, they had been willfully oblivious to the fact that people made of *flesh* and *blood* would suffer the consequences of their grand schemes.

Although he could hardly stand to look at it, Chase picked up the severed appendage and walked back through the hole in the wall.

He had a mission to finish.

Epilogue

Because none of their cabins, including Brewster's, was large enough to contain four people, the team met in the hold of the boat, in the space next door to the lazaretto. Before a word was spoken, in response to two fingers lifted by Brewster, Alex Michaelides—the new Number Two—and Frankie Farmer—the new Number Three—closed and locked the watertight doors at either end of the compartment, sealing in whatever words were about to be spoken.

"By now the man we took from the Spanish geriatric hospital last night has been wondering for many hours where he is and who's got him," Brewster said.

His air was professorial, reasonable, judicious. He was explaining to a class what to expect when the imaginary curtain behind him was opened and the monster in his shackles was revealed to them.

He continued, "Actually, thanks to Chase's tenacity, he's probably guessed. However, no matter who's got him, he knows his situation is not good. Because of the heat from the bulb inside the room, which is tiny, he will be very hot. He will be thirsty. He may have fouled himself. None of this comes as a shock to him. He knows we're trying to scare him, to break him down, to make him think he deserves worse than he's going to get. He's an expert, one of the most experienced people in the world when it comes to processing suspects. He probably thinks we're amateurs compared to him. Nevertheless, now come these amateurs, who've got the power to set him free and also the power to torture him. He probably expects torture. He tells himself he's prepared for the worst but he knows he isn't, because while he himself has never been tortured he has tortured many others and he knows that no one can stand up under torture. He may defy us, he may tell us what we want to hear, he may say nothing. Naturally he won't tell us the truth under any circumstances. His truth is not our truth. You've got to realize he doesn't think he ever did anything wrong. To him, being nailed in a room with a hot electric bulb shining on him, shining in his eyes, is a crime against humanity. To him, the only thing he ever did in his life was what was right. He followed a virtuous calling. This person is an idealist. He has always been an idealist. He likes himself, he admires himself because he has ideals. Why else would a person have ideals? That's the most important thing about him. Remember that. Now come with me."

In the lazaretto the silence, except for the thump of the diesel engines deeper in the ship, was almost as complete as the darkness. The boxlike room, glowing through its many cracks and fissures as if light were seeping through the very pores in the wood, seemed to be rigged as a mock-religious experience: Lucifer imprisoned and giving up his light.

Followed by Chase, whom he ignored, Brewster strode across the deck and flung open the judas hole. A wave of heat came out of the aperture. The Mirza uttered a little groan as if grateful for the cooler air that flowed inward. Through the judas hole Chase saw that the Mirza was wide awake, with intelligence in his eyes. He dripped with sweat, some of it faintly bloody. He covered his sexual organs with cupped hands.

Brewster, standing well back in the darkness and off to the side where the light from the room could not reveal him, studied the Mirza at length. Then he closed the hole and, taking Chase by the arm, drew him away from the door. In a voice so low that Chase had to lean in to hear the words, he said, "Your blood tests came back. No trace of the Thiopropofal was found. Verena was probably bluffing. Anyway, you've been cleared for the field again."

"What if the solution is such that tests don't necessarily reveal its presence?"

"All agents are walking time bombs, Number One. At risk for capture, interrogation, breaking under pressure and revealing the very thing they were created to protect. It's all part of the game."

"Comforting thought."

"You've seen worse than any agent I know and still haven't broken. Perhaps one day something *will* come along that proves to be your match, but it hasn't yet. And I have a gut feeling that, whether the drug is still in you or not, it'll be something far worse. Something we're absolutely unprepared for. That's just the nature of the lives we lead. Anyway, this is something for one person to do. Mind if I go in first?"

"Fine, chief. Go first. Just leave something for me to talk to when you're through."

Brewster entered, sat down so that the light shone directly in his face, and let the Mirza look at him for a long moment.

Then he said, "Life is long, Duque Joaquin Marcario Lope de Vega. You are in American hands."

Standing in darkness outside the room, Chase could see Brewster's face by the light from the judas hole, but not the Mirza's. The two were talking to each other in English, Brewster's voice soft and reasonable, the Mirza's changing by stages from shrill anger to bluster to a reasonableness so studied it seemed to be a mockery. Finally, only the Mirza talked, a long soliloquy Chase had heard before—his childhood, his schooldays, his army service, everything but the parts that had put him into that room.

For a long time Brewster did not interrupt. Finally, hours after the conversation began, he began to confide. He spoke in low tones and the Mirza replied in kind. Chase caught a word here and there. In the final hour, Brewster and the Mirza whispered to each other, parties to an understanding so secret, so delicate that no one else on earth could be privy to it.

At last they shook hands. Brewster exited, pointing a finger at the door. Before stepping into the light, Frankie and Alex covered their heads and faces with black hoods and offered one to Chase. He said no. Frankie shined a flashlight into the Mirza's face. He blinked and raised an arm to shield his eyes, but he wore a pleasant expression—the vestige, Chase supposed, of the look of deep sincerity he had been wearing to win Brewster's trust. Brewster pointed another finger and Frankie and Alex poured water over the Mirza, emptying three buckets over his head and flinging the last bucket at his fouled buttocks and groin. A towel flew through the darkness. The Mirza snatched it from the air and draped it over his head and shoulders like a monk's hood.

They were on the foredeck, looking out on international waters. On the deck above, officers and seamen were at their stations on the bridge, but the rest of the deck was deserted. Frankie and Alex covered the Mirza, still wearing their black hoods. The Mirza tugged his white towel into place and bowed his head. They looked like mummers posing for a Lenten procession.

From the moment Frankie and Alex put on their hoods Chase had believed that Brewster was going to let the Mirza live. If he was going to die, why protect their identity? Let him live for what purpose, live where, live how, live why?

At the other end of the deck, Brewster whispered to Chase, "Okay. I'm going to tell you everything."

"Fine. But please remember that I already know the story of his life. There's no need to go over it again."

"So what interests you?"

"His future."

"Easy," Brewster said. "He thinks we're going to put him back on shore. He's going to work for us—make that pretend to work for us."

"Just how tempted are you, chief?"

"What I want to do is try him in open court. But as you already know, the problem with the Mirza is he can't be tried for his crimes. He's killed everybody he ever met in his life except you. You're the only person that's seen him in action. As far as we know, nobody else who ever saw him lived to tell the tale."

"So my role as you see it is to identify him in a court of law?"

"We both know that can't happen. Anyway, what charge would be enough? What sentence?"

Chase said, "Chief, stop. If nothing is enough to even the score, tell me, please, what you plan to do with him."

Brewster said, "I'm going to let you talk to him. Then we'll decide. Right now it's your turn." Brewster whistled and when Frankie looked up, pointed a finger first at Chase, then at the Mirza. To Chase he said, "Go on. Take your time."

In the bow of the ship, the Mirza was crouching now. Chase stood over him. He said, "Stand up."

The Mirza rose to his feet. Swaying a little, he stood at attention, heels together, back rigid, eyes straight ahead. His posture was a confession that he wished to make a good impression. He was at his captor's orders. However, now that the moment for interrogation had come at last, Jonathan Chase had no questions for him.

In loud Spanish Chase said, "Where is your army of ghosts now, old man?"

Even louder, as though he had a greater right to the Spanish language than this impostor, looking Chase straight in the eye, the Mirza replied in English, *"Everywhere!"* His tone was prideful. Brewster was right: this man liked himself. He was proud of his memories. Chase had no intention of doing what he did half a second later, no inkling even that he was going to do it. As if someone else were using his body, without forethought, without emotion, Chase picked up the Mirza and threw him over the side of the ship. The Mirza was so light that Chase half expected him to drift on the wind like a large insect. Instead he fell like a bag of bones, white towels fluttering away in the night, and made a phosphorescent splash when he hit the water.

No one cried "man overboard." A searchlight came on and swept the water. Chase expected to see nothing. But the circle of bluish light found him and blinded him.

The Mirza was alive, thrashing as if trying to swim the butterfly. His movements, wild and uncontrolled, resembled the gestures he used to make when having one of his tantrums. If he was screaming, no one could hear him. The thrashing, frantic at first, slowed as the cold took hold of him, and after a few seconds, not longer than that, he sank beneath the surface, creating a dimple in the water that sealed itself almost at once. No one but Chase had moved or spoken. For several minutes the light stayed on the spot where the Mirza had drowned, but no boat was lowered, no life preserver flung. No effort whatsoever was made to rescue him. At length the searchlight went out. The diesels throbbed, the screw bit into the sea. The USS *Shangri-La* shuddered and made way.

Not much had happened. Not much had changed.

"My God, how I loved her," Chase heard himself whisper.

MULHOLLAND BOOKS

You won't be able to put down these Mulholland books.

A SINGLE SHOT *by Matthew F. Jones*

THE REVISIONISTS *by Thomas Mullen*

BLACK LIGHT *by Patrick Melton,
Marcus Dunstan, and Stephen Romano*

HELL AND GONE *by Duane Swierczynski*

THE HOUSE OF SILK *by Anthony Horowitz*

ASSASSIN OF SECRETS *by Q. R. Markham*

THE WHISPERER *by Donato Carrisi*

SHATTER *by Michael Robotham*

A DROP OF THE HARD STUFF *by Lawrence Block*

BLEED FOR ME *by Michael Robotham*

GUILT BY ASSOCIATION *by Marcia Clark*

POINT AND SHOOT *by Duane Swierczynski*

EDGE OF DARK WATER *by Joe R. Lansdale*

Visit www.mulhollandbooks.com
for your daily suspense fiction fix.

Download the FREE Mulholland Books app.